UNTOLD
DAMAGE

UNTOLD DAMAGE

A MARK MALLEN NOVEL

ROBERT K. LEWIS

MIDNIGHT INK
WOODBURY, MINNESOTA

FIRST EDITION
First Printing, 2013

Book format by Bob Gaul
Cover design by Kevin R. Brown
Cover art: Badge © iStockphoto.com/DNY59
       Pistol © iStockphoto.com/Garret Bautista
       Spoon © iStockphoto.com/rusm
       Syringe © iStockphoto.com/malerapaso
Editing by Nicole Nugent

Midnight Ink, an imprint of Llewellyn Worldwide Ltd.

This is a work of fiction. Names, characters, places, and incidents are either the product of the author's imagination or are used fictitiously, and any resemblance to actual persons living or dead, business establishments, events, or locales is entirely coincidental.

Library of Congress Cataloging-in-Publication Data
Lewis, Robert K.
  Untold damage: a Mark Mallen novel/Robert K. Lewis.—1st ed.
    p. cm.
  ISBN 978-0-7387-3576-4
1. Ex-police officers—Fiction. 2. Drug addicts—Fiction. 3. Murder—Investigation—Fiction. 4. San Francisco (Calif.)—Fiction. 5. Mystery fiction. I. Title.
  PS3612.E979U58 2013
  813'.6—dc23

                          2012032825

Midnight Ink
Llewellyn Worldwide Ltd.
2143 Wooddale Drive
Woodbury, MN 55125-2989
www.midnightinkbooks.com

Printed in the United States of America

For Dawn

Gold in Peace, Iron in War.
— SFPD motto

ONE

MALLEN WOKE UP WITH the needle still in his arm.

Waking up with the pin still in him was something new. First time, actually. Made him think of how vodka was the last drink a chronic drunk can take. Because their stomach's given out from all the abuse heaped on it. Vodka was the last stop before a coffin. The last line in the sand, crossed. That bit of knowledge was just like waking up with the needle still in you. He yanked it out, threw it onto the scratched coffee table.

His throat was parched, tongue feeling five sizes too large and covered in matted fur. He checked the small, yellow-purple bruise the size of an ink drop. That would be a bad one. The skin in the crook of his elbow was tender to the touch. He could imagine his veins collapsing like subway tunnels during a quake.

Outside rain started up, beating on his window. Sounded like it would be another mother of a storm. The city'd been battered all week by a rain that felt like God himself was trying to power-wash away all the putrid stinks of the city's soul. *Good luck with that one, God.* He rose off the couch, padded barefoot across a wood floor strewn with dirty clothes and empty ice cream containers. Peered out the grimy window. Yeah, it would be a depressing day for scoring. Dreamo would for sure be in his office, as per the usual. At the Cornerstone. The dealer had better attendance than most CEOs out in the real world.

There was a knock at the door. Hard and loud. It was a cop knock, one Mallen knew very well. He snatched up his rig, then went and deposited the needle, rubber tubing, and bent-back spoon under the sink, in an old B&M beans can. He went to answer the door.

The plainclothes cop standing there tried valiantly to hide his shock when Mallen opened the door, all faded black clothes and shining eyes; he failed way past miserable. Mallen recognized him right away, since they used to sometimes work together a long-ass time ago. They'd even gone drinking together. Talked over cases together.

Police Inspector Oberon Kane stood in the dingy hallway, his gray tweed sport coat a nice match for his mostly gray, shoulder-length hair. He wore glasses now, simple wire rims that made Mallen think of John Lennon. Even though he had Oberon by three inches in height, the man had always seemed taller and bigger. Like how somebody might imagine Teddy Roosevelt. The finishing touch was a salt-and-pepper goatee. Overall, the cop seemed more a philosophy professor than a homicide detective.

"Well, well, well," Oberon said, "The rumors weren't true, after all. You're alive."

"You can call it that, sure."

"May I come in?"

"What for? I haven't done anything. Haven't even been outside for a couple days."

That didn't seem to be the answer Oberon wanted to hear. He pulled out a worn notebook in response, along with a red and silver Parker pen. "Would you rather step out into the hall and talk to me, Mark?"

He didn't want Oberon playing hardball with him. The fact that Oberon had that luxury pissed him off. However, he stepped aside to let the cop in. He was way too aware that his place was like the places they both had walked into, years ago now, ready to arrest the addicts and thieves that lived there. Oberon glanced around at all the kites hanging from the ceiling: diamonds, boxes, and delta-style kites were suspended in the air like fossils fixed in amber.

Oberon pointed at one that rested on the table, half-finished, its chopstick skeleton like whale bones on a beach. "Interesting hobby."

"It's for Anna. Her birthday…" he trailed off, realizing with a sick feeling that her birthday had been yesterday. He'd been high longer than he'd realized. What happened to the days? They seemed to all run together now until they were a tangle of coarse string wrapping him up. Choking out what was left of his life.

Oberon opened the notebook. It was then he caught a look at the crook of Mallen's right arm. His gaze then traveled up to Mallen's face. Like he was seeing him for the first time. Mallen put his left hand over the track marks, trying to hide them, only drawing more attention to them. Oberon glanced around the room again, like it all of a sudden made sense.

"So, at least some of the rumors *were* true, it would seem," Oberon said softly as he busied himself with some notes in his book. The old cop's voice held that note of sympathy that Mallen was very familiar with and hated worse than the thought of getting clean. "Since you left the force, or before?"

"Why are you here, Oberon?"

"Am I going to find any drugs here? Any needles?"

Mallen went and sat down on the couch. The thin cushions lost the battle against the worn springs. "Come on, why are you playing it this way? We always got along, didn't we? I'm a citizen now, sure. Just over about four years now. But you know me, I'm not a bad guy. I don't look to get over on people and scam 'em, you know? I shoot my drugs and mind my own business."

Oberon jotted something down in his book. Glanced again at the unfinished kite on the table. "How long have you been making the kites?"

"Since Anna was born."

"I never knew that about you. About the kites. How old is she now? Nine?"

"Yeah, nine." A brilliant nine, too. Her smiling face appeared in his mind's eye. Pale eyes, a cleft in her chin she got from him. The image didn't make him feel any better. It only heightened the shame at being what he now was: a junkie. A burnout. A lowlife who did nothing with his days but shoot drugs, then go out and find some more. It was a cycle he'd gotten used to. One he performed without much complaint or effort. It just happened, and he went with it. It was easier than fighting. The thoughts of the needle and its chain to him started The Need growing again. It began as a dull pressure just above his stomach, like someone gently twisting his guts. He knew it would begin radiating outward from there, following his nervous system, stabbing as it went.

"You see her often?" Oberon asked.

The question drew his thoughts back to the here and now. "Not as much as I'd like. Chris and me, well … you can see it, I'm sure."

"Yes, I can see it." He changed the subject. "You asked why I was here. Well, first I need to ask you a question."

"Business call, Obie?" He tried to lighten a mood by using the nickname he'd had for the cop, way back when. It didn't work. The air continued to feel heavy and troubling, gray and suffocating. "Like I said," he added quietly, "I've been here all day."

Oberon jotted it down, then said, "When was the last time you saw Eric Russ?"

"Eric? Jesus … well, I guess not since I left the force. Damn, man … haven't thought of him for some years now." How long had it been since they'd gone through the academy together? Ten years? More? He smiled as he thought back to them running the obstacle course together, competing against each other in pistol competitions. Always taking each other on in the self-defense drills. The nights drinking beers under the north windmill in Golden Gate Park. Then it was being rookies together in a city that chewed them up and spat them out by the dozens. He'd made undercover work his thing about the same time Eric had gotten his first promotion. Eric had opted to stay in uniform and his squad car, and at first Mallen couldn't understand that. But then, after awhile, he heard that the citizens on Eric's beat were talking about him. What a good cop he was. How much he cared. How he would go the extra mile for a citizen, if he could. Mallen understood then that Eric just liked being a beat cop, one who knew the people on his beat. To him, Eric had been "old school" that way, always reminding him of Joseph Wambaugh's Bumper Morgan.

"Why are you asking about him?" he said to Oberon. "He's not in some sort of trouble, is he?"

"No, Mark, he's not in any trouble. Not anymore. Officer Eric Russ is dead. Found this morning with a hole in his head, complement to the ones in his arms." Oberon's expression softened. "Sorry, I know you two had been friends."

Mallen's mind reeled under the news. Eric had still been a cop the last he'd heard. His mind went from there to the needle, hidden in the empty bean can under his sink. His mind needed to get away. Now. *Eric.* "I ... I don't understand. Shot?" he said, and then it hit him what Oberon had said. Hit him harder than a Millwall Brick to the face. "Wait ... wait a minute. You said holes. In his arms."

Oberon kept his eyes steady on him, and Mallen knew he was being read. "Russ was found in an alley, two blocks from where he'd been staying, at eight this morning. The bullet entered the back of the head. Looks like the shooter stood about ten feet away."

All he could do was keep shaking his head in disbelief, like a windup doll stuck in gear. "Wasn't," he finally managed to say, "wasn't he married? I thought I'd heard that. To ... Jenna, yeah? That was his wife's name, right? Jenna?"

"Yes, he was still married, but only just so. He'd ... had trouble, Mark." Another glance at the crook of his right arm. "Like yours. They gave him medical leave two years ago, so he could get his life back together. It didn't work, and he ended up leaving the department. Seemed to hit rock bottom but then appeared to be getting better by all accounts. For the last six months, at least."

"He was one of the best Police I ever knew. How the hell did he get involved with shooting dope?"

Oberon looked down at his notes as he said, "I'm not sure."

"Not sure? Or won't say, Inspector Kane?"

"More important to you, Mark, is why I'm here."

The way he said it resonated. It was a tone he'd heard cops use a lot back in the day. The room got a little tighter, matching the tension in his chest. Had the impression he suddenly held a live wire in his hand and was about to fall into a pool. "Okay," he answered, "why are you here, Obie?"

"Russ had your name and address in his pocket. His writing. He also had two vials of heroin."

"My name and address? You sure?" Then he got it, Oberon's being there. "No," he said. "You think the vials came from me, right? Or that we were shooting buddies? Is that what you think?"

Oberon said nothing, and said it all by doing so.

"Look," he continued, "I swear I haven't seen Eric since…since I left. Seriously, I hadn't seen or talked to him since leaving the force." It was all moving too fast, sliding away from him, and he was losing his grip. "No…no leads at all other than my info in his pocket?"

"None yet. The ME is going to post him later today."

Oberon's voice was beginning to fade in his ears. All he could hear was this rushing sound in his head, like high-velocity water through pipes. Took him a moment to recognize the feeling attached to that sound: anger. He was angry. At himself. Wished he could've done something to help his old friend in some way. If he'd only known somehow that Eric had been in trouble. If he'd been clean, been living a life that helped others, still been a Police, he could've done something. Anything. He wished then, more strongly than anything he could ever remember wishing, that he could've stopped the train Eric had been traveling on. A part of him suddenly wanted now to stop that train for himself, too. He knew it wasn't going to happen, though. All the anxiety, the conflict, only heightened the desire, The Need. The rig beckoned. The siren's call to a lonely sailor, adrift on the ocean.

"Well," Oberon said as he looked at him a long moment, then closed his notebook, "I can tell you that his family is of course torn up about it. You knew them pretty well, didn't you?"

"Yeah. Hal and Phoebe were nice people. Always had their door open for me."

"Too bad you can't go see them," the cop said as he moved to the door. "Offer your condolences."

"Too bad I—" Oberon had done it well. Shamed him in a slick way. Maybe it was the cop's way of trying to help? *Fuck him*, Mallen thought. *Nobody helps anybody anymore.* "Maybe I will, yeah? You can't stop me from doing that. No law broken in going to visit an old friend's grieving parents, right?"

All Oberon did was nod his head. Like indulging a small child's fantasies. "I'll let you know when the funeral is. Maybe you could send flowers, Mark. Been good to see you." And with that he left, quietly closing the door behind him.

Mallen sat there, staring stupidly at the door. His world had just exploded. His carefully preserved world. *Fuck people*, he thought as he turned and marched to the sink. Reached under and pulled out his rig. Remembered then he was going to go score some more today. Cursed. Better get it the fuck over with, before the weather got even worse. Maybe being outside would help his head. As he got ready to leave, he couldn't get the news of Eric's murder off his mind, or the shaming that Oberon had given him…

Well, that's why you shoot up, asshole. To keep the shit off your mind.

TWO

THE COLD, BRUTAL WIND hit Mallen like a pissed-off nun's slap on Sunday as he came out of his building and headed west on Eddy toward Polk. The collar of his dingy overcoat was pulled up against the elements, not that it did much good. The rain seemed to find its way into every opening. Every torn seam. He was drenched before he got half a block from his door. As he trudged along, he thought of Eric. They hadn't spoken for a very long time. Why would Eric have his address? What would have been going on in his head? He racked his brain for the street Eric's parents lived on. Somewhere out in the avenues. Out near California and 6th? Maybe 4th? He'd know the place if he saw it.

There was a rumble of thunder overhead. Angry and bitter. He figured to go see Eric's parents once he was done with Dreamo. Yeah, that would work. However, for the first time he could ever remember, he wasn't looking forward to copping. The feeling surprised him. For just over four years now it had been all about copping the next high, or about protecting the current stash from prying eyes and sticky fingers. A dope hound's world was all about sleeping with one eye open and one hand on the stash. Whatever it took to protect the e-ticket ride to that distant, golden shore.

Sirens erupted nearby, filling the air as they approached. Two black and whites tore around the near corner. Shot past him, all Code Three. Stopped at a building down the street. It was hard to fight down the urge to walk back, see what was going down. The siren acted on him like some bullshit Pavlovian experiment. He stood and watched for a moment longer then turned away and headed down the street.

The inside of the Cornerstone was darker than usual. Funereal in its inky, still dimness. The bar felt to him like a holding cell in Hell: easy to get into, but leaving was a whole different matter. A large, dark mass came down the bar toward him. Took him a moment to realize it was Bill.

"Jesus," he said to the bartender, "turn on some lights or something."

Bill put a huge, meaty hand on the bar. "You got a problem with the dark? After all those dark alley deals you did as a cop?"

"I keep telling you I was never a cop. Only a junkie on vacation." He said it with a smile, but it always kept him on edge. People around the neighborhood knew he'd been a cop. It couldn't be hidden, not here. You never knew when that bit of noise would carry to the wrong ears and someone might decide it was time to come for a pound of flesh. Over the years he'd arrested a lot of guys, burned a lot of people, shattered a lot of people's faith in their fellow man. Again, he asked himself, for the three millionth time: why didn't he leave and go to another town? And again the answer came back, as it always did: Chris and Anna.

"Dreamo in his office?" he asked. The bartender indicated the back hall with a tilt of his bullet-like head.

"Thanks." He walked to the back, noticing a few shadowy figures sitting in the corners. Pale hands wrapped around glasses, heads close together as they whispered to each other. Tenderloin lifers, doing deals; people whose entire world was lived out in that strange isosceles triangle of San Francisco: the bottom demarcation line being Market Street, the western border stopping at Van Ness, the top running no farther north than Bush Street. That one small area of real estate known as the Tenderloin held, per capita, more child abusers, drug addicts, thieves, and just all-out bad people than any other part of the city.

The hall was illuminated by a single naked bulb that turned the graffiti carved into the old wood walls to a sort of bas-relief. Ancient runes, carved by drunken ancestors. The men's room door was slightly ajar. He thought he could hear soft breathing coming from inside.

"Dreamo? It's Mallen, man."

"Yeah. Enter, my child," came the thready reply. He could tell instantly that Dreamo was already loaded.

He pushed into the small restroom. Decades of pen work and phone numbers made the walls a swirling nightmare under the hard light of the bulb over the sink. There was the sharp crack of glass under his boots. Bill hadn't swept in here since the Clinton administration, at least. Dreamo was in the second stall, the one against the wall, lying back against the stained porcelain toilet tank. The dealer looked even more high than usual. *Must be some good shit.* The crook of his arm suddenly itched—a metal detector sensing gold.

11

Dreamo pushed some of his sagging blond mohawk back away from his face. It reminded Mallen of a tired bird's tail. "Hey, Mal. You don't look so good. What's up?" he rasped.

"Nothing man. It's nothing. Just got some bad news on an old buddy is all. No worries."

"No shit? That's fucked up, man. I hate it when shit happens to people I know, or used to know. What happened, man?"

"He was shot. Killed."

"Damn," Dreamo said as he adjusted himself into a more comfortable position. "'I care not; a man but once; we owe God a death.' That's Shakespeare, man, you know that?"

"No, didn't know that. Philosophy was never my strong suit."

Dreamo snorted with laughter. "Fuck man, why would it be? It's all horseshit. I just know it's from fuckin' Shakespeare because one of my other customers told it to me. Mal, you kill me, sometimes." He straightened up. Tried to erase some permanent creases in his shirt. It was his "getting down to business" move that Mallen knew very well. "How much you lookin' for?"

For an answer, Mallen reached into his pants pocket. The severance package the PD had given him when they told him to leave—paying him off with the air of getting an unwanted baby aborted—was something he was thankful for every first of the month when the check came to his PO box. Hell, he'd actually been thankful every day of his misbegotten life. He would never forget Captain Stevens's look when they made the offer to him to go away and keep his mouth shut. Stevens looked like he wanted to puke. Nobody at City Hall and none of the brass wanted anyone to know, especially the fuckin' press, that they'd lost an undercover cop to the very world they were so desperately trying to get rid of.

Mallen shook his head then, trying to keep thoughts about the past from running away with him. He pulled off a couple twenties. Hopefully there was enough to make it to next month. He'd noticed lately that he'd been running closer and closer to the bone as the months went by.

Dreamo attempted to whistle with amazement at the money thrust at him, but it only came out a leaky steam pipe. "Man, you should really talk to my friend. Dealin's the way to keep shootin' and livin', my friend."

"I don't want to. Quit asking."

"I could get you some real weight. Could push it for you."

"Yeah, push it right into your own arm. Just give me three, okay?"

Dreamo's only reply was a shrug. Pulled out three small glass vials each the size of a .45 slug. "And the Lord said, 'Let There Be Junk!'" he said with a laugh that mutated into a jangled giggle. Mallen sometimes wondered if the insane edge to it was forced for effect.

"You know," Dreamo continued, "society is lucky to have us, Mallen."

"Oh really? How so?"

"We're the bell curve. We show society how bad it can get. And because of that, they subconsciously bounce off us, higher than they would go otherwise. If it weren't for *us,* there would be no *them.*" Another broken giggle.

"Dream on, Dreamo, dream on," he replied, shoving the vials into his underwear. No way anyone would ever grab him that close to his dick. Or at least it hadn't happened that way yet. But as he stood there, the feeling that it was all wrong somehow struck him, struck him right down to bottom of his soul. The whole transaction bugged him for some reason. Like he was an actor in a play he didn't really want to see and couldn't enjoy. Maybe it was just the beginning of the comedown off the junk. Maybe it was waking up with the pin still in his arm.

Maybe it was hearing about Eric.

He'd turned to the door to leave when Dreamo spoke again, his voice having receded even further away into what the dealer always referred to as the Users Realm. Dreamo would be asleep soon, he knew, dreaming again. Golden thread and silver needles, weaving images of sunshine and shadow.

"Dude, just remember this," Dreamo rasped. "We show 'em how bad it can be. We're the monsters."

THREE

Mallen stood outside the Russ house, huddled up in his coat in an attempt to keep out the harsh, cold wind coming from the north. Gazed up at the off-white stucco row job, complete with flower baskets along front windows. He'd been supremely proud of the fact that he'd remembered where it was. Proud as if he was a kid, wanting a fuckin' gold star for the day. *Is that what it's come to?* he suddenly wondered. *Remembering where a fucking house is located now merits pride? Jesus H. Christ…*

The place looked as cared for as the last time he'd been there, long years ago. Would they even recognize him? Would he really want them to? The longer he stood there with the ocean wind creeping into the very fiber of his being, the more he wanted to turn away and leave. The vials of H in his shorts seemed to be like a neon sign in his pants, he was so self-conscious of them. *You don't need to involve yourself with their world,* his junkie monkey chattered at him. The world had shown him it didn't need his involvement. It could get on fine without him, thank you very much, so go home. But then he found himself putting his boot on the first step, and then the next. And the thing that made him do it was remembering what Oberon had said. Eric had been an addict. Had been trying to kick it. But it was the *why* of Eric writing down his name and address that was the clincher. Mallen ran his fingers through his dark, tangled hair, trying to neaten it. Took a deep breath before knocking on the front door.

After a moment, the door was opened by a woman who he knew was about sixty, but looked seventy. Phoebe Russ. Her eyes were past tired, moving quickly beyond extremely exhausted. She folded a strand of gray hair out of her eyes to tuck it behind her right ear. "Yes?" she said, "Can I help you?"

"It's Mallen, Phoebe. Mark Mallen? Remember?"

She did. Looked at him again. Couldn't hide the shock on her face. "I … I'd heard you left the force."

"Did, yeah." There was a silence that started up. One that made him wish he'd kept away. "Heard about … what happened. Just wanted to come by. Offer my condolences. To you and Hal. I was really sorry to hear that Eric had … had trouble."

"Thank you, Mark," she replied, then shook her head with tired exasperation. "Where the hell are my manners! Please, please come in."

She opened the door wider to let him in. He found himself in an entryway that hadn't changed much since his last time here. On his left was the living room, through a wide, high arch. Great room. Had always been one of his favorites in the place. Now it seemed filled with a heavy, sad air. On the mantle was an 8 1/2 x 11 black-and-white photo of Eric. Taken in full uniform. Eric's death already felt like it'd woven itself into the very fiber of the house.

16

Phoebe led Mallen back to the large, eat-in kitchen. The round wooden table that sat four was still there, right under the large windows that overlooked the backyard. It was late into winter, the flowers nothing but stalks. She gestured for him to sit. "Coffee?"

"Sure. Thanks."

She retrieved the bag of coffee from the freezer, filters from the pantry. Set the machine up. Hit the On button. Put a pint of half-and-half on the table along with a sugar bowl. Sat opposite him. The silence grew uncomfortable. She seemed to want to say something but instead kept tracing invisible designs on the table with her index finger.

"If there's anything I can do to help," he found himself saying, "just let me know."

She failed to hide her skepticism, though she tried. Another curb stomp to his soul. He'd broken bread with these people, bled with their son. It took him a moment to regroup. Took all his failing inner strength to find his voice. "I spoke with Oberon Kane."

More designs traced. "Oh?"

"Yeah. He filled me in on Eric. A little. Told me...about some of it."

A moment. Then a nod. Eyes were wet now.

"I had no idea he...was in trouble," he continued. "Oberon, well, he told me that Eric had my name and address in his pocket."

Phoebe got up from the table. Went to the coffee machine. Stood there, still as stone, for ten very long seconds. Poured two cups. Came back. Put them on the table. "I'd heard about you, Mark," she said, anger creeping into her voice. "I'd heard about how it'd turned out for you. What you gave up. Your family. Everything." Glared at him. "I figured he had your name and address in his pocket because you were selling him that stuff he was putting into his soul. That you were his dealer. Making money off of other people's addictions? That's what you are, right?"

Finding his voice was like finding a needle in a haystack. "No, Phoebe," he replied with as much conviction as he could grab on such short notice. "I never dealt to him. Hell, I hadn't even seen him in years. Didn't know about his addiction. I'm telling you the truth: I didn't deal to him. Ever. To him, or anyone else."

"You only take it, right? Isn't that right, though? You shoot it, don't you?" Angry. So angry. He understood that, and there was enough of him left to know that she wasn't angry at *him,* but at what he was. At the brand he bore: *junkie.* He waited her out, wishing he'd never come, knowing that was a bullshit feeling.

After a moment, she relaxed. Shoulders sagged. Wrapped her hands around her coffee cup. "I'm sorry," she said quietly. "I know you haven't been around. He mentioned you a lot, though. Missed you, actually."

"He did?"

She looked right at him. Looked right into him. "Yes. He did."

He filled his coffee with a lot of sugar. Partly to stall for time so he could collect his thoughts. "Wish I'd known that."

"I don't know why he had your address, Mark," she finally said. "We had no idea about his starting up again. About him ... going back."

"How's his wife taking it? Jenna?"

A nod. "About how you'd expect. They weren't really together, but ... they were still close."

He stared at the black, oily liquid in his cup. "How's Hal taking it?"

For an answer, she indicated the door behind him. Hal's den. "He's in there." Tears started. Hard. He didn't know what he was really doing, but he got up and went to her. Put his arm gently around her shoulder.

"I'm so sorry, Phoebe. I'm going to miss him, too."

He could feel her nod. Let her go. She wiped at her eyes. He went and pulled a tissue out of the box that had always lived on the kitchen table. Handed it to her. "I'm going to go talk to Hal, okay?"

She nodded absently, eyes staring down into the cup in front of her. Maybe she was watching some old memory of her son as a little boy. Before he ever became a cop. Or an addict.

The den door wasn't shut all the way. Mallen wondered how much of their conversation might've been overheard. The huge old desk was still there, taking up one entire corner. The blinds were drawn tight, leaving the light from the outside world dull and gray. Old bowling trophies glinted in the weak light.

Hal Russ sat in the big faded leather easy chair he'd owned since way before Eric had been born. The man only appeared as a vague shadow in the dimness. Head was down on his chest. Like he was sleeping. There was a slight glint from a half-empty bottle on the side table near the chair. He thought Hal might really be asleep, but then the man spoke.

"Mallen," he said quietly as he raised his head. His voice was wasted. Tired and thready, like from shouting at the world. "Wondered if you'd show. Hoped you would, actually."

"Yeah?"

"Yeah. You went through the academy with him. That bonds guys together, doesn't it? Like going through boot camp."

"Very much like that, true."

"He'd be glad to know you came by," Hal said, adding, "I heard about … your troubles. Eric had kicked it, you know? Worked hard to do that."

19

"Well, he had that strength, and then some."

"He did," Pride there now. But it sounded like being proud of the *Titanic*.

Mallen walked over to the bottle. Glanced at Hal, who nodded. "Be my guest, Mallen." He poured a half glass of whatever it was. Didn't care at this point, just needed it. The vials were yelling at him for attention. He wanted to quiet them. Needed to, while he was here.

"Hal," he said, trying to keep his voice even and strong, "he had vials in his pocket, along with my address. We hadn't talked for a long, long time. Have to wonder if the police will be coming up with leads. You know why he'd have my address in his pocket?"

The man's soft chuckle filled the space between them. "You know, you still sound like a cop. I think that makes me happy, Mal."

"You can take the junkie out of the cop, but you can never take the cop outta the junkie. Or so they say, anyway." He made a silent toast, regretting his choice of words. To his surprise, Hal held up his glass, and the two men drank one in silence.

Hal then adjusted his large stomach. "So, you came by to offer condolences?"

"Yeah. And any help you might need. You know, if he wanted to talk to me, well..." he took another sip of his drink, "well, to be honest, I wish I hadn't missed out on the chance." And he was being honest. The longer he stood there, the more he wished he hadn't missed out on the one last chance to talk with his old friend. Maybe he could've... but no, that was for people who could actually do shit. Accomplish things. Not for junkie burnouts. "I guess I'm just looking for answers, like the rest of the fucking world."

"Answers," Hal echoed. "I heard those were extinct."

"Maybe," Mallen responded as he took another sip from his glass, feeling the alcohol in his system now. "But I recently heard the state of their demise has been greatly exaggerated."

Hal laughed silently. Held up his drink in another toast. Drained it with a gulp.

"I'm getting the impression he was trying to turn his life around," Mallen said.

"Had," came the firm, definite response. "He *had* turned his life around, damn it. Was doing fine. Just fine. Working on getting back with Jenna. Looking for work. Everything."

"What do you think happened then? An old score, settled? The vials suggest—"

"I know what they fucking suggest!" The yell echoed out in the room, swallowed up by a deep silence. Then Hal filled his glass again, from the nearby bottle. Shrugged. "I still can't—will never—believe it."

And why would any parent believe it? If it'd been his Anna? Taken way earlier than she should've been? He shuddered then, as though the arctic air had suddenly blasted through the windows. "Was there anything going on with him lately?" he said. "Anything…out of the ordinary? Had he mentioned me to you or Phoebe at all?"

Hal's soft chuckle filled the room. "You really can tell you used to be a cop, kid. Ever miss it?"

"Only when I get a speeding ticket."

"Come on, do you?"

He didn't even bother trying to play it off. "Yeah, I do."

"I can tell." Hal took another sip, then continued, "No, nothing. I'm telling you, Mallen, if my son had something going on with him, he never told me."

Mallen finished the rest of his drink. The Need was preying on him now, stronger and stronger. And he found himself hating it more and more, along with the rest of his life. "Thanks for the drink, Hal. If you need any help with anything, just let Oberon Kane at the department know. He'll find me."

His hand was on the doorknob when Hal's voice cut through the gloom. Choked with emotion. Raw. Bare. "Mallen?"

"Yeah?"

"Thanks for caring."

He nodded, not sure if Hal could even see it. Left. Phoebe still sat at the kitchen table. It looked like she hadn't moved at all. Her eyes were red and moist. She daubed at them with a crumpled tissue.

"I was … hoping to get Jenna's address," he murmured, instantly ready for Phoebe to shoot it down. "Thought I could go and offer my condolences. She came along just before I … left. But I'd like to, just the same. If it would be all right." And his soul cringed with the begging quality in his voice. More so because he knew that was the truth of his position.

Phoebe sat there thinking about it longer than he'd hoped she would. In the end, though, she heaved herself up like her soul weighed a thousand pounds. Went to a scratch pad attached to the refrigerator door by a magnet shaped like a rainbow. Scribbled an address down on it. Came and gave it to him. Jenna was over on California, just east of Hyde.

"Don't … don't make her feel worse, Mark," she said as she handed it to him. Then pursed her lips, regretted saying it. The words stung, but what could he say? To her, he was a walking disaster zone. Barely kept together by the very thing that was tearing him apart.

"I'm really sorry for what happened," he told her quietly, his face hot with the effect her words had on him. "I wish there were … answers … for what happened to him."

She was about to reply when she stopped. Like she'd just remembered something.

"What is it?" he asked. It was like the old cop motor had suddenly kicked on. Rusty and broken, needing oil, but the damn thing still fucking ran.

"It's just something he said to me the day before … it happened. I wondered about it at the time, because it was so out of character for him."

"What did he say?"

"He told me that people really did have a personal devil. One that followed you until it killed you."

That didn't sound at all like the cop who would storm into any building, no matter how dark and dangerous. "Any idea what he meant by that? Maybe he meant his addiction. Did he explain it at all?"

"Never had the opportunity. Hal came into the room then and said he needed help with something down in the garage. I'd forgotten about it until now, actually." She gave him a wan smile then. Glanced around the kitchen, as if looking for something she'd lost. "You know," she said, "it feels like we won't be able to live here anymore. We were going to leave this house to him. Now it will always make me think of him."

Mallen didn't know how to answer that. After a moment, she showed him down the hall to the front door. Then she left him there to find his own way back out into the world. He watched her for a moment as she retreated down the hallway, back toward the kitchen. A dim, lonely figure, vanishing into the gloom.

FOUR

MALLEN CAME IN, LOCKED his door. The bus ride home had taken way too long. It was all he could do to not scream at everyone and leap out the window. He'd never been like other junkies. Never carried his rig with him. Shooting was for home, not in some fucking alley somewhere. Maybe that was why he never went out much the last four years or so. It was safer at home. Going outside was like navigating a minefield. Fuck that.

He went quickly to the north corner of his room. Moved aside the stained leather chair. Grabbed at the bottom trim, right where the walls met. There was a barely perceptible vertical line in the trim there, about eight inches out from the corner. Dug his dirty fingernails behind the slim piece of painted wood and it came away. Behind it was a small, rectangular compartment. His little safe deposit box. Inside was his life savings: $345 in a tight roll, banded with a few red and green rubber bands. No matter how hard it got, or how bad The Need was, that roll was never touched. The aim was to one day give this tiny nest egg to Anna. He tried, as much as he could, to add a little bit to it each month. Sometimes he was even successful. The fact it existed made him just a little more hopeful, like maybe it would somehow make everything okay.

He stashed two of the vials inside the compartment, keeping back the last one. The trim was returned to its original place. He rubbed over the line a little to make sure it didn't stick out. It was this very trick, the hidden compartment, that blew the Geddes case for him. At least he'd learned something from that.

The rig was retrieved from the can under the sink. He set the shot, the junk turning to that all too familiar mercurial liquid as the fire made contact with the spoon. The air filled with a smell he now long associated with the cookies his mother had baked for him on Sunday afternoons. Back before he knew of a world that contained the words *junkie*, *felon*, or *failure*. He tied off. The needle went in with the ease of a high-gloss kiss.

In the back of his mind, like one of those noisy, crazy assholes sitting at the back of the bus, was a voice very much like the voice of someone who no longer tries to be heard, but *will* be heard. It kept screaming at him to stop, stop, *stop*. A friend was dead. Someone that had mattered to him. And there was a reason he was dead. Murdered. It made no sense, but Eric had been *murdered*. And then the man that was attached to the arm that was now attached to the needle realized that he needed to fucking do something about it. *Had* to. But then the golden horse hit his veins, galloping in and acting like the transit police, effectively kicking that voice off the bus.

And then the dreams took hold again. Surfed him up into a sky of his own making while he ran below, holding the slim string that connected them together. They ran in lockstep for what seemed like hours, him and the kite. Then he floated in a golden pond. He sighed as he curled up, back in the womb. It was safe. No more blown life, no more worry, no more failed marriage...no more anything. There was only the warmth, and the floating.

A knock sounded in the deeps. Someone banging on the outside of a submarine. A huge bell. Maybe it would go away and leave him alone? No, there it was again, getting louder. Insistent. Made his head hurt. He curled up tighter, put his hands over his ears. The knocking turned into a pounding and someone, a man, called out his name. He drifted away...but it called again. Eric's voice. Then there was a prowler car radio. It couldn't be, but it was. Buzzing at them, telling them of crimes committed. He was sure he could smell cooking heroin. The hammer of a gun was cocked back, sharp and loud. The gun fired, and the back of his head exploded in numbing pain, his neck snapped from the velocity of the bullet and he was falling and—

He woke up bathed in sweat. It was night now. Dead night. Someone had their radio turned up full blast. Some Spanish rap song. Other than that, the noises outside seemed muffled. A spasm of coughs wracked his frame. Lungs hurt, and he wondered if pneumonia was setting in. Some of the other junkies he knew had gotten it recently. The wet weather, the constant low vitamins. Enough to make anyone sick.

He sighed as he sat up, rubbing at his face. It still tingled, like a hand does when blood starts circulating again after you've fallen asleep on it. Looked over at the coffee table. The needle rested on the twisted spoon handle, circled by the rubber tube. Some sort of strange, abstract art installation.

And the needle ran away with the spoon... and his life. He put his head back on the couch. Why did it feel like everything that was his life had suddenly gotten even worse? A tension began to grow inside him. It grew deep down inside, deeper than muscle or even bone.

Cut easily through the junk, working and working to build that tightness there, brick by brick. At first he didn't recognize what it was, because it had been years since he'd last felt it. It pushed and tugged and kept working on him, the pressure increasing until he felt he had to scream.

It was the sense that *he had to do something.*

He had to find out what happened to his friend. Why would Eric have turned to drugs in the first place? And once he'd gotten his head out, why would he go back? Eric just wasn't a quitter. Why the fuck did he have *his* name and address shoved in his pants pocket? Was it some sort of message? Was Eric going to come to him for some sort of help? His friend must've been pretty fucking desperate to come to an ex-cop junkie for aid. What did it all mean?

Whatever it was, there was no doubt about one inescapable fact: it wasn't going to let him go until he found out.

But...but then there was his present state of imprisonment.

His weakened, starved soul.

A growl of impatience erupted from deep inside. He wanted to jump up off the couch, right then and there, but it was as if the cushions were magnets, holding him in place. An angry shout echoed in through the window from outside. A horn honked. Out there was a world in need of help, but he was in here, in this shitty room, unable anymore to even get up.

That thought sickened him worse than any of the bouts of withdrawal he'd caved to over the years.

He needed to get up.

FIVE

"GET OUT OF THE *car, hands where I can see them!" Mallen yelled at the black Ford Crown Victoria stopped approximately seven yards away. The rear and rear-side windows had been tinted dark to almost midnight-black. Mallen had his sidearm in his left hand, right hand supporting. Just like they'd taught him. His arms instructor had tried to get him to use his sidearm right handed, just like they'd tried to make him use a pencil right handed back in kindergarten, but he just couldn't work it. Just like back in school. He'd had to get a specially made "lefty" firearm, the safety on the right side.*

Mallen stood behind the open driver's side door of his prowler, body angled to provide as little a target as possible. Again, just like they'd instructed him. Sweat ran down his back, under his body armor vest. He hated being weighed down with so much crap, but this was part of the job. The belt alone—holding his taser, his .40 caliber, cuffs, pepper spray, radio—felt like it weighed over ten pounds. Would he ever, ever get used to carrying all this junk?

The driver's side door of the black vehicle opened. A man slowly came out of the car, hands up and in front of him. Big guy. Must be six three, at least. Mallen's mind, now trained for situations like this, registered all the facial features that would be necessary if he had to describe the man: Hair: short and black. No beard, moustache trimmed just above the lip line. Weight: about two-ten. Dressed in black hoodie and black, military-style pants. Heavy work boots also black. All of this was registered in only a few seconds, but Mallen had been born with a photographic memory, compliments of his police-man father, Ol' Monster Mallen.

"Turn and place your hands on the roof of the car!" he barked, using the low-timbered call they'd taught him about. A deep voice was an authoritative voice. Keep it low, keep it loud, they'd told him. The man hesitated, and Mallen could swear the bastard smirked. Like he didn't believe that Mallen would do anything other than just sit there and wait.

Mallen came out from behind door of his cruiser, repeating his command. "Turn and place your hands on the roof of the car, NOW!" For effect, he moved his crosshairs from the man's chest, to his face. Not regulation, but fuck it: he needed to prove a point here. That HE was in command of the situation, not the suspect. Take control immediately, they'd taught him, or else with each passing second control moves more and more into the hands of the suspect and or suspects.

The man did as he was told, turning and putting his hands on the roof of the car. Mallen moved forward, and as he approached, he shifted his sidearm to his right hand, reaching around for his cuffs. He'd been instructed to circle around and come at a suspect from directly behind, but it was a lot of ground to cover and he wanted this guy in cuffs quickly. Time was of the essence.

Mallen was just parallel with the left rear side window when he heard the sharp click of a shotgun hammer coming down on an empty chamber, followed by a woman's voice that said, "BANG! You're dead, Cadet."

The suspect, Lt. Fred James, shook his head at Mallen as the other instructor, who'd been hiding flat on the rear seat of the car, exited the vehicle. She was Cpl. Lisa Adams. "Where was your blind spot, Cadet?" she asked.

"On my right, back seat of the suspect's vehicle, Ma'am."

"And why was it a blind spot?"

"Due to the smoked windows, Ma'am."

"And you didn't check that because?"

"I forgot to."

"And that's why the city would be paying for your funeral." She turned to the assembled group of cadets who had been watching the exercise. "Never forget to check your goddamn blind spots! Everything this cadet did was fine, if he'd had a death wish! Next!"

Mallen could feel his face burning red. Tried not to look at the other cadets as he moved his way to the back of the crowd, all of whom would soon face the same scenario, but with a slight twist to keep them off balance. Maybe there would be no second person. Maybe there would be two other people in the car beside the driver. Maybe the driver would exit the passenger side door. Maybe he wouldn't come out right away, or at all.

He found himself standing next to a cadet he'd seen before a couple times but had never spoken to. It'd never been that easy to speak to other people anyway, and since he'd signed up to join the SFPD, he'd found this trait magnified. Everyone had families. He had no siblings. His mother had been dead a long time, his father lay dying of

Alzheimer's in a "care facility" up in Redding, where it was more affordable. Where the police benefits went further for a retired cop.

The cadet looked over at him. Smiled as he nodded. Mallen couldn't remember the guy's name. He was a few inches shorter than Mallen, maybe ten pounds lighter. Blonde crew cut. Didn't strike him as police material any more than he felt at the moment, but he'd seen men and women who he hadn't thought of being police material kick some serious ass on the obstacle course and in HTH combat drills.

The guy looked at him then. Grinned. "I would've made the same mistake. I was watching you, and the suspect's size would've made me hone in on getting him under restraints as soon as fucking possible."

"So," Mallen smiled back, "you'd be dead, too?"

"Deader than road kill." They both laughed then, and Mallen held out his hand. "Mallen. Mark Mallen."

"Nice to meet you, Mallen. I'm Russ. Eric Russ."

———

Mallen turned with the defense pad held high, knowing that Eric always went for the head. Sure enough Eric, baton in hand, went to town on the pad, laying in some good blows that would've busted a perp's body in half. Mallen had begun to think that maybe Eric had some pent-up anger he needed to let go of. The drill sergeant called time thirty seconds later and everyone relaxed, Mallen pulling off his headgear, wiping sweat from his eyes.

"Switch!" the sergeant called suddenly. There were a couple groans from the crowd, quickly silenced. No one really wanted to be singled out. Mallen tossed the pad to Eric and pulled his baton from his belt. Even though he hated carrying the belt at all times, especially

31

in HTH training, it did get you used to the weight, he had to admit. He laughed about it to Chris once, saying he felt like Batman, wearing his utility belt. Not highly original.

He laid into the heavy padding covered in thick, fake leather. As he went through the drill, Mallen wondered what he'd feel if he ever had to beat on someone in this manner. He usually tried to keep those thoughts away. He wanted to help, not hurt, people. Would he really be able to?

A strap on the pad Eric held up suddenly snapped. Just worn equipment. The pad drooped at the worse possible moment as Mallen swung down. He ended up catching Eric in the headgear, headgear very much like what boxers wore when they trained. His blow sent Eric staggering backward. A whistle blew and everything stopped.

To his surprise, Eric began to laugh as he pulled off his headgear. The gear had done it's job, but there was a little bit of shock in Eric's eyes, in spite of the laughter. There might be a slight bruising, too, just above the right eyebrow.

"Eric, sorry man," Mallen said.

"Lame," Eric replied with a grin. "You have no arm strength, man." Then he laughed again.

SIX

Oberon stood in the dank underground parking garage, the air bitter, cold, and damp, smelling of motor oil and urine. It was a quarter after two in the morning. Red and blue lights bounced and ricocheted off the dull concrete walls. Made the place look like a poor man's disco or some sort of sad rave. He sighed, knowing it would be many long hours before he saw a bed.

The reason for that thought lay at his feet. The body of a man, early thirties. Brown eyes that stared sightlessly at the ceiling. Military cut dark hair. The body had landed on its side from the force of the bullets shot into it. Two entry wounds, circular and ragged. Smallish caliber. Both into the back, left side, just behind the heart. The muzzle burns on the back of the man's shirt seemed a black exclamation point to the entire scene.

He looked over at forensics tech Veronica DeJesus, busy working the body, too involved to even glance up at him as he squatted down next to her, his knees castigating him as he did so. "How are your children doing, Ronnie?" he said. "Matt ever figure out how to snow-board?"

"Unfortunately," she said, "he did. Already broke his ankle."

"Ah, to be young again." He looked closer at the entry wounds. No, not a big gun, but used by an effective shooter. Execution style, too. One would've been enough, but two? Either it was the twitch of the trigger finger, or a pleasure shot. "Has a wallet been found?"

Veronica nodded. Indicated the victim's hands. "Still got his wedding band. Not very high end. Pinky ring has a good stone in it, though. Maybe the shooter got scared."

"No other marks on him?"

"Just the two holes."

This building rose twenty-five stories above them. He'd seen the registry—some of the floors carried at least seven businesses. He sighed as he stood, knees again yelling at him. "I'll get some uniforms to canvass the building. This gentleman will probably turn up an employee."

Veronica got in closer to one of the entry wounds. Studied it for a moment. "I can have make and model of the weapon tomorrow."

"So soon? My, I had no idea that forensics was so well funded. Your department is a veritable bank vault, it would appear."

"Funny. I just don't want to be home."

"With a son nursing a broken ankle? For shame, Mother DeJesus."

"With an ex-husband who now sees himself as Florence fuck-ing Nightingale."

"Ah. The clouds part," Oberon replied, then walked off to take another look around the crime scene.

———

It took only until eleven a.m. the following morning to find out the victim's name. An officer making the rounds of one of the floors had walked into a small software start-up on the seventh floor. The photo of the dead man's face matched one of the employees.

The victim's name was Carl Kaslowski. He had a small jacket, which topped out with a short stint in Folsom that ended a bit over a year ago. Drug-related. Like so many. Seemed the man had been turning his life to something other than incarceration since then, judging by his job, his clothes, and the way the people he worked with spoke of him when they heard the news. The officer gave Oberon the address where the man had lived. The Outer Sunset. Near Taraval and 33rd. Oberon wasted little time in getting to his car and pointing it toward the ocean. This was the hardest duty there was: questioning a loved one left behind. Sometimes he really hated being a Police.

The fog was in as he drove down Lincoln Way, making the left onto 33rd. The sky above was gray and bleak. A heavy scent of rotting seaweed swept in from the ocean. The address he'd been given belonged to a nondescript multi-unit building in the middle of the block.

Kaslowski's new widow opened the door at Oberon's soft knock. She was a short woman. No more than twenty-two or -three in years. She silently let Oberon enter then excused herself for a moment, answering the sound of an infant crying in the other room. All the furniture was IKEA, from a few years back, judging by its condition. Mrs. Kaslowski then came back into the room, baby in her arms. Sat on the couch, holding the infant tightly as she rocked it gently back and forth, a wan expression on her face.

Oberon sat on a nearby chair. Gazed for a moment at Kaslowski's now fatherless child. "Boy or girl?"

She cleared her throat. "Girl. Carlie."

"How old?"

"Four months."

He pulled out his battered notebook and opened it. "I am very sorry for your loss, Mrs. Kaslowski. I want you to know that I will do everything I can to find the person or people responsible. If you would like me to come back at a better time, I certainly will."

She dismissed that. "What did you want to ask me?"

"The people employing your husband thought very highly of him. They told me he was very dedicated. Often worked late."

"He worked hard."

"Well," Oberon smiled, "with a lovely family to support, who wouldn't?"

"Who would kill him?" she said, breaking down, the tears suddenly streaming down her cheeks. The baby picked up on it. Began to whimper. Oberon got up, came over.

"May I?" he said, indicating the baby. Mrs. Kaslowski nodded, and he carefully picked Carlie up, cradling her gently. Cooed at her as he bounced her softly. *And life is given to none freehold, but it is leasehold for all,* he said under his breath.

"What?" Mrs. Kaslowski replied as she wiped her eyes.

He smiled at her. "My apologies. Holding infants for some reason brings out the philosopher in me. It's a quote from a Roman poet named Lucretius. You mind if I hold her for awhile?"

"No," she replied with a small smile. Oberon stood there for a moment, cooing and tickling Carlie until she was giggling and staring up at him like he was the biggest thing in her universe. After a minute longer, he handed her back to her mother.

"Shame I can't write and hold an adorable baby such as that at the same time." He sat back down. "Now, can you tell me, was your husband having any troubles lately? Anyone you—or both of you—might consider as an enemy?"

She thought for a moment. "No."

"You sure?"

A nod.

"I know about his time inside. Men inside sometimes make enemies that follow them outside."

She glared at him then, if only for a moment. "I knew they would use that as an excuse. Why waste time on someone like Carl, right? Figures." The bitterness in her voice was thick. Strong.

That pulled him back a bit. "I'm in charge of this investigation, Mrs. Kaslowski. I assure you, whether your husband was rich man, poor man, beggar man, or thief, I will find his killer. A man—a family man and by all accounts a good man—has been tragically taken from this world." He leaned forward. Said quietly, "I will find his killer."

She wiped at her eyes. "Thank you for saying that. I believe you, you know? Thank you." Gazed out the window as she continued, "He only got out last year, but had been working his ass off trying to make it go. Worked so hard to stay out and change his life. A friend of his got him in contact with that office. He studied computers and accounting. Everything. They took a chance on him. And he slaved to show them they'd made the right choice. And now . . ." She wiped at her eyes again.

He'd have to look again at Kaslowski's jacket. Maybe that would turn up something. "Had your husband been acting differently lately? At all? Even if it might seem trivial, it might be very important."

She thought about it for a moment. There was no sound in the room except the infrequent noises made by Carlie as she wriggled in her mother's arms. "He did get a phone call a couple days ago. It upset him."

"Did he say why it upset him, or who it was from?"

"No, he wouldn't tell me. He just got quiet. That was his way. When confronted with a problem: go quiet. I tried to get him to talk, because he seemed pretty upset. It was no good. That was unusual, actually. I could usually get him to talk, eventually, but not when it came to that call."

Oberon wrote all this down. "Did the call come to his work? Here? His cell?"

"Here."

He finished writing his notes. Put the notebook back in his jacket. "Thank you very much for your time, Mrs. Kaslowski," he said as he rose. Went to the door. "If I need more or have news, I'll be in contact." At the door, he stopped and looked back at her. At her child. "I *will* be in contact," he said, then left.

SEVEN

MALLEN FROWNED AS HE looked at his needle-ridden reflection in the mirror. Hair like an overgrown brillo pad. Deep-set gypsy eyes. Well, once they'd been puppy dog eyes, but that was about ten years ago. A Roman nose, broken only once. Before Chris, before the needle, he'd never lacked in opportunities for dates, thank you very much. But now? Well… The sport coat and trousers, threadbare in places, were baggier than remembered. If the shaving job he did had been a blow job, he would've asked for his money back. At least there was still the cleft in his chin. *Haven't lost everything.*

He sat on the edge of the bed, gave his scuffed shoes a quick shine that didn't do shit for them. There weren't two socks in the whole place that matched or didn't have holes. Ran his hand through his tangle of dark hair as he tried to neaten it, but stopped then. Stopped dead, like he was an actor caught on stage forgetting his lines.

What the hell am I doing? I can't go see Eric's widow.

What the fuck was he thinking? What was he really going to be able to do? Why was he even considering doing anything at all? Let the cops do their job. The tension set off The Need. A fix. Now. Yeah, just fix a small shot to take the edge off. *It'll help me calm down*, he thought, *make it easier to see Jenna.* That brought him up: was he still thinking of going to see Jenna? The battle was tearing apart his mind, and his soul.

A giant cramp racked his body. Bent him up like a hairpin turn. His stomach was on a rampage. He *had* to fix, and bad.

But he couldn't.

It was the first time since getting hooked that he felt that way. The thought entered his consciousness like a sudden and unwelcome party guest. *Fuck being a pallbearer; I'm in some agony here.* The rig was in the coffee can. He stumbled across the cold floor. The sweat across his back made him shiver. He set the fix as fast as his shaking hands would let him. The sharp odor of Butane filled his nostrils as he held the lighter under the spoon. *Soon*, his mind crooned, *soon…*

There was the sudden explosion of a car back-firing outside. Sounded just like a Glock.

Eric's gun.

It had been his gun, too, until he switched to something easier to hide: a Heckler and Koch M7. Insanely, he still missed that gun. He'd never forget the day he had to turn it in. Like saying goodbye to one world, turning the corner into another.

His hands began to shake, crouched there on the floor with the spoon and lighter in his hands. Sweat dripped into his eyes. The world went wavy. It didn't feel like it was his choice when he put the rig down and stiff-legged it to the window like an old man without his walker. He needed air.

Gazed out at the street. A typical Tenderloin street. Filled with people struggling, people hustling, people fronting. They were all fighting something. Addictions. Evictions. Unemployment. Their family. Their past. The government. Hell, even the whole world. There was a major part of him, however, that no longer felt a part of what he saw down there in the street. A junkie walks alone, they always say. *Four years is a long stretch, man...*

He was hit with another spasm of pain. A real bad one. Like being folded up with a vise clamping down on him. He was barely able to make it through the agony into the bathroom to splash water on his face. Could hear the needle, hear it softly crooning to him from the other room. The siren's call.

One that wove its way inside...

Relentless, unforgiving.

Unable to keep the song away from him, he went back to the main room. The needle pointed right at him, the spoon glinted in the light. Winking. Crying for him...

Just a small one, man.

———

Shooting just a little turned out to be a fucking brainstorm.

It took the edge off but still left him able to function. He felt invigorated as he decided to just walk up Polk Street toward California. Hell, why ride that shit number 19 bus? He again took out the address Phoebe had written down, forgetting her last words to him. Well, Jenna lived in a nice part of town. California was a good street. Close to Whole Foods, bars, some good places to eat. Some bars. Far enough away from the shit, but not north enough to where you got charged both nuts for rent. Should he bring flowers? Didn't people do that, when they went and visited people who had lost someone? He used to know this stuff. Anyway, he figured he'd go and tell her how sorry he was. Maybe he could learn a little about why Eric had

41

done what he did. It really broke his heart that Eric was gone. Yeah, maybe Jenna could help him make sense of it. Good plan.

He was sweating in his old car coat by the time he made California and turned right at the Out of the Closet used clothing store. The weather had turned cold, bordering on nasty, but he felt hotter than usual. Probably not the greatest shit that Dreamo had ever sold him. That was unusual. He huffed his way up the street, passing the old, now closed Lumiere on his left. Crossed California to the north side, wishing he had time to step inside the Hyde Out. Nice place to drink, even if it was too well lit for his tastes.

The building Jenna lived in was usual for the area: built long ago and covered now with stucco. He hit the buzzer to number 12 and waited. There was no response. He swore under his breath; he should've remembered to ask Phoebe for Jenna's phone number. That would've made this entire episode a lot easier. Glanced at the front door. Didn't look shut all the way. Looked like the lock wasn't set well in the door anymore. Loose. Probably knocked that way from years of tenant abuse. Could he be that lucky? He pushed on it and, sure enough, it opened. He went inside.

The lobby was carpeted in a modern pattern made up of green and blue rectangles. The walls were stark white with the old, fancy trim painted yellow ochre. A brief recon showed him four flats on the street level. He went to the elevator and pushed the Up button. The elevator clanked its way down to him. Got in. There were only three floors, so he pushed 3. *Four times three is twelve, so number 12 would be on the third floor*, he thought, stupidly proud of his deduction skills.

After a brief ride, he slid aside the doors and walked out into the hall. *Nice hall*, he thought. He needed to move. Get out of the Loin. That would probably help him quit the junk. If he had a better environment, he bet he could quit it easy. He just needed a change of scenery.

After a glance to his left, he figured Jenna's place would be on his right. Probably toward the back. He moved down that way, the sweat starting to dry under his arms and across his back from his long walk. He hoped he didn't look too scummy. Wondered what Jenna would be like. What kind of woman would Eric be serious about? Someone with a big heart, that was for sure. Someone who gave a shit about stuff.

He got to her door and knocked, the door pushing back silently. It was quiet beyond. Still. Another old feeling woke up in him then after a long-ass time asleep: the feeling that he needed to proceed with caution. More old cop instincts kicked in as he pushed gently on the door. "Hello?" he called loudly. "Jenna? My name is Mark Mallen. I was friends with Eric, back in the cop days. Hello?"

No answer. He pushed the door open a little more, and out of another old habit, hid a bit behind the wall to the right of the knob as he did so. Peered through the doorway. The place had been ransacked. Real tore up.

"Shit." He tried to take in as much of the room as he could from his vantage point. Stuff was thrown everywhere. "Jenna?" he said again. Figuring taking one step inside wouldn't set the world on fucking fire, he moved through the doorway. Place looked like a one bedroom. On his left was the living room. Ahead was the dining room area, and off that was the kitchen. A hallway opened directly on his right. He took another step forward. There was the crunch of broken glass under his boot. There was a framed photo nearby, the glass broken and gone. It was of Eric and Jenna, taken on some beach somewhere.

Mallen couldn't help himself. Picked it up. Eric looked happy. So did Jenna. She had intelligent eyes. A kind smile. Pretty lady. He and Chris had looked that happy, too, at one point in their story together.

He stole another glance around the room. There was a desk in the living room. Seemed to be the main focus of the search. He went over. *Old habits die hard*, he thought, remembering back to all the tossed rooms he'd ever investigated. What could someone be looking for? The laptop was still there, on the floor where it had been tossed. Not a burglary. Then he picked up a drawer that had been thrown on the ground. The only thing left in it was a business card that had caught in the side, where the bottom and back met. He pulled it out. A counseling center for drug addicts and ex-cons. Phoenix Today was the name. On impulse he put the card in his pocket. Maybe he could call them, get some help. He turned back to face the rest of the room but couldn't shake the feeling there was someone else there. Went quietly to the hallway. Noticed a few dark droplets on the wood floor. Blood. Put his back to the wall even as his mind shouted at him to just get the fuck out and call in a 911. No one in the bathroom; it hadn't been touched. Moved to the bedroom. The door was partway open. He pushed on it.

And there was Jenna, lying on the floor. On her right side, facing away from him. Mallen went to her. There was an ugly welt on the side of her temple. Blood had seeped out of her mouth. "Jenna? Jenna? You hear me?" Checked for a pulse. Thready. "Jesus," he said as he got up, glancing around for a phone. He found the bedroom extension and picked it up.

"Freeze, asshole. Put your fucking hands on your head and turn toward me," said a heavy male voice behind him.

Mallen froze then, realizing that he was now living the most fucked up day of his life in recent memory. He hadn't heard them at all, either. *They must be doing some great stealth training nowadays.*

"Do it!" the voice barked at him. Typical cop voice, one he knew how use himself, once upon a time. He knew there would be a Glock pointed at his back, safety off. As slow as he could manage, he put his hands on his head and turned around to face the cop. There were two of them, actually. Both were young. Big and young. "Now, wait a minute, guys," he said to them, "I just got here. Her name is Jenna Russ. I was friends with her husband—"

"Shut up. Step toward me," the officer in front said. Mallen followed the order. "Turn around," the cop said.

Then he made a mistake. He later blamed it on the junk. "Now, look man, I just—" He didn't get to finish because the second cop swooped in and spun him around to the wall. Smashed him into it. His right hand was wrenched behind him and he heard the jangled clink of the cuffs as they came out. He heard more than saw the other cop go to Jenna.

"She's alive. I'll get an ambulance," he said. Pulled out his radio. Spoke into it urgently as he requested the paramedics, stat.

"Look," Mallen said, panic setting in as his other hand was cuffed. All his life as a civilian, he'd never gotten arrested. He'd always stayed as far off the radar as he possibly could. All it took for him to break out in a sweat was the mental image of him walking through booking, then to the holding tank. *Maybe it's what you need, junkie,* said a quiet voice inside him. He was shocked the junkie part of him didn't protest more. "Look," he repeated, unable to remember ever feeling so fucking desperate, "Call Inspector Oberon Kane. He knows me. Call him, please. He'll help straighten this out."

"How do you know Inspector Kane?" the cop who'd cuffed him asked. The man turned Mallen around, pushed his back into the wall.

This was it. He wondered if he was still known around the department. Maybe in the four years he'd been gone, they'd forgotten mostly about him. "I know him because I used to work with him sometimes. My name is Mallen. Mark Mallen. My old badge number used to be 0412. Come on, man, please? Just call him."

The two cops looked at each other for a moment. A siren grew in volume. Approached quickly, then cut off. The paramedics had made good time.

"Mallen, huh?" the first cop said. "Yeah, I heard about you from my sergeant." Looked him up and down. Not impressed. "Take this fucker downstairs and put him in the back of the cruiser."

———

He had to sweat it out for about an hour. All that time, he sat in the back of the police cruiser, trying to ignore the looks from the locals and other officers that had arrived. One of them, a plainclothes detective, smirked at him as he passed. His hands were going numb from the cuffs. He kept flexing his fingers, sitting sideways in the backseat to keep the pain to a minimum. It was hot, too. Stuffy. All the windows were up. Partway through his time in the car, he watched Jenna get wheeled out on a gurney and into the back of the ambulance. With a roar of siren and lights, the vehicle tore away up the street. He hoped she was going to be okay.

He glanced again out the window, trying to not see the stares, glancing constantly around to avoid the eyes trained on him. He felt like a circus act gone wrong. Someone had snapped the high wire. His knives had killed the beautiful assistant.

And that was when he saw them.

At first he didn't recognize the two men standing there in the crowd. And he, or the junk, couldn't be blamed for that one, as it had been four years and some change since the last time he'd seen them. Had to admit that the last time he'd been around them hadn't been a fucking heartfelt goodbye party anyway. He'd never been on great terms with either of them. Never liked them, and they'd never liked him. Just a "junkyard dog" thing, he'd figured. And then when he knew for sure, he didn't want to admit it was really them.

Jas and Griffin.

Soldiers he had run with, back when he'd been "under the waterline," or undercover in the drug world. Guys that he'd seen many times take orders from Franco, the man at the top, to make sure some dope-stealing son of a bitch never stole again. Sometimes it would be an order to stomp a rival that was showing too much attitude. And they'd been good at their trade.

Very good.

Jas was just standing there. Staring right at him. Griffin, just as Mallen had remembered, was on guard duty, eyes scanning up and down the street. Like a secret service cat watching over the president. He felt suddenly that he was living a nightmare, that a day this bad just *had* to be a dream, and all he had to do was just wake the fuck up.

He looked away, bit his tongue, hoping that it wasn't real, knowing he was being lame. Looked again into the crowd. Yup, there was Jas. Mallen wondered what Jas was thinking right about now. Mallen had dropped out of that world when he'd been kicked off the force. Would they know now about who his real employer had been? They would wonder, sure. Might do some digging. Hell, he'd made some enemies on the force, too; cops that would be only too happy to give over the truth for some bread. Probably be fuckin' eager.

There was nothing worse or more unsafe than being an undercover man, uncovered.

If Mallen had been sweating before, he was *really* sweating now. He worked to keep his eyes level with Jas's, and it took every bit of the last shreds of his manhood to do it, but he did. He even nodded at the man, trying to be all, "Fuck, man…look at my sitch, will ya?"

But Jas just shook his head. Grinned like a death's head. Turned and walked away through the crowd, Griffin in tow.

So. They did know what he'd been. And Jas had just handed out his death sentence. Mallen knew then, at that moment, that he'd have no peace anywhere in town. Not until those two were either brought in or put down.

A unmarked brown sedan then pulled to the curb. To his ever-lasting relief, Oberon got out. The detective didn't look too happy. Oberon was about to go into Jenna's building when he spied Mallen in the back of the black and white. He came over and opened the door. Mallen took a deep breath of fresh air.

"I heard where you were found. And under what circumstances. Just what were you trying to accomplish?"

"I was just coming to see her to offer my condolences, man."

"And?"

He caught the look in Oberon's eyes. "Yeah, okay," he replied, looking at the ground. "I wanted to ask her if she knew why Eric had my name and address on him when he was killed."

Oberon looked at him for a moment. Shook his head like a disapproving parent. "I better go up there and see what I can see. Don't go anywhere," he added as he shut the door and went into the building.

Anxiety crawled inside Mallen's chest, choking his air. The wait seemed to go on forever. Finally Oberon returned. He again opened the door, then indicated Mallen should step out of the car. "What's going on?" he asked.

Oberon didn't reply right away. He put a hand on Mark's upper arm. Guided him over to the brown sedan. Opened the back door. "Get in," Oberon said in a flat tone.

"What? I didn't do anything!"

"*I* know that. But those Police up there told me they found you standing over a woman who had been beaten into unconsciousness. Her apartment has been torn apart with a great degree of violence. Like someone was looking for something. Like maybe a junkie, looking frantically for money, or maybe his dead friend's stash. They know about Eric's struggles, as well as your history. They found prints, too, Mark. Would some of those be yours?"

The temperature in his face skyrocketed. He was sure he was beet red. All he could manage was a sad nod of his head. Oberon cursed under his breath. "Some of them will be, yeah," he replied. "But come on, it's all horseshit! So my prints are there. Okay. That's not proof I was the one who beat her and tossed the place!"

"Like I stated, I know that," Oberon replied calmly. "But they have enough to hold you, if only for twenty-four hours. And, Mark, they're very intent on doing so. The only thing I could do was call in an old marker and ask them to let *me* take you downtown and have you booked. That way, I know for sure you won't be put anywhere you're not supposed to be. You know what happens to Police that go inside. Even ex-Police."

Oh yeah, he did. He'd heard the stories. Every cop knew those stories. "Thanks for standing for me, Obie. I'll find some way to pay you back."

"You can pay me back by staying out of my quickly turning white hair," Oberon said as he put Mallen in the back of his car and shut the door.

His mind raced. Panic was firmly in place now. The Need was already awake, crying for its needle. He was going away for at least a day. *Maybe that's not such a bad thing,* whispered the quiet voice inside once again. He found himself not disagreeing with that voice as much as he thought he would. Maybe this was it. Maybe this was the real bottom of the well. He had to admit, his crash-out appeared pretty fucking complete.

Oberon got behind the wheel. Started up the sedan. "You were a great Police back in the day, Mark," he said quietly. No masking the disappointment there.

Mallen thought back to those days, his time carrying a badge. Yeah, he'd been good, all right. Lots of times better than good. And then he suddenly realized he wanted to be good again. At something. Anything. But he never would be, not if he stayed hooked. And there it was: the abyss standing between him and his life. Between being a junkie, and being clean. The addiction was a huge chasm, and he needed to get over it to the other side. Could he possibly find a way to jump that gulf? Images of Anna and Chris came to him. His throat was tight. Constricted. But he knew what had to come next.

"Do me a favor," he told Oberon. "Tell them to put my booking jacket on the bottom of the pile for a couple days."

There was a pause before Oberon responded, like he wasn't sure he'd heard right. "Excuse me?"

"Just do it, will ya? Might be the only way for me to get clean. A few days in jail. Then maybe I can actually try and do something good for a change."

Oberon looked at him in the rearview mirror. Searched his eyes for a sign of truth. "You mean it," he said, stating the fact that Mallen felt growing inside.

"I have to do something. Maybe this is the time."

Oberon nodded. "I'll make sure you're out in three days, okay?"

"Thanks."

"You want me to sign you up at a clinic?"

Methadone. *Same shit, different day*, he thought. "No," he replied, "I know me. It wouldn't work. Thin edge of the wedge."

"Okay," the detective said as he turned the vehicle onto Hyde Street. "Let's get it started then."

———

Oberon led him into central booking. Mallen hadn't been there in about six years. That last time had been while on a case. Captain Oxford badly needed to talk with him. The top heroin suppliers were watching him all the time, so jail turned out to be the safest place to hold a long discussion. Plus, it made his cover look all that more solid. Stuff like that happened every once in awhile, by arrangement. He'd get picked up and taken in for questioning. Sometimes he'd even take a couple body blows from a fellow officer. Anything to make his cover tight like a drum head.

The walls were still the same dull institutional color. The constant white noise of prisoners yelling, doors clanking open and shut, and names being called over the PA system filled the hot air. He followed the yellow line, Oberon guiding him by the elbow.

"Look," the cop said in a voice only he could hear, "I'm not booking you, okay? You're being held on suspicion of burglary. If I can pull this off, you'll get to even skip the lovely cavity search."

"Oh man," he answered, trying to sound upbeat, "and that was the part I was looking forward to."

He glanced around at the cops and criminals. There was a face or two that he recognized, on both sides of the law. Those that he once worked with seemed to quickly shutter their eyes and look right through him. The criminals he knew winked or nodded in brotherly affection. He was suddenly so tired of it all—the shitty apartment, the threadbare clothes, the constant scrounging. Not least, the junk. He wanted out. As far out as he could get.

Well, let's see how far that can be.

———

The pain began within hours. The sweating, spasms, vomiting, and the runs. Oberon hadn't been able to keep him in the holding cells. They were too overcrowded. The best, last resort had been to get him into the drunk tank. How he'd done that, Mallen couldn't figure out. Probably had to call in yet another marker. The list of how much he owed Obie was quickly growing out of control. In the drunk tank he'd be safer, left mostly alone to sweat it all out. After one bout of passing out from the agony of The Need, he found someone had taken his shoes. His pants were probably safe from suffering the same fate only because he'd thrown up all over them. Another prisoner—one of the trusties who walked around mopping the corridors and doing general cleaning—had given him a towel at one point to help him wash up some. He was a short, wiry-looking guy. Latino. Intelligent eyes. Black hair shaved close to the skull. Small mustache and thin goatee. Looked to be about twenty-five or so. Forearms sleeved with jail tats. He even brought Mallen some water to keep him hydrated. When Mallen asked why he was helping him, the trustie just pushed up his left sleeve. Showed him the track scars in the crook of his elbow.

"The Lord tells us to look after each other, my brother," the man said to him. "Simple as that, *vato*." He then rolled up Mallen's coat for him. Stuck it under his head for a pillow.

"Thanks, man," Mallen told him. "What's your name?"

"Gato. My friends call me Gato."

"What are you in for?"

"B&E. Been here a year. I'm almost home, man, and I ain't never coming back. Had enough of this shit. Be out tomorrow night. Free to fly."

He relaxed his neck muscles. Seemed like the first time in years he'd done so. The gesture of Gato rolling up his coat for him made him feel, if only for a moment, less alone. It was a gesture he wanted to remember for the rest of his life. "You know a bar called the Cornerstone?"

"Yeah, man. I used to hang there, once in awhile. Why?"

"The name's Mallen. When you get out, go there if you need anything. Any help, or anything. I used to be good at helping people. Might be good again, I hope. Leave a message with the bartender. Bill's his name. He runs the place. I'd like to do what I can for you."

Gato put out his hand. "Thanks, bro. There's a good heart, beatin' in that chest of yours."

Lifting his hand was like lifting a concrete block, but he managed. Gave Gato's hand a weak shake. The trustie then picked up his mop, put it over his shoulder. "Try to keep in your mind what my *padre* always used to tell me," Gato said. "Sometimes the darkest moments of our life give us the brightest chance at our redemption."

Mallen liked that. Smiled the first real smile he could remember in a long time. "Keep your head down, brother."

"The Lord looks after me. I'm good," Gato replied as he genuflected. He then left the tank, the door clanking shut behind him.

Mallen closed his eyes as another spasm of cramps racked his body. He was on fire. Breathing was hard. It felt like he'd vomited up every last bit of liquid he'd ever drank. Even his eyes burned. Every time a cramp hit him, it was a giant's fist low in the stomach. Cries were ripped from his cracked throat; he moaned that he wanted to die. He was only vaguely aware of the answering catcalls and laughter from the drunks around him.

One time he woke up and found himself staring up into the pockmarked, scabby face of a bearded man who smelled of sweat, old wine, and urine. His coat was in the man's hands.

"You won't be needing this, friend," he told Mallen through a grin of yellow, rotting teeth. "You look like you're gonna be dead, so I'll give this a good home."

Mallen tried to rise, but no go. He could barely move his mouth to speak. "Take it with my blessing, asshole," he muttered. He turned over and tried sleep, but couldn't. His dreams were filled with visions of Eric's body lying in an alley, hypos sticking out of his arms, chest ripped open by bullets.

———

Someone was shaking him awake. He groaned as he opened his eyes. Retched at the smell of dried vomit. Took him a moment to realize the smell came from him.

"God, I need a shower," he said to no one in particular. A young uniformed police stood over his bunk. The kid was picture perfect, not a hair out of place or blemish on his uniform. Had *rookie* written all over him.

"You're correct there, Mallen," the kid said. "You smell worse than a bucket of rotting meat. Come on, you're outta here."

"Been three days?" Felt like he had fallen into a black hole for at least a month. As he sat up his vision cleared. He was weak as a baby. How the hell could he get home, or find a meal? Could he even eat? His stomach felt like it was mostly holding its own. Maybe he could.

"Yeah, three days. Inspector Kane wanted me to give you a message: go home, get some rest, and he'll see you later. Can you make it?"

He stood up, wavering on his feet. His apartment was a long-ass way away. Getting on a bus looking and smelling the way he did wasn't an option, no matter how sick he was. He didn't want to be seen by anyone for awhile. "I don't know."

"You got some money on the books. You can catch a cab outside."

"I do?"

"Yeah, we booked it in when we booked you."

Obie. "Okay, thanks. Yeah, that'll be fine."

"Come on then, life awaits."

EIGHT

MALLEN WATCHED AS CHRIS *picked up her bowling ball, went to the line, got set, then proceeded to throw another gutter ball. Her list of curses would've sent a sailor running for cover. He laughed as he got to his feet to take his turn. "I told you," he said as he picked up his bowling ball, "try not to cross your arm across your chest."*

"Oh bite me, Mr. Bowler Man," she said with an answering laugh. He'd always loved how competitive she could be, in everything. Back in college, she'd always competed with him and the other students. Even in bed, it seemed she was competing to see who could have the biggest orgasm. That part, he had to admit, he didn't mind at all.

Eric sat at the score deck. He yelled at Mallen, "Try to keep it in our lane this time, man!"

He laughed at that in reply. Mallen was killing them, as he knew he would. His dad, Ol' Monster Mallen, had been a great bowler, and had taught him all he knew about it. Monster could've gone pro. Had bowled semipro at a couple points in his life but had chosen to knock down bad guys rather than seven-ten splits. But even in something like bowling, the old man had done what he'd usually done: taught his son to never settle for anything less than perfection. Fuck that "second best" crap. All that training and yelling had made Mallen a pretty fair bowler.

Now he set his feet, glanced down the lane, chose that sweet spot on the first set of arrows painted on the lane, and let her rip. The ball sailed down the lane like a laser-equipped missile. The clash of the ball hitting the pins, resulting in a nice, clean strike, drew a wave of groans from Chris and Eric. He smiled as he went and sat down next to Chris, resting his hand on the nape of her neck. He glanced over at Eric.

"Okay, punk," he said in his best Dirty Harry voice, "your move."

"I find myself suddenly hating bowling," Eric said as he got up and went to take his turn.

———

Mallen worked his way through the heavy Friday night crowd in the emergency room at SF General. He'd told Franco only that something had come up, that it involved a bitch he cared about, and that she was sick, taken to the hospital. Franco had been pissed and a bit wary. There were big things going down, and the drug dealer was feeling pressed, from what felt like every point on the compass. He was getting edgy, paranoid, sometimes reminding Mallen of Hitler in his bunker. That feeling was filtering down to everyone in the upper echelons. So this needing to go and see Eric couldn't have come at a worse time, but what the fuck was he going to do? Not go?

He had to.

Eric had been shot trying to stop a liquor store holdup. Called in as a 911, first cop on the scene. Being in the vanguard was the short straw, and that was a fact. Mallen didn't know what had gone down. All he knew from the coded text was that Eric had been shot, and taken to SF General. He had Chris to thank for telling him that much. The brass wouldn't have risked it, but she would know that he'd want to know as soon as possible. Eric's mom would've called Chris, he knew, totally freaked the hell out.

And all Chris had texted was: B1978, X'D @ SFG.911

Mallen got to the reception desk. There was an older guy behind there, with sort of mad-scientist hair and geek glasses. Dark blue, polyester suit jacket. Name badge said Wiggins. "I heard a policeman was brought in. Eric Russ. He okay? I'm a … a friend."

The man looked him over, only a little longer than he should, only because Mallen looked the part of drug-dealing associate. Maybe the guy thought Mallen was here to finish the job, Mallen couldn't say. "Look," he added, very quietly, "I'm a friend. I need to know if he's okay."

The man studied him a few seconds longer, and Mallen wanted to break his face open for making him wait while Eric might be dying. The man named Wiggins looked at his screen. Tapped a couple keys, almost like he had nothing else to do with his day, said, "He's in surgery."

"So, he's alive?"

A nod.

Now Mallen had a quandary. Sit and wait, or go away? He shouldn't be here, he knew, and every moment he was here was dangerous.

"Mark," Phoebe said as she came up, Chris in tow. Chris's look said it all: Oh shit, what the fuck are you doing here? But there was that tiny curl of the lip, the one that always drove him crazy. She was glad he'd come, even though it was dangerous. As Phoebe hugged him, he heard Chris say in a soft voice, almost a whisper, "How's my knight in shining armor?"

"Still around," he replied as Phoebe let him go. He looked at her. "What's the word? The guy at the desk said he was in surgery." He looked around then. "Hal," he said, "where's Hal?"

"He's outside the door that leads to the operating rooms," Phoebe replied.

Of course. Where the hell else would Hal be, with his son in his present situation? Hell, the guy would be pulling out the bullet himself, if he could.

Chris came and put her arm around Phoebe's shoulder. Said, "Phoebe? Can you give me and Mark a moment? I'll be right back."

Phoebe nodded, clutched Chris's hand. Went and sat in one of the neutral gray chairs made for people who had to wait to hear either good news or bad.

Chris watched her until she was out of earshot, then walked to a drinking fountain. He admired her for that, knowing his job, dealing with it, working with him on it. She'd been a great cop's wife. He followed. Watched her take a long drink from the fountain.

"Do you know how he's really doing?" he asked.

"From what the doctors told us a half hour ago, it looks positive."

He could actually feel his entire body relax. When was the last time that had happened? It seemed so long ago now. "I better go, ya know?"

She nodded, automatically checking up and down the hall, like she could see who was bad and who wasn't. "You okay?"

"Yeah. Stevens tells me they're getting ready to move in. Soon. Needs me where I am a little longer."

"A little longer," she echoed.

"Anna? She okay?"

A smirk. "She's taking after her father. Corralled some kids in daycare and told them to come clean about the crayons they'd been holding back. She's a regular Kojack."

"That's actually your side of the family, not mine. Mine are drunkards, liars, and cheats," he said, then quickly swooped in for a kiss. Yeah, it was dangerous, but damn if he didn't miss his wife. "I'll be home soon as this detail is over, I swear. Stevens promised—"

"I know what he promised," she replied. "When he makes good on those promises, then maybe I'll like the asshole."

"Give my best to Phoebe. Tell her I'm sorry I couldn't stay longer. Thanks for the text, and let me know if it goes bad," he added as he gave her shoulder a reassuring squeeze, then turned and walked out through the sliding glass doors and back out into the night.

NINE

MALLEN WAS SEVEN FEET from his door when he realized that something was wrong. It wasn't the sobriety, which felt like an uncomfortable new suit and probably would for some time. No, his door looked different. He approached slowly, checking up and down the hall as he got closer. The lock had been jimmied. Gashes in the wood. Scratches all along the jamb right at lock height.

The street must've heard he'd been locked up and came to pay their respects by robbing him. Joke was on them. He studied the knob for a moment, half just for shits and giggles. Maybe there might be a visible print. Habit, he guessed. Strange how old habits that'd lain dormant for years could suddenly appear out of nowhere thanks to not having a high on. He wondered what other shit was lying dormant that he'd forgotten about. Quietly turned the knob, went inside.

The first thing he noticed was the small white envelope on the floor. To the left of the door. He picked it up and opened it. Eric's funeral announcement. Funeral had been two days ago. He'd been getting clean just as Eric had been getting put in the ground.

How fitting, in its way, maybe? He made a note of the cemetery. Down in Colma. He'd have to bring flowers. Put the envelope away as he then saw the state of his apartment…

Everything was all over everything. All the kites, Anna's kites, had been trashed. Nothing but sticks and torn paper. The first thing that struck him was his anger. Deep and cutting. Whoever did this would be really fucking sorry. They were just kites, man. Why fuck 'em up? The second thing that struck him was that it was just like how it'd been at Jenna's. The same level of violent destruction. They'd even found his little safe-hole in the floor trim, the money tossed all over. Whoever had been here, it certainly wasn't some strung-out motherfucker looking for shooting money.

And the vials were still there, too. In the corner near their hiding place, appearing as if they were cowering, only waiting for their papa to come home and rescue them. His eyes riveted on them. There was nothing else in the world at that moment. Nothing else in the entire misbegotten universe. The Need laughed as it sat on his shoulder, directing traffic to clear the way for him to get to them quickly. He went. Stiff legged. Weak willed. Suddenly drenched in sweat. *The vials…*

And he put his hand on them. They folded into his palm like kittens into a warm blanket. He stared at them. No sound. No world. Grasped them tightly. Went to under the sink. His rig was still there. He grabbed it up…

And he threw the vials down the sink drain. Needle, too. Ran scalding hot water as he flipped the disposal on. There was an incredible screeching noise as the disposal chewed up the metal and glass. He threw the rubber tubing and spoon in the trash, but only after breaking the spoon in two.

Then it was done. A corner turned. *Fuck that shit*, he thought, still sweating, still breathing hard.

But he'd done it.

—————

He got out of the shower, wiped the steam away from the fogged-up mirror. Careworn eyes stared back at him. Could it really have been four and a half years since he got the boot off the force? He thought back to that first day in Narco, and how he'd walked in through Captain Stevens's door like he was walking to his reward. Thought he was so super cool, just like Al Pacino in the undercover cop film *Serpico*. No one was ever going to trip onto who and what he really was.

Then there was the time he'd always blamed for his falling into the world he'd been in for the last four years. Of course he now realized there was nothing to blame, no one to blame, but himself. He'd been in real deep cover, moving up the chain toward a major supplier the entire law enforcement world of California wanted, dead or alive. One of the top guys in Northern California. A slip of the tongue or a hairline crack in the persona you created, and everyone would guess you were a cop. You'd be dog food within the hour. He was getting more and more stressed by the constant threat of being found out. The men at the top didn't do too many drugs. They drank, maybe did some coke or weed, but they kept it in order, under control. It was the conversations about shooting up or being high that worked on him the most. Mallen had only ever smoked weed or drank, and that had been back in college. He'd been constantly worried that he wasn't coming off as a guy who'd gotten high tons of times in the past. There was only one way to really know how it felt. Only one way to carry it off convincingly. Just like an actor would, he figured. A guy had to dive in and live it, right? Experience it. No way Monster Mallen's son would ever take a nosedive and lose his perspective. Not a fuckin' chance.

Of course it hadn't work out that way. And that one moment led him to here: standing in front of the mirror, clean after four and a half years. Those years worked out to about 1,460 days of shooting, give or take. The number alone stunned him. He'd never really thought about it in those terms. Junkies only thought minute to minute, moment by moment. Hours and days were for other people.

He quickly got dressed, pushing away images of needles and The Need. His suit was too big for him now, so he tossed it in the trash. He was no longer a junkie, but he could no longer go back to what he was, either. Instead he changed into his regular clothes, the only ones in the place that were still mostly clean: black sweater and jeans, old army boots, and his only remaining coat—a black wool car coat he'd found draped over a garbage can. The cuffs were worn and the bottom button was missing but, all in all, it was still serviceable. Had to laugh when he was finished tying up his boots and stood there, all in black. Was he in mourning for his now-gone junkie life, or the life he'd had before that?

Would he ever know the answer?

———

It was cold outside, though it was just early afternoon. Clouds hung heavy overhead. Made the sky a dull, flinty gray. A wind picked up, blowing in from the west. It tried to creep in between him and his coat. What was he going to do? The apartment was no good. Had to stay out of there, at least for the short term. Staying clean was all about racking up days, and days start with hours, even minutes. If he could take it hour by hour, one by one, he might just make it.

Mallen glanced up and down the street as he pulled out his last pack of cigarettes. People always told him it was harder quitting smoking than quitting junk. He'd have to put that to the test someday. Lit a cig, if only to stall for time. In the end he decided to go down to the Cornerstone. It was nearby. Yeah, Dreamo was there, but he'd stay out of Dreamo's realm. He just wanted to sit and be quiet. There were so many things to think about. Anna. Chris. Eric. He thought for a moment that maybe he should go to another bar, but then realized there just wasn't any *other* bar for him. He knew Bill, and Bill knew him. He could steer clear of Dreamo. The guy wouldn't take it personally, that was for fucking sure. Well, okay ... maybe he might, a little.

The street felt flat to him as he walked. Probably from seeing it not high. Colors seemed a bit more dull. People seemed a lot more angry and put out. He laughed as he caught himself thinking, *and people don't shoot because ...*? But he knew why now. The air did smell better, even with the exhaust fumes and moldering garbage rotting in the gutter. Okay, he could do this. Again, not one day at a time, but one moment at a time.

He made his way to the Cornerstone. A drink would help. Fighting fire with fire, sure, but baby steps, man, baby steps. One day without a needle was a day won, and that was a fact.

He'd never really noticed before how beat-up the bar looked. Hadn't really come on his radar. He entered and let his eyes adjust to the dimness. The regulars who haunted the place were like dark statues as they sat on their stools. Heads were downcast or staring over at the TV in the upper corner of the room. He went and sat at the far end of the bar, nodding at Bill. The bartender came over, a welcoming smile on his face. Stopped suddenly. Looked him over for a moment. A soft whistle escaped his lips.

"Jesus fucking Christ. Heard you were arrested, Mal. Now I know it's true."

"Yeah? How you know that?"

"You're clean," he replied and laughed in his dry, smoker's cackle. "You did the jail clean, right? Smart man."

"Didn't know it had a name."

"Ain't no original thoughts under the sun, boy-o. I thought them all ages ago." Bill seemed genuinely happy that he was clean. That meant something to him. Another thing he wanted to remember. "Now, what would you like to drink?" Bill said, like some wizard that has all secrets at his command.

"Scotch on the rocks. Double."

Bill went and fixed the drink, Speedy Gonzales quick. Put it in front of him with a flourish. Finished it off with the rare bowl of Chex Mix. "First one's on the house, Mallen."

"Thank you, sir," Mallen told him, meaning it a hundred percent. The drink felt good. Relaxed him. Would it be a slippery slope? All he had to do was imagine Anna, and the answer was a very strong no. *One fucking moment at a time, asshole.*

He was half-through his drink when Bill came back over. "So," the bartender asked quietly, "how does it feel?"

"Feel?"

"Yeah. Being off the stuff."

"Well," he said after a moment, "it's like having a hard-on, but also knowing that you have VD. You want to, but you can't. Well, *shouldn't* would be more accurate, yeah?" He smiled at Bill's raucous outburst of laughter.

"Mal," Bill said after he calmed down, "you better not god-damned go back on the horse because you are *way* more fucking funny this way!" Then he remembered something. Mallen could almost see the man's mind snap an imaginary finger at the memory. Bill went over to the cash register, some ancient beast the previous owner had left behind when the bar had been sold to Bill over fifteen years ago. The man fished through a wad of notes and old receipts, came back with folded piece of notebook paper. Handed it to him. It had his name scrawled on the outside. He didn't recognize the writing. Took a sip of his drink then opened the paper.

Written in block letters, in pencil, the note said: *Vato—My friends inside told me you were now outside. I am praying for you, that your veins run red and clean now, not dirty anymore. If you need help to stay clean, or anything, just call me: 415-555-1929. We were put on this Earth to help one another, as my madre always says. Best, Gato.*

Mallen reread the note again. He wasn't sure what he was feeling, but he could swear it was a mixture of amazement and gratitude. So, good people *did* still exist in this fucking place. That was great.

"You got change for the phone, B?" he asked.

"Yeah, of course, Mal." Mallen dropped a dollar onto the bar and Bill gave him the quarters. He slid off his stool and went to the phone at the back of the hall. He grabbed the receiver and was about to put the quarters in the slot when he began to wonder how Dreamo was doing. He wondered, too, how the dealer would appear to him, now that he was clean. Couldn't hurt to just pop in and say hello, right? Just see how the guy was doing, how business was, and maybe—

"Mallen!" Bill called from the bar. "The fucking phone only works if you put the money in, okay?"

He glanced over at Bill, shaken out of his thoughts. The universe did seem to be trying to keep him clean. Least he could do was play along and see where it would take him. He dropped the quarters in the slot, realizing he would need a cell phone again, if he was really serious about rejoining the world. He dialed Oberon's number first. He wanted to know how Jenna was doing. No answer, so he left a casual message, asking Oberon to let him know about Jenna, if she was still in the hospital, if there were any developments on Eric's case. Tried to make it sound like that's all it was. But it wasn't just that. No, he was still bugged about Eric having his address in his pocket. Why would Eric want to see him enough that he would ask around for his address? He'd been living pretty deep on the downlow, and very few people actually had an address on him. The cops did, naturally. The union did. Chris did, just for emergencies, like if something had happened to Anna. (She would at least try to get in touch with him, even if she didn't really want him seeing her.) People on the street knew him, sure, but they wouldn't have his *address*. Probably would only be able to give a street name to Eric, not even an actual building.

There was something going on. He could feel it, just like he could feel all his old cop instincts coming out of its owner-inflicted hibernation. Follow-up was called for, and that was a fact. He felt that the timing of Jenna's break-in, along with Eric's death and the facts surrounding it bore closer scrutiny. He needed to know why Eric had sought him out, and if it was indeed tied up with the reason he was killed, then maybe he could help solve a crime. Been too long since he'd done that, and that was a fact. As he he stood there, he realized now how much he'd missed solving crimes, helping people.

It was time to do that again. At the least, if he were running the fuck around all the time, looking for answers, it would help to keep The Need out of his head.

Then he made another decision. One he hoped would pan out. He was going to trust someone again. Trust that what they'd said, they'd meant. He would need more than just a cell phone if he were going to search for the answer to the puzzle of Eric's death and his connection to it. He would need help. He dropped the other two quarters into the phone and dialed Gato's number. It rang four times, and he thought it would go to voicemail, which would've been a bummer, as he wanted to keep the momentum going, but then he heard Gato's voice.

"*Hola*," Gato's voice said.

"Gato, it's Mallen. Remember? The guy you helped in the drunk tank? I got your note. Thanks for that. It's appreciated, you know?"

"*Vato!*" Came the enthusiastic reply. Seemed like a day where his heart was just going be warmed up, no matter what. "I'm happy you called me, bro." Then his voice got a little more quiet. "You okay, man? You having ... a struggle?"

"No, no, man ... nothing like that. I just ... I, um ..." He'd never been good at the actual asking for help thing, and now he found himself struggling with how to exactly phrase what only moments ago seemed like such a good damn idea.

"Mallen," Gato said, "just spit it out, bro. We're among friends here, okay? For reals."

"Well," he replied, "I do need some help, actually, but I'm not sure where to start. It would be better to do this as a face-to-face."

"Just tell me where you are, bro, and I'm there."

He smiled at how definite Gato sounded. "Thank you, Gato. I'll make it up to you, man, trust me."

"Ah, forget that. Where are you?"

"At the Cornerstone."

"I'll come and get you out of there, away from that Dreamo dude. I know about him. I can be there in fifteen. Be out front," and the call was over. Mallen put the receiver back on the hook, said his good-byes to Bill, finished his drink, and went outside to wait. So, Gato had wheels. That would help. Sure seemed that things were all falling into line. And in a good way, for a change.

———

Mallen paced up and down the sidewalk in front of the Cornerstone as he waited for Gato to appear. There was a rumble of a very large engine and he turned to see a tricked out 1965 Ford Falcon Futura Sprint, painted a pearlescent white, pull around the corner and glide to the curb. Gato grinned at him and reached over to unlock the passenger door.

And that was when he heard another sound. Tires screeching as rubber burned. He looked back up the street just as all hell broke loose. A black Escalade with tinted windows, passenger side window down, rushed toward them. A gunshot exploded and he felt the slug sail by his right ear and hit the Cornerstone's brick facade, rico-cheting off. He dove for the sidewalk as the Falcon's door kicked open. "Bro!" Gato shouted. "Get in and down!"

He threw himself into the car as another shot rang out, followed by the roar of the Escalade's engine. He glanced just in time to see the huge vehicle tear away down the street, heading toward Van Ness, probably to get lost as soon as fuckin' possible. Gato shoved the Falcon into gear and tore away, the back tires screaming.

"*Mierda*!" Gato said as he tore around the next corner, heading south down Hyde. "Was that for you, bro? I don't think I know anyone that carries a Magnum."

Gato was right. It had been a Magnum. A .44. Been a while since he'd heard one, but once you'd heard the gun in real life, you never forgot it. And the fact that it was a .44 meant only one thing: Griffin had pulled the trigger. Jas had to have been driving, just like he'd always done back when Mallen had known the two killers. Jas always drove, and Griffin always rode shotgun, his silver .44 tucked neatly under the seat. The pride that fucker had carried over that big gun would be hysterical if it'd been any other guy. Griffin was way too big, way too Dirty Harry, and way too on edge. He suspected the bastard of being manic-depressive. It would answer a lot of questions regarding how the man operated, that was for sure. Jas, on the other hand, had always been the smooth one, the one to offer up a smile as he gave you a choice: your life or your balls. Griffin was like looking into a pit of crazed hungry dogs.

The Falcon crossed Market Street, continuing south. "Well, thanks for picking me up, Gato," Mallen said, forcing a smile. The adrenaline was draining from his body, leaving him feeling ragged and shaky. Been ages since someone had shot at him. "I thought you'd enjoy the little hello gift I rigged for you. Hope you did."

Gato laughed softly. "So, what was that about, bro? Do you know?"

"Yeah, unfortunately, I do." They were cruising the 'hoods for him. That would make his life infinitely more uncomfortable and problematic as he searched for the answers to Eric's death. He explained to Gato who Jas and Griffin had been to him, and in doing that, he also had to explain how and why he'd known them in the first place. If he were going to ask this man for help, he had to be a hundred percent up front with him.

Gato listened to it all, nodding from time to time, glancing at him when he told about his years undercover, and how he fell. It felt good, actually, to say it all out loud. Cathartic almost.

"So," he said when he was done, "I totally understand if you want to pull out, Gato. I'm sure you didn't expect this when you wrote me that note. Really, I would understand."

Gato turned the Falcon off of 8th Street and onto Kansas, heading toward 16th. He expected Gato to pull to the curb and tell him to get out. Instead, Gato said, "Friends always show their love. What are brothers for if not to share troubles? That's from the bible, bro. My *padre* tried to weave those words into my soul, you know?"

"Well, it sure looks like he did a good job. He should be proud."

———

Gato had insisted on taking Mallen to Gato's place. Even though Mallen had tried to persuade the man he was quickly learning to regard as a friend that it could dangerous for him, Gato had just shaken his head, telling him that this is how it was going to go down.

It turned out that Gato's place was also his mother's place. Gato and his mother lived in the Mission, off of 24th and Valencia, on the top floor of an old but well-kept building. The Mission district was one of the more troubled parts of the city, as bad as the Tenderloin, but different. Fewer sex offenders here, more gangs. More shootings here, less hard, biting grimness. There was also more unity here in the Mission, like everyone trying to work together to make a go of it. In the Loin, it felt like every man for himself.

Gato's apartment was a large three-bedroom, decorated with a lot of religious imagery. Gato had explained to him on the way over that his mother was very devout, going to Mass every Sunday since she'd been a young girl, over fifty years ago. Esperanza had welcomed Mallen warmly, a woman with now graying hair, coffee-colored eyes, and a beautiful face. There were a lot of care lines in that face now, and a certain amount of sadness, but he could see that when she was younger, she would've been a woman so lovely that men would've easily dueled each to the death for her affections. Esperanza had looked him up and down after Gato led him in through the door, smiling at him, saying only, "*Mi hijo.* Always picking up strays. This one seems to not eat any better than the others. We'll fix that." Then she went off into the kitchen.

Gato had waited until she'd left the room before saying, "You can sleep here safe, bro, trust me. In the morning, we'll get going on helping you with finding out what happened to your friend. You know where you want to start?"

"I think so," he replied as he sat on the couch. If Jenna was out of the hospital, then he had to talk to her first. "Eric had a wife. They seemed mostly on the outs from what I've heard, but I need to talk to her. See what she knows." He leaned back, closing his eyes for a moment, feeling spent. He'd barely slept the three nights he'd been sick in jail, barely ate. He needed some rest, along with a good amount of food. Being clean seemed to be bringing back his appetite. Food and rest would have to be priority number one, no matter how much he wanted to be out on the hunt for answers.

But before that hunt resumed, and after he recharged his batteries, he needed to do one other thing. Something more important than any of it.

He had to see his daughter.

TEN

ANTHONY SCARSDALE ZIPPED UP his fly. Gave the long-legged hooker on the bed a well-earned tip. Grabbed his coat, left the motel room. He felt good. Drained from top to bottom. *What a mouth she had*, he thought as he walked down the street to the bus stop. He ignored the requests for change from the homeless and offers of crack from the dealers. Decided to stand at the bus stop and not sit when he noticed someone had vomited right in front of it. Went as far as he could upwind from the large splash of pale liquid and what looked like a half-eaten hotdog. *Some fuckheads are really fucking disgusting*, he thought with a shake of his head.

He didn't realize that he was being followed. Up the street half a block sat a small two-door hatchback the color of old memories. The bus finally came, and he got on. Flashed the driver his mother's handicapped pass he'd taken out of her purse earlier in the day while she napped. Went and sat all the way at the back, still thinking about the hooker. Grinned as he remembered how her eyes got so damn big when he pulled off his pants. She was really impressed with his dick. She loved every last thing they did together. He liked trying to make it nice for them, what with them having to fuck all damn day with a bunch of guys who were probably total fucking losers. Him, he just didn't want the attachment of a full, or even part-time, relationship. This way was easier. Less complicated.

After the forty-five-minute bus ride, he got off at his stop. Went the three blocks to his mother's house. It was nice being home, but part of him wanted out. That of course meant getting a job, and no one was hiring. Well, not hiring him, at least. Not with his history. At least mom had set up the garage room nice for him.

His mother's house was a faded pink row job deep in the Outer Sunset. Out far enough where the salt air rusted everything that had any metal in it. Scarsdale let himself in the door next to the garage. Went past his mother's old brown Buick. Frowned as he passed the rust bucket. She needed a new car. But of course she'd never put out the dough for one. She never put out money for anything nice or fun. The idea of finding her bank book and just going out and buying her a new ride had crossed his mind, but he didn't want her to explode and kick him out. He needed this roof over his head. And the allowance she gave him. Just enough for drinking on weekends and a hooker every ten days or so. Life could be worse. Heck, it *had* been worse. More simple, sure, but a hell of a lot worse.

He had no idea that the hatchback had followed him all the way home and was now parked at the end of the block. It would be there for another hour before the driver realized Scarsdale would not be going out again, and so drove away.

ELEVEN

Mallen sat on a bench at the Marina Green and watched the bay. The morning sky was gray, heavy. He had to admit, however, that it never looked so damn beautiful. Maybe being clean could do that for a guy.

Gato had been up already, ready to go, when he'd woken up on the couch. After a much-needed shower, Esperanza cooked him some breakfast, and then he called Chris to see if she could swing a visit between father and daughter. She'd given him some attitude about his request at first. It wasn't a scheduled visit day, plus it was way last minute. He knew she'd have every right to go tell him to fuck himself. In the past he'd never cared about making all the visits all the time anyway. Of course she wondered why all the urgency. In the end, though, and probably because of something in his voice she'd picked up on, she said she'd do it. Gato even drove him over, Mallen telling him thanks, and that he would call once he was done with his visit. He was just getting out of the car when Gato stopped him. "What is it?" he said.

For an answer, Gato reached under the dashboard, right below the glove box. There was a soft click of metal and he came out with a small automatic. Mallen recognized it as a .22 caliber. A Walther P-22.

"No," Mallen said, "I can't take that."

Gato shook his head. "You're not thinking this through, *vato*. Those *pendejos* after you are armed for bear. This isn't much, but it might save your life."

"I can't walk around with a stolen gun in my pocket, man!"

"Mallen," his new friend said, stern like he was a schoolteacher trying to explain the obvious, "you think I'd let you do something like that? You think I'm that dumb? This little one is registered, trust me. It won't show up as stolen. It will show up as a black hole. As a fantasma."

He looked down at the small black weapon. It'd been how long since he'd carried a weapon? Jesus...

But there it was. He couldn't argue with the fact that he would feel much safer with it on him. He'd have to risk it. With Jas and Griffin out there? Hell yeah, he should fucking be armed. He took the gun. Put it in his coat pocket. Smiled. "Thanks, man. I don't know how you manage your life, but I'm certainly glad you manage it in the manner that you do."

Gato started the Falcon. "Call me," he said as he put the car in gear and Mallen shut the door. He watched the Falcon rumble away, wishing they'd never stopped making cars that looked that cool.

He went over to the nearest bench and pulled out the bag of bread crumbs Esperanza had given him at his request. As usual, there were a lot of seagulls mulling about, looking for scraps. Out in the ocean, he caught a glimpse of a sea lion's head as it came up for air. Probably one of the colony that lounged and slept over at the docks by Pier 39, one of the ones that had turned into an attraction there years ago. A few families were out, walking along the path that led from Fort Mason all the way to the yacht slips, and then beyond to Chrissy Field. Only a handful of cars were parked in the lot. The occupants looked like they were either napping or partying. He sat there and fed the pigeons, watching them fight with the seagulls, as he waited for Chris and Anna. He'd thought about finding a kite on his way here. Gave it up when he realized he didn't want Anna to fly any kite he didn't make. Soon he would start again on that special kimono kite. Then they would come down here, in the sunshine, and fly it all day.

He heard a car pull up behind him. Turned to see Chris's steel gray BMW. Anna was out immediately, running to him. "Daddy! Daddy!" she screamed. Her hair was longer than he remembered. More honey colored. He was so glad she didn't get his dark hair and eyes. Both were just a shit brown. Her eyes though? A beautiful blue-silver.

He got down on one knee. Embraced her tightly. It was going to be okay now; he was holding his little girl.

"You didn't shave!" she squealed as he rubbed his cheek on hers. She giggled. Tried to get away. He straightened up as Chris approached. Her hair was now cut in a short bob that accented her sharp features. Looked like she still worked out. A stab of regret got him then—he'd really screwed it all up. All he could do now, he figured, was to just be there for them. If they'd allow it.

Chris studied his face as she approached. "You look … different," she said in a guarded tone. He'd let her down so many times. Couldn't blame her if she couldn't believe him capable of change, or ever getting clean.

"I am," he said with a definite voice.

She stared at him for a moment. He held her gaze.

"What happened?" she said.

"Long story. Safe to say, I've had a life-altering series of events take place."

Worry crossed her face, and she leaned down to talk to Anna. "Honey, why don't you go sit on that bench for a moment?"

"But I want to see Daddy," she replied.

"It's okay, babe," he told his little girl. Handed her the bag of bread crumbs he'd been feeding the pigeons with. "Why don't you take over for me?"

She smiled. Took the bag. "Don't let them poop on you," he warned.

"Daddy, you're gross!" she told him as she went to the bench.

After she was out of earshot, Chris said, "Life-altering events?" Added in a voice just above a whisper, "AIDS?"

"No, not that," he replied. Wondered if perhaps one day that might be the case though. He should get tested. "Something else. I can't get into it right now, but I'm finally on the right path, Chris. Really."

Studied him for a moment. A faint smile of relief there. "I'm glad for you, then. You had me worried there. I always wanted her to grow up with you in her life. You know that."

"I do."

She paused. "How long has it been?"

"Long enough for me to believe it'll take."

"That's good, Mark. Real good. I hope so."

On an impulse, he reached out. Took her hand for a moment. "I'm sorry, Chris. About everything. I mean that. If I could go back, make different decisions? I so would."

She seemed stunned by the heartfelt tone in his voice. Took her a moment to answer. "Thank you for saying that. It means a lot, to hear that. Thank you. Are you sure you can't tell me what happened?"

"It's about Eric."

"Eric? I didn't know you two were talking."

"We weren't." He then told her about Oberon's visit, and his visit to Hal and Phoebe's. Chris went and leaned on the hood of her car, arms across her chest, shaking her head in disbelief.

"I can't believe it. Eric? Eric got into the same trouble you did? I had no idea. Why? How'd that happen?"

"I don't know. Hadn't heard a word about it, at all. Oberon didn't say, either. I'm actually surprised you didn't know. I thought you and Phoebe were close."

"We are. Well, were, I guess. She'd stopped calling a while back. Stopped returning my calls. We hadn't spoken now in years, but I just figured that … well, it was because of you and … what happened." She kicked at the gravel. "I need to go see them."

"I'm sure they'd appreciate it."

A nod. She looked over at their daughter. He knew what she was thinking: what if they one day lost Anna? "I'll see them today," she said firmly. "Do what I can."

He'd always loved that about her. That she could be so strong when the chips were down. Again the stab of regret. Like a spear in his gut. He'd lost a great partner in this woman.

"Look, I'm going to go talk with her for a bit, okay?" he said.

She nodded again, then reached into her bag. Pulled out a paperback. "You have your time with her. All you want. I'll be over there at the next bench." She started to walk away. Stopped. Turned back. "You need anything? Clothes? A job?"

"I've sorta got a job right now, actually, but thanks."

She looked shocked at first. That tiny smile curled the corner of her mouth for a moment. That smile always got to him still, right to the bone. "Well, keep up the good work," she said.

He went and sat down next to Anna. His daughter laughed as he grabbed her up. Squeezed her tightly, spilling the crumbs all over the ground. Made every pigeon and seagull in the area extremely happy.

TWELVE

Chris had offered to drive him back to his place, but he declined. Told her he needed the exercise. Truth was, they'd never been to his street or his place, and he just didn't want them to see it. She probably had an idea, of course, but he just couldn't do it. Didn't want Anna to see the Loin, that was for sure.

He had Chris drop him off over on California, in front of Grace Cathedral. It was all down hill from there, anyway. Kissed Anna goodbye, told them both he'd see them soon. Stood and watched Chris drive away down the street, his daughter waving at him from the back window.

The walk felt like nothing. He couldn't remember ever feeling so fucking good. Like he'd made a significant move to getting his normal life back. One more step in what was sure to be a long-ass journey.

Mallen walked the blocks at a brisk pace. Just another guy hurrying on his way home, or maybe to a drug deal. As he neared his block though, he slowed, beginning to walk a patrol pattern that would keep him moving against traffic on the one-way streets in this part of town. Saw no black Escalades, and no sign of Jas or Griffin on the streets.

Once he got to his building, he went quickly inside, jogging up the stairs instead of waiting for the derelict, practically useless elevator. Couldn't remember if the building even had an on-site manager anymore. It'd been so long since he'd last cared about the state of anything, or anybody. Now he was beginning to wonder. The elevator. The halls. Eric. His broken-down studio. *It isn't too late,* he told himself. There was time to fix his life. Start over, now, before he was swallowed up and shit out the other end.

He came in and shut the door. Took off his coat. Tossed it over the edge of one of the folding chairs at the card table. He then quickly gathered up all of Anna's money, which he'd forgotten the last time he'd been here. Rolled it back up and stuck it in its hiding hole. Went and fixed himself a drink. The only thing he had was some cheap whiskey he couldn't even remember buying. Checked the freezer. No ice cubes. *Well, ice cubes just take up space, right?* He poured a double.

He tuned the cheap AM/FM radio he'd bought at a dollar store over on Pine Street to the college jazz station. Sat on the couch, trying to relax. Suddenly felt The Need. Badly. Took a drink. Took a breath. He told himself it would be okay. It would be … be a wave that he could surf, until he either made it to shore or wiped the fuck out.

Fuck it. It would be what it would be.

He'd just started on his second drink, way lost in a daydream, when a loud knock at the door startled him out of it. *That would not be Jas and Griffin*, he reassured himself. Those two would've just broken in, rained lead, and left. And if they'd gotten the apartment number wrong, oh well. Mallen looked around for a moment. Wasn't sure he was really in his apartment, he'd been so lost in his dream. He'd been imagining he was with Chris and Anna again. They were at Golden Gate Park, way out west near the soccer fields. There was a good wind. He and Anna were flying the kimono kite. A happy family. Could that happen again? Should he dare to hope?

There was another knock. Insistent. He could swear it was Oberon's knock. Got to his feet and went to the door to answer it.

It was Oberon all right. The first thing he noticed was how tired the detective looked. Mallen beckoned him inside with a smile. "Can I get you something to eat?" he asked. "I have some old bread that can made into old, dry toast. Maybe you want some vanilla ice cream?" Now that he was clean, he realized he would need to go buy some real, actual groceries at some point. The thought didn't thrill him.

"No coffee?" Oberon asked hopefully.

"Sorry. Not yet," he said with a grin. "Come back during the third week of my being clean, and I'll fix you a bacon and cheese omelet that would rival Han's over on Sutter." Went and sat on the sagging couch. "What brings you out this way? You look beat, Obie. Catch another case?"

"I was just in the neighborhood. Thought I'd drop by for a cup of joe."

"Oh yeah?" he replied, knowing full well that was bullshit. Oberon would come to it, in his own time.

It was then that Oberon noticed the state of the place. "What happened, Mark? You get into an altercation with your supplier?"

So *that* was it. Oberon had come by to see if he'd fallen back into his old ways.

"No," he replied. Pushed up his sleeves and held out his arms. "Go ahead, man. Check 'em."

"Stop," Oberon replied. "I came by yesterday to see how you were getting on after being released. Didn't find you home, and well … can't blame an old Police for feeling a bit cynical from time to time, can you?" He went and sat down in one of the rusty folding chairs that Mallen had at one time called part of his dining room set. "I'm very glad to see that it seems to be holding, Mark."

"Thanks. I have to say, Obie, that I owe it all to you."

"I will come and collect on that, one day, I assure you," the cop replied with a slight smile.

"And I'll pay off with a grin, trust me. Hey, you got my message about Jenna, right? She home okay?"

A nod. "Attacker struck from behind as she came into her apartment. Must've interrupted whatever they were doing."

Mallen wondered how much time to give her before he went and saw her. The more time he waited, the more she might forget, but he didn't want to push her, either. Not with Eric's death so raw and recent. "I know you, Obie," he said, "I know that look. You caught another case. A bad one."

"I must being going through some sort of karmic comeuppance. Just a nice young man with a wife and new baby at home. Takes two in the back as he's on his knees, probably begging for his life."

"Not your week, is it?"

"Son, not my lifetime."

"Anything to go on?"

"Nothing. Everyone liked him. He'd done time, in Folsom, but was actually turning his—no, *had* turned his life around. I'll just have to keep digging."

"You need a partner."

Oberon laughed, but there was no mirth in it. "That would be taken under 'budgetary consideration', I'm sure."

He found himself happy to be talking to a cop about a case again, after so long. "Were there any signs of torture? Like maybe a vendetta getting paid off? Was your victim beaten at all before he got it?"

"Like I said: he was married."

Mallen laughed. "The confirmed bachelor rears his ugly head and spits at the world. Nice."

Oberon bowed from the waist as he got to his feet. "'I have always thought that every woman should marry, and no man.'"

"Woody Allen?"

His friend registered a look of disappointment on his face. "Disraeli, of course." He passed by Mallen's coat hanging over the edge of the other chair, accidentally knocking it to the floor. The coat landed with a dull thump. All he could do was watch as Oberon picked up the coat to put it back, only to have the .22 Gato had given him fall out onto the floor with a crash that sounded like the shot heard round the world.

Oberon slowly bent down. Picked up the pistol. Eyed it for a moment. Smelled the barrel. "Well, at least it hasn't been fired recently. Would you like to explain this here, or downtown?"

"Come on, it's not mine. I'm just holding it for a friend."

"For shame, Mark. That was quite poor."

"It's the truth. Well, mostly the truth. Look, it belongs to a friend. He's going through some things. I don't want him to get into trouble, so I took it from him." His insides cringed at the lying, but he didn't know what else to do. He thought about telling Oberon about Jas and Griffin, but there was a little voice inside that told him to keep quiet, that he could work it all out on his own. And that voice also told him that if he involved Oberon, then he knew there were other people on the force who would think badly of Oberon for helping him in the first place. He couldn't do that to his friend, not when he was so close to retirement. He knew full well how the hard the game was played in the department. No, he couldn't do anything that would maybe, even slightly, hurt Oberon.

The cop stared at him for a moment, then back down at the gun. "And you're just keeping it in your coat pocket for safe keeping? Is that what you're telling me?"

"This just happened. I haven't had a chance to find a safe place for it."

Oberon dumped the coat on the couch. "I know a very safe place for it." Checked it for bullets. Whistled softly. "And fully loaded, too. How joyful."

"Look, just trust me on this one, okay? I'm just trying to … help out a certain man who is now not among the living. That's all."

"Ah!" Oberon responded. "You mean like when I helped you to the extent that I risked my pension to have you put in the drunk tank so you could clean the junk out of your veins? You mean like that?"

He looked Oberon dead in the eye as he said, "Yeah. Just like that. Trust me on this one, okay? I won't let you down, Oberon. I won't."

There was an uncomfortable silence as both men looked at each other, trying to gauge what the other one would do if things ran one way or another. After a long moment, Oberon came over. Handed the gun to him. "I'm trusting you, Mark, more than I've ever trusted another human being in my life. If that gun comes onto my radar again, especially if it was used in a crime, I will fall on you like the devil himself. Are we clear?"

"Completely."

"If Mother Mallen could see me now," Oberon said as he shook his head and went to the door, "she'd have my hide for letting you keep that thing. Don't make me regret it, Mark."

THIRTEEN

"You're making me regret this, Mark," Chris said quietly as she stirred the cup of coffee in front of her. "Can't you go back to regular police work?"

They sat in the diner that belonged to the Seal Rock Inn, a small motel way out at the west end of the city, overlooking the Pacific. They sat huddled together at a small table, the one farthest away from the windows. The meeting place had been his call, one he'd made on the fly. It wasn't great, and he couldn't be seen being here for long, not in this place, not with a woman who was so obviously not a hooker or a pusher. But she'd sent the text, using the code they'd together set up before he went underground. She'd sent him the code that meant it was desperate, and he'd texted back to meet at the first place he could think of that would be safe, using the least amount of time.

"Look," he told her, "I'm close now. I'm moving up the chain. I'm close."

She shook her head. "When you said you wanted to be cop? Back after college? I thought you'd be in homicide or something, capturing murderers. Maybe even moving up, getting promoted, so you wouldn't even be out on the streets with all the crazy, dangerous people."

"I know," he answered. "But to get to that, I need to make a case for myself and my abilities. That's this work, Chris, the work I'm doing now." He sat back. Looked out the windows at the ocean. What he wouldn't give then to just be on a boat with her and Anna, sailing away to a new life.

"What if something happens to you? What if something happens to Anna, and I can't reach you?" She shook her head. Took a sip of her coffee. "It's too dangerous. I'm not sure I'm cut out for you being on this duty."

"Come on," he said, reaching out and stroking her hair, "you know that even if I agreed with what you were saying, you know it wouldn't be right away, right? I just can't… disappear. And do you think Stevens, or the guys above that fucker would let me just walk away? Now? I can't, Chris." He took her hand. Held it to his chest. "I promise you, once this case is over, I'll see what I can do to get pulled… to other duty. But right now? Right now I need to bring in these guys and send them to jail." That's what Monster Mallen would've done, and that was a fact.

She looked into his eyes then. Really studied them. He'd let her into his life more than any other person that he'd ever known. Even more than his own parents. If there was one person who could read him, it would be her.

After a long moment, she looked away. Took a sip of her coffee. Looked out the window. "Okay, Mark," she said, "I'll wait for this to be over."

FOURTEEN

SCARSDALE FINISHED HIS LATE lunch. Put his plate in the sink. He'd hear about it if he didn't.

"Don't forget to wash the dishes!" his mother yelled from the den. He sighed heavily. Hopefully loud enough that she'd hear. Turned on the water and proceeded to quickly wash the chipped plates, old glasses, and mottled silverware. In a small act of defiance, he left a string of spaghetti on the plate he'd used. *Have fun chiseling it the fuck off, Ma.*

He decided to go to the bar, the house suddenly too small to hold him. Went downstairs to his room. Put on some different pants. Combed his thinning hair back. Dug out the free sample of men's cologne he found in last month's *Penthouse*. Reached under his shirt and rubbed it all over his chest and stomach. You never could tell: maybe he'd be able to score a bitch for free. Stranger things had happened. Left the house. Walked off down the street.

The Cove was located fifteen long blocks from the beach, but the decorations tried hard to make you think the surf was washing up on the doorstep. The place was thinly populated. Mostly the usual crowd of burnouts and old Chinese men. That depressed him, as that meant there'd be no way to pick up some tail. All the women who usually drank here knew him.

He went to the bar and ordered a beer. Sat there for about an hour, first drinking his beer, then moving up to shots of whiskey. It was toward the end of that hour that he figured out his problem. It didn't make him happy, but what else was there to do? Yeah … the only way out was to start dealing again. Fuck his mother. It would be *her* fault if he got caught again. Determination filled him up. Fuck it. The best way to get the stake he would need would be to steal it from her. He took another shot as he wondered how to go about doing that. Goddamn it … it would serve her right, the bitch. Why did women have to be such bitches all the damn time? He wasn't a bad guy. Only had a bad hand dealt to him. If his father had stayed around, maybe it would've been different. But hell, could anyone blame the guy? Look at what he married. Poor, stupid asshole. He was getting more and more angry the longer he sat there. Now he really wanted to find a hooker. Didn't have the dough, though. So, like an ultimate defeat, he hoisted himself off the barstool and left.

It was late afternoon and cold. Fog was rolling in, sending wisps and tendrils down the street, ahead of the main curtain of gray he could see heading into the city. He had no idea what time it was and didn't really care. The ocean air cleared his head somewhat. He decided to walk for a bit. Turned west, heading down toward the beach. Maybe he'd run into some people partying there, and they'd invite him to join in. That would be nice. He could tell them horror stories of prison. They'd think he was a tough motherfucker. The chicks there would dig that. He'd be "dangerous." That usually excited the bitches.

He walked slowly, hands in pockets, enjoying the air. Being locked up could do that for a guy. Make him enjoy the sea air more. His shoulders sagged at the thought of being inside because he really didn't want to start dealing again. Because that might land him right back in prison again. Fuck that shit. He'd had enough of prison to last him a lifetime. And he liked fucking girls, not guys. Fucking guys to unwind was not something he wanted to do again, ever. The beach was coming up ahead, and he smiled. It was freedom, the beach. That's what it meant to him, anyway.

He didn't notice the two-door sedan pull to the curb ahead of him. He was lost in thoughts of freedom and women. When the blow slammed into the back of his head, the only thing he could think was that he was about to be mugged.

FIFTEEN

MALLEN LEFT HIS PLACE after having another drink, deciding he needed to get that cell phone. He had just enough to buy a phone and still make it to the first of the month, if he was careful. He rued the cost of the phone, but if he got a cheap burner, that wouldn't send him to the poorhouse.

He went over to the corner liquor store. Seemed every corner in this area had a liquor store on the corner. The Indian man behind the counter eyed him dubiously as he entered. Watched him approach like he was watching a rabid pit bull come over to him.

"Just need a cell phone, man," he told the guy.

The man nodded. Silently went and unlocked a case behind the counter. Pulled out a burner and then looked over his shoulder at Mallen, a questioning look on his face as he pointed to the top-up cards. Jesus, couldn't the guy even bother to fuckin' speak? Mallen just pointed to the cheapest card. The man grabbed one and the phone and held onto them as he rang them up on the register.

"Also need a pint of Jim Beam, thanks," he added. The reaction was like he'd begged the guy to blow him. There was even a sigh as the man pulled the pint off the shelf, acting like it weighed a thousand pounds. Held that, too, as he rang it all up. He was definitely *not* going to put any of it down until he saw the dollars. Mallen threw down a couple twenties and only then was able to pick up his new phone and booze. The man behind the counter didn't even say thank you.

As soon as he was outside, Mallen broke out the phone and booted it up. Stuck the bottle of JB in his right coat pocket, the gun again residing in the left one. He topped up the cell and quickly dialed Gato's number. Got voicemail and left his new number, telling Gato to congratulate him for joining the twenty-first century again.

He was half a block from his house when he heard a voice behind him say, "Hey man, you got a cig?"

The voice was recognized immediately, just as he immediately recognized the fact that he was too slow as he spun around, hand digging for the gun in his coat pocket. He never saw Griffin's huge fist as it rocketed in, smashing him in the temple, stunning him as he fell to the ground. Griffin grabbed up a handful of his collar and yanked him halfway off the sidewalk. As his vision cleared, he noticed that Griffin now sported a scar that ran down the side of his face.

"You look even more like Frankenstein now, Griff," he croaked at the huge man. Griffin looked like his wiring shorted out for a second, he was so fucking surprised at Mallen's not whimpering for mercy. Maybe that's what he expected from someone he thought was a junkie.

That didn't stop him from slamming Mallen in the mouth though. Mallen tasted blood. A lot of it. He spit it out before he choked.

"Hey, Mr. Undercover Man," Griffin said to him, then bounced Mallen's head off the sidewalk. Mallen's vision went like snow on a

TV screen for a second. He thought he was going to die. That the silver .44 would come out now and he'd be shot in the head and left for dead.

But then Griffin said to him, "Hope you're doing well, Mr. Undercover Fucker, because me and Jas have a lot of fun in store for you. Prepare to enter hell, you lying sack of shit." This was followed by a series of blows Mallen no longer even felt because he was numb all over from the beating he'd already taken. He couldn't even register the fact that he wasn't going to die today.

SIXTEEN

ANTHONY SCARSDALE NO LONGER had to worry about money. He lay on his back, sightless eyes staring up at the foggy sky above the crumbled ruins of the Sutro Baths, a huge indoor pools facility that opened in 1896 only to burn down sixty years later. Anthony had been found lying on the edge of the cliffs overlooking what was left of the old baths' concrete foundations. A woman out jogging with her dog on the path above had spotted the body. There was a bullet hole in the back of Scarsdale's head, the blood having stained the dirt and pine needles black.

Oberon stood next to DeJesus as she went through her routine and wondered briefly if his comment to Mallen about karma had been correct after all. Watched as DeJesus pulled Scarsdale's wallet from the corpse's back pocket, then hold it out to him. He took it in a gloved hand. Riffled through it. Inside were sixteen dollars, an ID, and a business card for a parole officer named Denise Lewis. There were also a few scraps of paper with phone numbers or email addresses scrawled on them. No names. He looked down at the body.

There was no blood pattern around to indicate that Scarsdale had met his end here. The fallen, dried pine needles created a carpet that hid all signs of passing. He was probably shot somewhere else and dumped here. And pretty quickly, too, if he was still bleeding from the wound enough to pool under him like it had. The kill site couldn't be too far away. He'd get some uniforms to search around.

Oberon glanced again at the parole officer's card. Jotted down the name and phone number. "Madam DeJesus, can your office let me know as soon as possible if this bullet is from the same weapon that did in Kaslowski?"

"Sure thing. Looking at the entry hole made me think the same as you."

"That, and the fact this gentleman here might also have a history that involves one or more of our criminal institutions." He pulled out a plastic bag and put the wallet inside. Logged the time and date on the outside. He handed it off to a nearby forensics tech and then walked over to the edge of the cliff overlooking the ocean. Pulled out his phone. Dialed Denise Lewis's number. Waited as it rang.

"Officer Lewis," said the voice on the other end of the line. Crisp and businesslike.

"Hello, this is detective Oberon Kane, SFPD, Homicide. Are you assigned to an"—he checked the name he wrote down—"Anthony Scarsdale?"

There was a sigh. "What did that asshole do now?"

"Well, he got himself killed sometime last evening."

After a moment she said, "I can't say I'm surprised by this."

"Oh? And why is that?"

"I guess I just didn't believe he'd make it on the outside. He was having trouble finding work. Was unable to make any sort of connection with the right people. That usually leads to a return to prison."

"What did he go in for?"

"Assault and battery, with some drug dealing thrown in for shits and giggles. Went in an addict, came out clean-ish, as far as I know."

"Was his victim a woman or a man?"

"A woman. He had a lot of trouble forming relationships with them, from what his psych eval said."

"Where did he serve his time?"

"Folsom."

That tugged at him. How could both victims have criminal records *and* serve at the same facility? It could be a coincidence, but then again…

"Can I have a look at his file? I'd like to spend some time with it."

There was a pause on the other end. "Well," she said, "if you don't mind signing a paper taking responsibility for it while it's in your possession, then sure."

"I'll be by your office in about an hour."

"Okay," she said and hung up. Was there a connection between the two killings? It was a theory he was certainly going to entertain, as it would make his life easier, and he could use a little of that right about now. He walked back to the body to see if DeJesus had anything else for him.

———

Mallen slowly opened his eyes. Took a moment for them to come into focus. He'd been propped up against a building. About six feet away he could make out a splatter pattern of blood. His. The side of his face was on fire. His left eye was already swollen up, the vision not super clear. The right side of his rib cage felt like an elephant has danced on it. He carefully sent signals out through his body. They all came back: no broken bones. That was something anyway.

There was a homeless woman standing nearby, leaning on her shopping cart. She looked about forty, but if she'd been on the streets for any length of time, she could actually be twenty. Stared at him as he tried to get to his feet and failed.

"You're Mallen," she said matter of fact.

He nodded his head. Regretted it. "You the one that propped me here?"

"Yeah."

"Thanks. How you know my name?"

"You arrested my brother once. Years ago. I was a teenager then."

"I did? What'd your brother do?"

"Dealt drugs."

He checked to see if his wallet, phone, and gun were still on him. They were. So was the bottle. He looked over at her curiously. "If I arrested him, why'd you help me?"

"He was also fucking me, that's why. Felt I owed you one."

Had Griffin missed the gun, or just not given a shit? *Probably the latter*, he thought as he pulled a twenty out of his wallet. One of his last for the month. The effort alone made every muscle in his body scream in anger. "You know what?" he said as he held it out to her, "I think I'm still in your debt." She came over. Took the bill. Folded it up very small, disappearing it inside one of the dirty and torn layers she wore.

"What's your name?" he said.

"Trina."

"Well, Trina," he said as he got to his feet with a groan, "you ever get into trouble with anyone, over anything, go to the Cornerstone. Talk to Bill. Tell him I told you to do it. He'll let me know."

"Okay," she said. With that she turned and pushed her cart off down the street. He watched her go for a moment. Got out his phone and dialed Gato's number. He got voicemail again, which made him nervous. Left a message about what had happened, and to watch his back as they might be looking for the Falcon and its owner too. Gave a description of Griffin. Then he tried to text him, but couldn't focus so well. Had to leave the message at "call." Well, so much for his little foray outside. The Need knocked at his door then, in response to the pain. He was already very fucking tired of feeling pain, and he'd only been feeling it again for like three or four days. Took a deep breath, reminded himself he'd gotten off easy, all things considered. Hell, if they wanted to play him like a mouse in a box, it would buy him enough time to figure out how to bring those two fuckers down, and hard.

He made his way back to the corner liquor store. There was a small section behind the counter filled with all sorts of first-aid and emergency supplies. *A guy could get in a lot of fights around here*, he mused. If the Indian guy behind the counter had thought before that Mallen was a piece of shit from the neighborhood, he only had his opinion reinforced now. Mallen asked the man for alcohol, bandages, and aspirin. He couldn't wait to get the chance to toast his recent success. Hell, he'd survived the first beating he'd taken in a hell of a long time. Why not celebrate that fact in style?

As he approached his building, his steps slowed, then stopped all together. Being in his place didn't seem like such a good idea now. As he stood there, he realized the best thing to do would be to just keep off the grid as much as he could. That would be tough, but if he made it hard for Jas and Griff to find him, maybe they'd just give up for awhile, give him some breathing space. The space he'd need to figure out about Eric. He turned and headed off to the Cornerstone. If it weren't for Dreamo's office being there, he'd be able to maybe sleep on the floor for a couple nights. As it was, he'd have to figure something else out. Maybe only for the short term, if he were lucky.

———

The Cornerstone wasn't very busy. There were only few people inside. Not even the regulars seemed to be in attendance. Bill sat on the last stool, looking dejected, a couple empty glasses in front of him. He glanced up to see who had entered his world. Went back to staring at his drink when he saw who it was. Mallen strode over. Slid onto the empty stool next to the bartender. "How're you doing?" he asked.

"Been better." It was then that Bill could really see the effects of Griffin's work. "Jesus, Mallen . . . what the hell happened to you?"

"Long story," he replied as he pulled out the alcohol and bandages from the plastic bag. Looked again at the sparse crowd as he made his way to the bar mirror to clean off the blood from his face. "What did you do? Raise prices?"

"I should be so lucky," came the reply. "As long as motherfuckers drop in and shove people around, everyone will stay away. You know how word spreads around this hood." Bill took a drag from his glass. "Come on, kid, what the fuck happened to you? You need a doctor?"

"No, I'm good. Just need to clean up." Bill's comment about people coming and shoving people around surprised him. The Cornerstone had always seemed to be neutral territory. No one ever seemed to pull shit in this place. "Who was playing the heavy hand, man?"

"Why don't you tell me?"

"Tell you?" The words were barely out of his mouth when it hit him. Jas and Griffin. It was strange though. Not like them to rile up the herd animals, even for sport. It bothered him they'd shifted from known tactics.

Bill nodded. "I thought you'd know them."

"Why's that?"

"They asked about you."

He tried to put up some indifference. "Yeah?" He threw a couple red-stained paper towels into the trash. Reached over and took Bill's drink away from him. Drained it, then pulled out his cigarettes. "What'd they ask?"

Bill leaned over the bar for the bottle of well whiskey and re-filled his glass. "Oh, they asked about what your favorite movies were, did you like walks on the beach, what size your fucking shoe was. What do you think they fuckin' asked? They wanted to know where to find you."

Mallen grabbed a nearby glass to use as an ashtray. "They can go fuck themselves," he said.

"I don't think that's in the playbook, Mallen."

"Probably right."

"Anyway, I didn't tell 'em nothing. What I could say? I don't know where you live. Never wanted to know."

Jas and Griffin would have to wait. Even if meant letting those two bastards run around after him, it had to wait. Mallen checked to see no one else was listening. Moved closer to Bill. Leaned on the bar. "B, I need to talk to you about something, okay?"

"Why? What for? What the fuck are you involved in? It is those two pricks, isn't it? Shit…"

"Unhitch your bra, all right? It's not like that. I'm trying to, well… find out what happened to a friend."

"You?" came the reply. "You have friends?"

He grinned, knowing that the bartender was just upset at being fucked with by guys he couldn't touch. That would've fucked with anybody, anytime. He told Bill what had happened to Eric, falling into drugs and then trying to get back out. Told him about how Eric had died. He told Bill what Eric's name was, described him. "You ever hear about another cop that went needle, like me? There can't be that many, right? You hear a lot, B. You ever hear the name Eric Russ?"

Bill gave it his best shot. Thought about it for a long moment. But in the end, he ended up only shaking his head. "Sorry, Mal. Only cop that did that I know of is—was—you." Bill looked down into his drink again, and Mallen could tell something was tugging at him.

"What? What is it?" Mallen said. "Something come to you?"

For an answer, Bill only glanced over his shoulder, over at the hallway that led past the bathrooms to the storeroom. "He might know."

Dreamo. Yeah, how funny that it would come down to that, right? Now he'd have to walk in there and ask his old dealer for a favor, rather than some vials of heroin. He would've laughed at it all, if someone had told him the story. *Shit. On. Me.*

"You think he might know something? Really?"

Bill almost looked hurt at the question. "You fucking think I'd even suggest it, otherwise? Look, if this guy Eric is as important to you as you say, well ..." He left the rest unsaid.

For an answer, he patted Bill on the shoulder. A brotherly expression, and he hoped it came off that way. He moved toward the hall.

"Mallen," Bill said.

"Yeah?"

"If you're not out in five," Bill said with a slight smile, "I'm not only busting in there to drag you out, I'm cavity searching you for drugs."

"At this point," he replied, "I'd hope you would, B." He then went to the men's room door and pushed his way inside. Glass, as usual crunched under his feet. He'd never realized the stink of the bathroom before. How it smelled like beer piss had somehow become a part of the very room itself. There was no air. Something else he'd never noticed before.

"Mallen," came the thready voice from the second stall. "Was wondering when you'd come back to me."

And it struck him how comical, and dangerous, it all had been. It was all crazy, like some sad, comedic play. He went and pushed open the stall door. There was Dreamo, sitting on the toilet seat, a couple scented candles burning on the tank behind him.

"Feel like I'm visiting an Oracle."

Dreamo did a slow double take at his face. "Dude," he rasped, "what the living fuck happened to you? You look like shit, bro."

"Not part of our story, man."

"Yeah, I hear ya," came the response. Dreamo then sat up a bit, and Mallen caught himself unconsciously reaching into his pocket for a wad of bills. Stopped his hand. *Look at me, Pavlov's dog.*

Dreamo caught the movement with his quick eyes. Eyes that could be so glassy and lazy but could also zero in on the smallest detail like a laser. "Ah," he rasped, "you're unfunded, man."

Mallen stood there, knowing that Dreamo was about to offer him that dark and deadly Holy Grail of the dealer/customer relationship: credit. It would be so easy ... so fucking easy, and then it would all go away and he could just—

The sound of a glass crashing to the floor in the hall cut through his thoughts. He heard Bill cuss, followed by the man's heavy step as he probably went to dig out a broom. Perfect timing again. He was starting to feel blessed, in a way, and that was a fact.

"No," he said then to Dreamo, "I mean … I mean that I'm not here for that."

Dreamo pushed the sagging mohawk out of his face. Tried to regard Mallen with clear eyes, but that was impossible. Shrugged.

"Another one of my flock has fallen," he said with sadness, but then Mallen caught the grin in Dreamo's eyes.

"You know a guy named Eric Russ?" Mallen said.

"Why? Why you want to know, ex-customer?"

Mallen leaned against the wall. Lit a cigarette. Blew the smoke at the ceiling. "Because I was a *good* customer, that's why. I'll never ask of you something I don't feel you can't answer safely. I won't ask shit of you if I know it will put you in dutch, okay?" And here he leaned in, putting his face closer to Dreamo's, so the dealer would see his eyes. "I'm clean now, yeah? There are bad things happening out there, to people that we both know, and the cops won't do shit. Maybe I can help them, right?" And as he spoke, he got it: maybe *this* was exactly the thing he needed—he'd help people.

As much as he could.

Any way he could.

It would help keep The Need away, and that was a fact.

He flicked an ash onto the scarred floor. "My dead friend? His name was Eric Russ. Was a good cop. A cop that cared. He somehow took to the needle and lost it all. Then got clean. *Then* got dead. You hear anything about it?"

Dreamo leaned back then. Leaned back against the porcelain tank. Studied him, deeper than any look of Dreamo's he could ever imagine. Nodded, in an almost approving manner. "I'd heard about this guy," Dreamo said. "It's not for me to say shit, right? If you're an ex-badge, and he is? Well, my customer's business is their own, right? I respect their privacy."

"That's what makes you … you," Mallen replied.

Dreamo straightened his Mohawk again. With dignity. "I'll see what I can see, okay, Mallen?"

He flicked the cigarette to the floor. Squashed it out. Nodded. "Thank you, Dreamo. I appreciate it." Went back out to the bar. Bill had been pacing nearby, like a worried expectant father.

Mallen smiled. "It's all good, B. Really."

Bill looked like he believed him. "Don't make me cavity search you," he kidded.

"What? And miss out on the high point of my day? You're a bastard," Mallen said in reply as he went to the bar and sat on the stool at the near end. Pulled out his phone as Bill gave him a shot of JWB. He figured Bill must be giving him the prize for not succumbing.

He dialed Gato again. Still no answer. No way he could run all over the city looking for him, either. He'd just have to wait it out, and he just fucking hated that fact. It was the control freak in him. That's what Chris had always called it, anyway. He found himself hoping that his newfound friend was alright. Wondered what it could be that could keep Gato from replying to his phone message. Had he decided it was just too dicey, after the gunplay from Jas and Griffin? He answered that with a shrug; hell, who could blame him, right?

Mallen's mind left Gato for now and focused on Eric, and what had happened to him. There *had* to be a reason Eric had looked him up, right? It wouldn't be to send him flowers, for fuck's sake. Pulled out his cell. Got Jenna's number from information. Dialed it. She answered after six rings. Her voice was thready, uncertain. "Hello?"

"Is this Jenna?" Had to work hard to sound chipper. That was made harder with his somewhat broken face and body.

"Who is this?"

"I don't know if you'll know my name, Jenna, but my name is Mallen. Mark Mallen."

There was a long pause. Long enough to make him uncomfortable. "Eric … he mentioned you. A lot."

It was always nice to be remembered. "Yeah? He talk a lot about those days?"

"All the time."

"I was …" he said, unsure how to state it. "I hoped I could come by. I know you've been through the wringer. I was the guy that … that found you."

"I know that, too. The police told me. Told me your name."

"I just want to talk to you for a few minutes. You know he had my name and number in his pocket?"

"I know."

"I wanted to talk with you about that. Face to face, not over the phone. But only if you're okay with it."

Another long pause. "I'm okay with it."

"I could be there within thirty."

"Pick up the directory phone when you get here. Dial four-zero." She hung up. He shoved the phone back into his pocket. Looked at his reflection in the mirrored wall that had been placed behind the bar back when the Bee Gees were on top of the world. He tried to make himself presentable, but it was hard with the fake gold "marbleizing" the mirror had been treated to. Tried to comb his hair with his fingers but gave that up. Finished by downing his drink and sliding off the stool. With a goodbye and thank you to Bill, he went outside, back into the world.

SEVENTEEN

MALLEN WALKED UP LEAVENWORTH, realizing he was more out of shape than he'd fuckin' thought. Felt at his sore jaw, at a loose molar way in back on the right. A coldness crept into his body as he thought back to the beating he'd taken from Griffin. It was the cold of wanting revenge.

But junkies don't seek revenge, a voice inside his head told him. Revenge would bring attention, and that would bring an interruption to the shooting.

But he wasn't a junkie anymore.

He was something else now. Something he used to be. Something complete. He was a man again. Now he could think of, and enjoy, thoughts of revenge. Because now he could act on them with the chance of actually succeeding. Junkies never won. He spent the rest of the time on the way to Jenna's picturing how much dental work Griffin would need when they crossed paths again. And he had to admit, that image warmed his heart.

A few minutes later he was in front of Jenna's building. He went to the intercom. Pushed the button next to Jenna's name.

"Yes?" came the tinny voice through the speaker.

"It's Mallen."

For an answer there was the soft click as the front door lock, which was now repaired, released. He pushed through the heavy, dark oak portal. Made his way up to apartment twelve and knocked softly on the door. It opened immediately, like she'd been waiting.

Jenna Russ stood there. Worked up a smile. A large bandage tightly hugged her right temple. She was pretty, in a midwestern way. Emoted personality like a firecracker. She looked him up and down. A faint smile played across her lips. "I wonder which of us looks worse," she said. Yeah, he'd figured right. Sounded like she was probably from Iowa.

"Me, I'm sure." He smiled back. "But only because I was uglier to begin with."

She stood aside so he could enter. The apartment had been completely scrubbed of any signs of the attack. He hadn't noticed his last time here, but the place overlooked the backyard garden of the building next door. That would've been an attraction for taking the apartment, no doubt. He went and sat on the couch as she lowered herself into a nearby overstuffed chair.

"You going to live?" he asked.

A nod.

"You didn't see the guy who did it?"

"No. He came from behind me. I'd just come in through the door. The police say I must've interrupted him while he was trying to find something to fence. I guess that's why he attacked me the way he did. Out of fear."

"Maybe so."

After a moment of silence, she said, "You look like you met my attacker's older, way bigger brother."

"Lost a bet, is all."

She paused. "He told me about you. Eric did."

"Yeah?"

"Told me you were a great cop but lived too hard."

"Sure feels that way now."

Another silence. She got up suddenly. Went to the kitchen. He could hear her fixing coffee. Maybe tea. He hoped coffee. She came back into the room then. "So, what did you want to talk about?"

"I hadn't spoken to Eric in a long time. Not since before I left the force. If I were still a cop, I'd be crawling the streets trying to find his killer. As it is, I'm just trying to figure out why he would have my name and address in his pocket. I feel like it was a message or something. Do you have any idea why he'd have my address? He would've had to ask around to get it. Dig a little."

If he'd been hoping for answer, he was disappointed, because Jenna just shook her head. "I have no idea. He'd been clean. Just got a job. Wanted to earn money to go back to school. Told me he really wanted to study psychology."

"Psychology?" That seemed light years away from the guy who loved jumping over walls as he chased a felon. Or the guy who lived and breathed sports like football and soccer.

"He told me he wanted to study what made people do the things they did. It was one of the things he most liked back when he was in school, studying for the police force. He just wanted to understand people, I think," she said as she twisted the wedding ring on her finger, a simple gold band. The kind someone gives to someone else when it's the message that matters, not the weight of the rock.

"He chose well," he said, nodding at the ring.

She removed it. Held it in her palm. "He did," she said in a hoarse voice. Didn't put it back on her finger. Put in her pocket instead. Tears formed in her eyes then and she broke down, sobs racking her body. Mallen figured he was like every other guy he'd ever met: never really knew what to do when a woman cried. He noticed a box of tissues on the table, so he snagged it up, held it out for her.

"Thanks," she said as she tugged a couple free. After a moment she was able to continue.

"How did you two meet?" It was weak, he knew, but he wanted to try to get her focused on the beginning, rather than the end.

She smiled as the memory came back to her. "We met at a concert at the Warfield. He was wasted, but we had a fun talk. I gave him my number. I didn't know he was using, not right away, but by the time I realized how bad it was, I was in love with him. He was so sweet. Then Folsom happened."

"Folsom?" He hadn't heard *that*. That was a hard place to go, especially for an ex-cop. *Damn*, he thought as he sat there. That was a hard ticket to buy.

She nodded. "Got caught with some heroin. Not a lot, but just enough to catch attention. Did about a year. I would write to him, and he'd write back. It was hard for him in there. Really hard. I sometimes wonder how he made it through."

No doubt about that, he thought. Jesus … it had been the fear of jail that kept him flying under the radar as much as possible the last few years.

"He would tell me stories about prison, but only rarely," she said. "Usually when he was feeling bad. He always had to watch his back in there. Was beat up a few times. Once *really* bad. Prison did to him what it does to a lot of men, I guess: changed him. He got quiet a lot, pulled away. I know he was thankful to get out alive, but he was really changed."

"Yeah? How exactly?"

Well," she continued, "he told me once that he wanted to write a book about his experiences, both on the force and in prison. Even had a title, *From Cop to Con.* I saw him jotting down a few notes once. The old Eric wouldn't have cared about something like that, you know? I tried to get him to open up, but after awhile of it not working, I let it be. Sometimes a guy has to work through it on his own, right?" she added with a half-smile. "I helped him any way I could. I loved him. He loved me, too, I think."

Mallen let the quiet fill the room for a moment, his mind filled with images of Eric fighting every prisoner around him, and finally losing. Made his gut turn over, his heart break.

"When I heard," she said, "about your address and name in his pocket, I figured you'd have an answer for me, not the other way around."

"Trust me, I wish I had. I'd rather give answers than go looking for them."

She smiled. "Yeah, he said that about you, too. That you liked having all the answers."

Got to his feet. Put his hands deep into his coat pockets. "Well, if there's anything you remember, call me, okay? If there was any-thing... weirder than usual, yeah? Even the smallest thing could lead something much bigger." Paused then, adding, "Or, even if you just want to talk about him." She smiled at that. Thankful-like.

He was at the front door, her following, when she laid a hand on his sleeve. "There was something."

"What?"

She didn't seem to want to continue, like she'd spoken impulsively. He let it ride, waiting a moment or two before gently pressing her to go on. "It was about three days before ... it happened," she said. "He was staying over—I mean, we weren't really back together, but maybe if we'd had more time ... Anyway, he had gone out for cigarettes. I was in the kitchen making dinner when he got back. I heard him go right into the bathroom and shut the door. Slammed it, actually. I had this really bad moment where I thought maybe he was about to shoot, you know? That he'd fallen back into it. I went to the bathroom door. Because it was so weird how he just came in like that without saying a word. I knocked. Twice. It was really freaking me out, but I also knew that people have struggles of their own. You know? We fight it all the time." She paused.

"Yeah, we do. Did he answer? Say anything?"

A brief nod. "I knocked a third time, but he still didn't answer. I called out to him. Nothing. Then I heard it."

"It?"

"Crying. I heard him crying."

Crying? *Eric*? Mallen had a hard time picturing that. "And he wouldn't tell you what it was about?"

A smile crossed her mouth as she looked at him. "You're a guy, right? Would *you* have told why you were crying?"

"Point to the lady," he replied.

"That's why I don't believe any of that shit about him dealing again. I don't care if he was found with bags of heroin on him. He was crying, Mallen. Sobbing. Like he was scared."

"And not scared of going back into the world that put him in prison? Maybe he felt he had no other way?"

For an answer, she only shook her head. Emphatically. "So. If you learn anything, you'll tell me, right?" she said.

"You'll be the first one to know." He went to her door. "Thanks for the talk," he said as he left.

EIGHTEEN

IT WAS THE FIRST time that Mallen had seen this much H outside of the stuff they'd showed him during his training, so he'd be able to recognize it. Six wrapped bags that strangely reminded him of six wrapped hoagie sandwiches. He'd been moving up in the ranks, slowly but steadily. He had been a wheel man for a little bit but had shown smarts during what had turned out to be an ambush, not a "meeting of the minds." He'd also had to stand guard, but only outside whatever building the meet was going down in. He'd done that with his usual attention to detail. No mouthing off or attitude. It was shit like that, just doing his job and paying attention to the details, that got him noticed for his current duty. It'd been a long haul, that was a fact, but here he was: inside with the buyers and sellers. This was his first eyewitness account to any sort of buy this large, but this was why he'd opted for the detail. Why he'd chased down the chance to do undercover work. This was Serpico. This was the French fucking Connection, man. This was the job. Right here, right now. He was inside. It'd taken a long time, but he'd made it. And now he was looking at a boat-load of death, sitting there on a folding table inside an abandoned store front in Potrero.

Jonesy, another soldier, stood to his right, shifting nervously from his bad leg to his good. Mallen knew it hurt Jonesy to stand for too long, victim of a stray bullet during some fucked-up assassination attempt on the boss man Franco that had ended with a lot of guys dead on both sides—and an unscathed Franco. Jonesy had taken one for the team, trying to defend his boss. Franco had granted him inner court after that, almost taking him to his breast. Mallen thought it was almost cute, in its way, how it really felt like some old world court, with kings, bishops, advisors, and, of course, pawns.

But he was no longer a pawn. He felt like a rook now. Maybe he could parlay that into becoming a knight. He stood there and looked down at the table containing enough horse to set him and Chris up for the rest of their lives in some South American country. He'd proven his worth, although not like Jonesy. No, he'd been diligent, smart, and had only spoken enough to give good advice when he knew for a fact that the department had told him when and where the raids were going to go down. He'd played it like he was just a whiz kid, moving with his gut instinct. He'd appeared to those around him as a guy who could see the playing field and adjust accordingly, even as the shit was hitting the fan. That had impressed.

And it had led him here.

Franco's buyer in this scenario, a guy named Two-Bit, checked the merchandise. Ran the test to see how good the horse could run. It ran quite well. Two-Bit nodded to his assistant, a huge black dude who ran by the name of Wall. Wall then held out a plastic Safeway bag stuffed with neatly counted out bills, rubber banded together in one-thousand-dollar amounts. The other side of the buy, the suppliers, were a bunch of little Mexican dudes. They sent one of theirs to collect the dough.

And that was when it all fell apart. Just as Wall let go of the bag and the other side took possession, there was the sudden concussive sound of a tear gas gun going off. Mallen knew it immediately, as he also knew immediately that shit had just blown up in his world. The cops were not supposed to be here. This wasn't one of the staged buys, set up so they could help him get higher up the chain.

This was now, as the colloquial phrase runs, fucked all to high heaven and back.

Suddenly it was every man for himself. No one wanted to be anywhere near the dope. Well, Mallen did see Jonesy stuff a kilo under his coat as he bolted for the door. Bravery and stupidity oft look the same, as another old saying goes.

Mallen ran for the nearest door, crashing through it full throttle. The damn thing almost came off its hinges as he charged ahead. The air was filled with yells and cops shouting their usual cop crap when they bust into a joint. "Down! Down! Down!" "Hands where I can see them!" "Eat the floor, motherfucker!"

He found himself running down a short hall, an old office door dead ahead. There would be some fucking anger over this, and that was a fact. He'd told his superiors to keep it cool, that he had it under control. Someone, somewhere, had fucked up royally.

The door broke apart like he was some superhero dude as he threw all his weight into it. A small office lay beyond. Maybe some manager's, at one time, now empty except for graffiti and garbage. There was the door that would lead to freedom, right there. He registered daylight sneaking in under the bottom. Grabbed at the knob, twisted, yanked, and the door flew open and then he was outside…

… and there was Eric.

Glock in hand, regulation pose down to the feet being one yard apart. Uniform was immaculate, as it always was. Badge like a mirror shining in the sun. Poster boy for what a cop should look like, be like.

The look on Eric's face would've made him laugh, if it were any other fucking time. Like Eric had just thought he'd bought a hooker on the sly, and that hooker turned out to be his wife living a secret life. Eric started to say something, but Mallen put his gun up, aiming right for Eric's face.

"Nope," Mallen said, "you're gonna need to take me in, or let me ride over you, man."

"But—"

Mallen strode forward, knowing there wasn't time, hoping for any extra seconds. He swung his gun at Eric's face. The barrel slashed a deep gash across Eric's cheek. Eric dropped his gun, and Mallen let his fall to the ground as he piled into Eric, driving a knee into Eric's midsection.

"Make it look good, man," Mallen whispered.

Eric gave him a good chop to the ribs. He thought that the rib might have actually broken, the pain was so heavy and intense. Then they were down on the ground, rolling in the muck of the back alley. It reminded Mallen of being back at the academy, when they'd have to try and disarm each other in a drill, or use each other as tackling dummies. They exchanged kicks and blows in the alley, some heavier than others, both knowing that Mallen's life now depended on it looking real. People had to buy into it.

Then Mallen felt himself hauled off of Eric and slammed against the hard brick of the building. He was turned around and shoved into the wall, blood getting in his eyes, his vision turning red and blurry. There was the sharp stab of the cuffs on his wrist. He was turned around and again shoved hard into the wall.

Eric walked up to him then. Winked, then slugged him hard in the gut. Not too hard, but just enough. Enough to make Mallen think his friend had enjoyed it.

"Come along now, little bad man," Eric said as he made a show of leading Mallen back to a cruiser, "and if you're really good, I won't face-plant you into the gravel and tell the judge you were so whacked out on smack you kept falling."

He tossed Mallen into the back of the car, the door slamming tight behind him. The windows of course had the wide metal bar across them to prevent anyone from escaping. On a whim, he angled around and gave the glass a few good slams with his boots. For effect, he told himself, but actually because he was fucking pissed that someone, somewhere, had fucked it up. Badly. It was entirely possible that Franco, already paranoid, would equate this outcome with Mallen being there. Maybe Franco would want to play it safe, meaning that Mallen would be put down like a syphilitic mongrel with three legs. He'd heard worse stories. Eric hit the bar welded across the window with his billy club a couple times. To "calm the passenger" as it was called. Then he climbed behind the wheel. As Eric started the engine, he said without looking at him, "Sorry man, we didn't know."

"You sure?" He didn't like it. The fact only reinforced his uneasiness. The raid had been planned without the knowledge of them having a man inside, or it had been planned because someone knew a man was inside. There was no third option. Either someone was incredibly fucking stupid, or someone knew he was there.

Eric glanced over his shoulder. "Yeah, I'm sure."

Mallen got better situated in the back seat. "This is fucked." He sighed. "Well, at least hit the AC, okay? Then take me down to booking. Call Stevens, tell him you 'caught a blackbird.'"

The cruiser was out in the street by this point. Eric did a double take back at him. "Caught a black bird? What the fuck kind of horseshit spy crap is that?"

"Hell, I just do what they tell me." Mallen gazed out the window for a moment, trying to guess at all the angles he'd need to cover to make Franco relax enough to keep him on the inside. Maybe he could use his being in jail until bailed out to lend the needed authenticity. Hell, could fuckin' happen. "Who set up the raid?" he asked.

"Dietrich."

That didn't make him feel any easier, either. That fucker was almost worst than Jas. Jas with a badge, for fuck's sake. Could it really be that way? Could he have been set up? But why? He wasn't even high up yet. He was still a street dog. "When was it planned? When did you hear about it?"

"Why?" Eric replied. "What's going on?"

"Just fucking tell me, man!" he yelled. He was feeling strung out, worn out.

Eric guided the car onto the next street. They were close to booking now. Had only a few minutes. "Just this morning," came the reply. Told quiet. Flat. "Everyone just looked at each other, and then we went out. We were voluntold, basically."

And that made him feel way worse than any other news could've. It was sounding more and more like someone either had it in for him, or at least wanted to send a message to Franco that people were in his tree, getting ready to shake his leaves.

Mallen lay back on the seat. Stared at the ceiling of the cop car. Something was going on. But what was it? He tried to get comfortable. Couldn't. If—if—he had been ratted out, then jail was the worst place for him to be. He'd be dead, right down there in the holding tank, maybe. He had to get a message out. But, to who?

"Hey," he said to Eric, "remember to call Stevens, yeah? And then call Chris for me, okay? Let her know when you dropped me off. Let her know what you just let me know."

Eric glanced over his shoulder. "What will that do? If it's bad, like you're saying, what the fuck will that do?"

"It'll go on the fucking record, if nothing else," he replied, but not with much heart. He knew he had to get ready. There would be signs ahead. He had to be ready to read them. Would he be put in solitary? Or with the rest of the dirt? Would Stevens get him out fast, or would he spend days behind bars?

Either way, he noted with growing anxiety, he'd have to suffer that lovely dance known as the strip search.

NINETEEN

OBERON ENTERED INTO THE small file-strewn office of parole officer Denise Lewis. She was a short, harassed-looking woman in her late thirties. Understanding the harassment was easy, judging from the mountain of files that surrounded her. Some of the file stacks he counted were forty high, at least. Had to wonder at the sheer magnitude of it all. Each case represented a person who would, or wouldn't, get their life turned around. Odds were they wouldn't.

He smiled pleasantly at her. "I'm Inspector Kane. Thanks for getting me the file on such short notice."

She looked him up and down for a moment. Gave him a shy smile. Leaned back and grabbed up a stuffed manila folder off a two-drawer file cabinet behind her. "I'm always happy to help one of the branches of justice, Detective Kane." She laid it on the desk right in front of her, next to the release letter.

"If you don't get it back to me, you'll have to buy me a drink," she warned.

"Well now," he said as he signed his name, "maybe I'll just have to grow forgetful." The file was thick. Scarsdale's past with the criminal justice system was lengthy. He started to flip through it. Found the usual: drug addiction and escalating crimes.

"How'd he die?" Lewis asked.

"Shot. In what looks like a very execution-style killing."

She pondered that. "He didn't seem like that type. Not the one for that level of enemy. He did have the drug background, of course. That's pretty much a given at this point. But still...his known acquaintances just didn't seem *that* hard-core."

There was no Kaslowski listed under known acquaintances. Well, it was a long shot it would be that easy. "He seemed to have not checked in recently. Was that normal?"

"We have them call in, and I hadn't checked the logs lately," she said as she looked down at the pile of forms on her desk. "But no, I wouldn't say that was normal. I know he was having trouble finding work. He was also getting down on himself. Liked to hide in bars. I believe he was seeing prostitutes. I tried to warn him off that once I found out, but you know how guys can be about their hookers." She smiled.

"As legend has it." If there was no connection in this file to Kaslowski, he would have to speak to people out at Folsom. Maybe they would have something. He tucked the file under his arm. "Thanks again, Mrs. Lewis. I'll only have it for a couple days."

"It's Ms.—Ms. Lewis. And I'll be waiting for that drink," she said with a wink.

———

Oberon took a sip of his coffee from the same mug he'd been using for the last ten years—an old off-white diner mug he'd found at a garage sale. A couple on his street had been selling their row house and moving to Marin. Well, the city isn't for everyone... Something about the cup had registered with him because it was the identical type of cup his father had drunk coffee from every morning of his life. That is, up until the man had died of a heart attack back when Oberon was just entering the academy as a cadet filled with hope and idealized visions of right and wrong. And in a sort of homage to the man who had shaped his life, Oberon always drank coffee as his father had: heavy on the cream and sugar.

He looked up from Scarsdale's file and over at the old proto-digital electric clock on his desk. The kind where the numbered tiles flip down with every minute. Somehow, way long ago, a cockroach had gotten inside the device and died. It's mummified carcass still lay there to this day, pressed behind the clear plastic, just under the minute plates as they plocked away the passing of time. Somehow, it all made sense.

It was late. Much later than he'd intended to stay. What kept him at his desk was that part of him enjoyed being there when it was quiet and still, as it was now. Most of the other detectives were out on calls or off duty. He looked once more at the computer screen. Just to be sure of his facts. Wrote some information down in his notebook. Turned out that Scarsdale and Kaslowski had indeed been at Folsom during the same period of time. Overlapped for just over fourteen months until Kaslowski was paroled. Scarsdale had served on, doing another ten months. Oberon had made a mental note to call Folsom after reading that bit of news, knowing he'd need to speak with the warden's assistant or anyone who would know if Scarsdale and Kaslowski ever mixed while they were incarcerated.

His phone rang then, startling him. His direct line. Grabbed up the receiver. "Inspector Kane."

"Well, I'll be damned. You work the same shit hours I do," said DeJesus with a yawn.

"So it would seem."

"I have something for you. Thought I was going to leave it on voicemail."

"Just pretend I'm a recording."

Soft laughter on the other end. "Okay. The bullet that killed Scarsdale and the one that killed Kaslowski came from the same gun. Same twist. Everything lines up."

Worst fears confirmed, or best-case scenario? He couldn't decide which at the moment. "Thanks, Ronnie. I owe you."

"You know it, inspector," came the reply, but he heard the humor attached to it. "Get some sleep," she said and then hung up.

This new fact made him very concerned. It was official: there was something going on. He leaned back in his chair. Wished for the seventh time this week that he'd never given up smoking. Okay, the same gun had killed these two men. So, what could the motive be? They'd both been in the same prison at the same time. Just coincidence? Revenge? Did they both know something? He sighed. Reached over and picked up the phone. He knew someone would answer, no matter what time.

Sure enough, after pushing 0 for the operator and giving his badge number to the computer, he got through to a live person. The phone line had the hollow sound of being tapped. The usual.

"Folsom admin," said the voice on the other end, which could've been one of those old gypsy fortune-telling machines you'd put a dime into and get your fortune.

Oberon told them who he was, gave his badge number again. "I just need to know if you have any record of an Anthony Scarsdale and Carl Kaslowski mixing while there in your care." He gave the voice the dates of their incarcerations.

"We'll have to check. What number can you be reached at?"

He gave them his cell, saying it was *very* important to his *murder* case. After the usual civilities, he hung up with a sigh. They were busy. His request wouldn't be a priority. Clicked off his lamp and sat there in the dark, thinking. Maybe if and when Folsom got back to him, there'd be something that would start the ball of thread unraveling. But what else could he do in the meantime?

TWENTY

MALLEN ROLLED OVER ON his cot as the call went out for everyone to leave. Such was life in a shelter. He'd used his rolled-up coat as a pillow for two reasons: One, it seemed a better alternative to the one he'd been handed; and two, it would keep the gun close to him. He knew that things went missing, and men got stabbed in places like this. Why risk it? When he'd been back in uniform, right before hitching up with Narco, he'd answered a call on a dead man in a shelter over on Eddy, near Larkin. Some old man, stabbed over twenty times in the chest as he probably lay there, sleeping, thinking he was safe. They never caught the killer or even figured out a likely motive, other than it had been "a street thing."

He'd walked around upper Knob for a while after leaving Jenna's apartment. Even stepped inside Grace Cathedral. Just trying to stay safe and put Eric's death, and his own new life, into some sort of perspective.

The attempt hadn't netted much resolution, but at least it was quiet inside the church, and he felt safe there. A feeling he hadn't felt since getting spotted by Jas and Griffin, and which was only reinforced by the beating Griffin had given him. It was as he sat there that he realized he would need a place to crash where he could feel safe. The local shelters offered that, if he got there early enough.

All in all, it hadn't been a bad night. The usual white noise of a bunch of men all corralled together. Very much what jail was like. He'd been lucky, having arrived just in time to be one of the last admitted for the night. Found a cot right in the middle of the room, one of the last not taken. Sleep had been long in coming—his mind refusing to shut up—but eventually it had, and he got about four hours of decent sleep.

And then the call had gone out for everyone to leave. The inside of his mouth tasted like something better left untasted. He wanted to shower. That was another newly remembered feeling, now that his veins were back to being his own.

In short, he realized he'd have to risk going back to his place. Hell, shouldn't Jas and Griffin have other things to think about other than one lone ex-cop, ex-junkie? He'd have to risk it.

———

Mallen had just put his boot on the first of the five steps leading up to his building's street door when the gunshots cut the air.

Must be a slow time down at the ol' drug den! he thought.

They exploded out of nowhere, heavy and concussive. The glass in the lobby door shattered into a thousand glittering shards. Knew instantly the bullets came from the other side of the street. Another volley, and he felt concrete and wood splinters rain down on him. There was the roar of an engine, an engine he now recognized, followed by the squeal of tires. He dove down behind a silver Jetta parked at the curb. Screams and yells from the citizens out on the sidewalks filled the air. It was the second time within days he'd been shot at. Must be some sort of fuckin' record.

"Everybody down!" he yelled, hoping people would duck out and run for their lives. Peered over the hood of the Jetta just in time to catch a glimpse of the black Escalade. A muzzle flashed, and the Jetta's windshield starred from a .44 slug. Griffin was feeling really determined in giving him a scare, that was for sure. And that's what it had been about, too: a good scare. They'd had the drop on him. Could've iced him right there, right then. But they'd chosen to blast away at everything *but* him. It was a follow-up to the beating.

He had to admit that it worked. He had to fight to stop the shaking. He'd been so freaked and out of practice he hadn't even remembered to grab his own gun. Not good. Those thoughts burned in him as he stood to watch the Escalade turn right at the end of the block and disappear.

Then he heard the sirens. The cavalry was on its way. Glanced over at the shattered lobby door. Well, they'd chosen a good position to fire from. If they'd meant to kill him, he'd be dead right now.

———

There had been no way to get gone before the cops showed. It was a "shots fired" call. That brought all the dogs running, ears pinned back. He'd had enough left as far as awareness went to run and hide the gun, sliding it under the gate that led back to the the trash cans the city picked up once a week. There was a dark patch of gloom there, just near the gate, and he'd managed to shove the gun deep into the shadows. All he needed was a bit of time, then he could go and retrieve it.

After arriving, the cops of course ran his soon-to-expire license. Of course. It was only five minutes later when a plain brown sedan rolled around the corner. He watched as Oberon got out and came over.

"Once again, you turn up a crime scene," Oberon said. He got the highlights on what had gone down from the uniformed officer first on the scene. Turned back to Mallen. Almost did a double take, as he only then seemed to take in the bruises and swelling on Mallen's face. He could tell by Oberon's expression that the detective figured there would be more to this situation than just some random shooting.

"Mark, you're a very lucky man," Oberon said. "It wouldn't have anything to do with your ... previous habits, would it?"

"No," he said emphatically. Hoped his friend would believe him. Obie stared at him a moment. At his eyes. Relaxed a bit. Yeah, he'd believed him.

"The officer told me what you told him. Now you can tell me the truth."

"The truth? What do you mean, man?"

"Oh, Mark. That was quite poor."

He nodded. "Okay, you win. Do we have to do it out here?"

"No, not really."

He led Oberon inside the building and up to his apartment. Had it really only been about a week since the cop had stood in the center of this room and told him about Eric? Felt like years. He pulled the Jim Beam from his pocket. Needed a drink after being shot at. *Who wouldn't?* he told himself. Downed it quickly then took another. Turned to see Oberon watching him. "What?" he said. "I just got shot at, man."

"Of course." After a moment, he continued. "So, what's it all about?"

"You know, I'm really lucky that guy was a bad shot."

"And why, if I might ask, is anyone shooting at a *recovering* junkie anyway?" He couldn't help but note the emphasis Oberon had put on the word *recovering*.

"Well, you said I needed a hobby, yeah?"

Oberon sighed as he shook his head. "You are a child of trouble, Mark. Tell me."

Mallen went and sat on the couch, bottle in one hand, glass in the other. Held the bottle out to Oberon. The cop came over. Took the bottle and found himself a not-dirty glass—no small feat. Filled it with a shot's worth. Slammed it down. Almost didn't cough.

"Well?" Oberon said in a choking voice as he put the glass and bottle back down on the kitchen counter. "What's it all about?"

Mallen took another slug from his glass. Looked down at the clean liquid in the dirty glass. Hoped it was a good visual metaphor for his soul inside his body. He sighed. Looked over at Oberon. "It's about Jas and Griffin." He then told Oberon about how they'd seen him outside of Jenna's the day he'd been arrested. Then how Griffin had beat on him. Then about the two shootings, one outside of the Cornerstone, and this recent one outside his place.

As he'd expected, Oberon wasn't happy. "You know, I realize you miss the force, but come on now. You're really pushing it."

"Look, I just wanted to know why Eric had my info in his pocket, that's all. I didn't ask to be seen outside of Jenna's, did I?"

Oberon sighed. Took the Jim Beam back off the counter. Poured a shot. This time downed it like a pro. "First the gun, now this. The next time you get off heroin, can you do it somewhere else, please? I have enough on my plate as it is."

TWENTY-ONE

IT WAS BAD AFTER Oberon left. Maybe it was the shooting on top of everything else. The Need started. A whisper at first, growing quickly into a steady nagging and tugging at his soul. He could swear that the crook of his right arm was turning warm. He took a hot shower, trying to scald away the growing creature inside him that wouldn't let him rest. It didn't work; he couldn't get his mind off the needle and the golden blood that ran through it. Got dressed quickly in old black combat pants and a turtleneck. Shrugged into his coat. Knew he was getting dressed to go and see Dreamo. Fuck Bill, right? It was his life, not Bill's or Oberon's. It was his. But then, his hand on the door, he stopped. Closed the door. Took his coat off. Went back to the couch.

He went through this little ballet at least five times. Even got so far that he had the door open and was standing there on the threshold of his apartment. It would be so fucking easy. He didn't even need to go to the Cornerstone. There were at least three other guys he knew of that would be flush with junk. Even some bad shit would be welcome at this point, for Christ's sake. He needed some relief. There'd been too much Life lately. Why did people do Life in the first fuckin' place, right? It was only filled with darkness, anger, and pain. It was pointless. There was just no reason at all he could think of to not shoot at that point. Hell, one of the reasons he'd checked out in the first fucking place was that there'd been too much Life.

No, man … that's not true.

That brought him up. Stopped him cold. No, that wasn't why he'd gotten hooked. He'd gotten hooked because he'd believed he was all Al Pacino Serpico and shit. That he could handle it. How could Ol' Monster Mallen's son fail to bring in the bad guys? Pops never had. And that was it. He shot to see how it felt, so he could "act" the part better.

Only, of course, it hadn't stopped there.

Looking back now, he laughed at how naïve he'd been in thinking he could handle it. How he couldn't see the obvious: that the first shot into his arm would bring him like a runaway freight train right to the day where he'd either die from it or get clean. How it would come right down to *this* inevitable moment: struggling to stay home, struggling to stay away from the people who would love to take his money and give him the key to oblivion.

So there he sat on his worn, broken-down couch, coat half on, sweat under his arms as he struggled to just sit right there and not fucking move. Not to the door. Not to his cell phone to call for delivery. Not to his wallet to check funding. He struggled just *to be*.

It was an hour later when he realized he'd won the battle, if not the war. He knew it because he suddenly felt completely exhausted. Spent. Maybe it was because of the battle he'd just waged. Maybe it was because of all the running he'd been doing since being cleansed of the crap he'd shot into his body over the last four years. And he knew that if running was one of the things he had to do to keep clean, that's what he'd fucking do. He'd keep up the pace of his life if that meant keeping the needle further and further away.

And almost like some sort of reward, his cell rang. It was the first call he'd received on the damn thing. He checked it and had to laugh: Gato. The universe was indeed trying to send him a message, and that was a fact.

"Gato," Mallen said, "thought you'd given up on me, man. Everything okay?"

To his surprise, Gato didn't sound like himself. "Long-ass story, bro. Got your message. What's up?"

He told Gato about the shooting and described the beat down he'd taken at Griffin's hands. His friend's voice got very quiet as he said, "Mallen. We need to fuck those guys up, man. Just say the word and we'll send them to the hospital or the morgue. Your call, *vato*."

"No, man, not the morgue," he said. "But something. I just have to figure out what that is. You free for a while?"

"Yeah," came the reply. Again, there was something off in Gato's voice.

"I mean," Mallen said, "if you're busy, man, I totally understand."

"No, man, it's not that. I'll come and get you. Call you when I'm downstairs. Where do you live, bro?" He gave his address and Gato hung up without another word. What had gotten into his friend? Was his mother ill?

———

His cell rang with the text that Gato was downstairs only twenty minutes after they'd ended their call. Mallen spied out the front door window for any black Escalades but saw none. He went quickly to

134

the Falcon double parked in the street. Got in and Gato sped away. Mallen immediately noticed that Gato looked like he hadn't slept in a couple days.

"I still have a license," Mallen said with a smile. "I can drive and you can relax."

Gato worked up a smirk. "Nobody drives this baby but her papa, bro. I'm good. Where we going?"

"Out to the avenues. I want to visit my old friend's parents," he replied. He needed to see if Hal or Phoebe had noticed the same change in Eric that Jenna had seen. Another reason also was that he wanted to see how they were getting on. To let them know he was still there if they needed any help. And he had to admit one other reason he had for going to see them: he wanted to show Phoebe and Hal that he was clean and was intending to stay that way. He gave Gato the address.

"I don't mean to make it seem like you're my taxi, G," he said. "Just leave me at the corner and we'll hook up after you've gotten some sleep."

Gato shook his head at that. "I need to keep my mind off of shit, bro. I'll hang with you."

"What's going on?"

Gato turned the car onto Geary. Flipped on the radio to an AM station that was playing big band stuff. "It's my sister," he finally said in a quiet voice.

"I didn't know you had one."

A nod. "She's . . . gone away. We don't know where."

"She a runaway?"

"No. She's twenty-one. She's driving *mamacita* crazy by doing this. I've been out trying to find her, or a line on her."

"Any luck, man?"

Gato's only response was a shake of his head. He looked suddenly very sad. "Don't know if I'll ever see her again, *vato*."

Mallen wondered if he could ask Oberon to check the PD's computers for him. He really wanted to pay this man back for his help in getting his life back together. "If there's anything I can do, Gato, just say the word, okay?"

A smile played across Gato's mouth. "Just like I said before, bro: there's a good heart beating in that chest. I'll let you know."

————

Traffic on Geary wasn't too bad this time of evening. Parking was a little worse, and Gato finally found a place two blocks away from the Russ house. "Really, man, you don't have to wait," Mallen said as Gato killed the engine.

"I'm good, bro. I'll be here."

"Thanks, G," he said as he opened door. "I might be about a half hour."

He got out of the Falcon and walked to the Russ house. It felt good to be out and in the open air, an air tinged with ocean salt. Wisps of fog were floating by above him as the day moved toward its end. He breathed deeply. He couldn't remember the last time he'd felt so good. Having beaten The Need earlier had really pumped him up. Given him the energy he needed to continue on with the fight, and with his life.

He turned the corner onto the Russes' street. Was two houses down when he noticed a man standing on the sidewalk across from the Russ house. Black dude. Seemed around his own age. Dressed in a black leather jacket and baggy jeans. Short hair, beard frizzy and unkempt. Was probably nothing, but his old cop sense had kicked on.

Why would the guy be standing right there, right opposite Eric's house? Looking at it?

Mallen decided to keep walking. Went to the end of the block and crossed the street so he was now on the same side as the man. The man did not notice him. He strolled back toward the man. Slowly. Casually. When he got closer, about three houses away, he ducked behind some stairs that led up to one of the houses. Watched the man from there.

This guy was obviously struggling with something. He'd look over at the Russ house, start for it, then stop. Pace a little. Weird.

Mallen watched for a little longer, than came out of cover and walked down the sidewalk toward him. Just another guy walking down the street. The man looked at him for a moment when Mallen changed course and headed over to him, staying out of arm's reach.

"Hey, how you doin'?" he said to the man, smiling.

The man nodded. "I know you?"

"No," he replied, "but I know the people in that house across the street. The one you seem unable to make up your mind about whether you should go up to or not."

The man looked him up and down. Studied his face. Like he was trying to see if he remembered ever meeting him. "No man, just waiting on a friend," he finally said as he walked off the way Mallen had come.

Mallen gave it a moment then went after him. There was something wrong about him. He was sure of it, with every bone in his body, every ounce of his being.

He tailed the man to the end of the block. The man turned the corner, heading east, and was lost from sight. Mallen raced forward, not wanting to lose sight of him.

Got to the end of the block. There was a pale green apartment building there, very 1930s in appearance. Pressed himself against the wall and peered around the corner. But then his world turned upside down as he was grabbed by a pair of large, strong hands. He was thrown to the ground with such force that all the air in his lungs seemed to momentarily disappear. A fist planted itself on the side of his head, and he saw stars. There was a part of him then, a part that had been locked up a long-ass time, that got angry. That anger was like a key turning in a lock. It was suddenly like all the training he'd ever forgotten took that moment to come rushing back in, fueled by the anger and panic at having to take another beating.

His foot lashed out with everything he had, almost of its own accord. There was the pleasure of hearing the man grunt with pain. He rolled away as the man lost the grip on his coat. Mallen got to his feet just in time to duck under another swing. He punched the guy hard in the stomach, then followed with a desperate fist to the groin. Hell, he wasn't in this for style points. The man bent nearly double. He took the opportunity to slam his palms onto the man's ears. Must've been like a bomb going off in the guy's head. The man went to the sidewalk, blood streaming from his nose. A couple pedestrians who were walking by slowed up. Maybe to watch, maybe to jump in. Hard to tell.

Mallen quickly frisked the man. Came away with a small automatic. A .22 Firestorm. Good little weapon. Nice stopping power. The discovery of the gun shooed the civilians quickly away. He dragged the man over to the apartment building. Propped him up. Removed the clip from the Firestorm. Ejected the shell from the barrel. Tossed the clip into the storm drain, putting the gun in his coat pocket.

As the man's eyes focused on him, a look of anger and embarrassment hit them. "What the fuck you following me for, man?

Don't like it when a black man comes calling on some white fucker's house?"

"Can it. Don't even bother playing that fucking crap. That's not why I followed you, and you know it. I followed because you wanted to go over into that house but couldn't bring yourself to do it. Why?"

No answer.

"Look," he continued, "that family? Been through a lot, see? Their son's been killed. He was a friend of mine. A cop, just like I used to be. We went back a long-ass way, okay? So you can't really blame me for being a bit edgy about it all, right?"

The man studied him for a moment. As if trying to read what he'd been told was true. Finally nodded his head. Relaxed. "Yeah, I can see why you'd follow me. I didn't handle it well, sorry. My bad. But I don't mean anybody any harm, man. You gotta believe me." He held out his hand. "The name's Leon Dockery."

Now it was Mallen's turn to see if he believed what he was being told. He had to admit that he did. Dockery didn't seem to be lying, unless he was a master of the craft. "Okay," Mallen replied as he shook his hand, "Mallen. Mark Mallen. So, what's it about? Why the pushme-pullyou act out in front of the house?"

At that Dockery shook his head. Started to get up. He helped Dockery to his feet, ready should the man try anything. But Dockery only pulled out a crumpled paper napkin. Wiped the blood from his nose with it. Straightened his clothes. A slight smile crossed his lips. "There, that's better for talking."

"Okay, let's talk."

Dockery shook his head. "I can't tell you what it's about, Mallen. I can't. It's for Mrs. Russ's ears only."

"Mrs. Russ? Why her?"

Dockery only shook his head in response. "Sorry man, I can't say."

"Can't? Or won't?"

"Both. But you have to believe me when I tell you that I mean that family no harm. No harm at all, man."

He stood there for a moment, again studying Dockery's face. Looked back at the Russ house for a moment. Dockery obviously knew about Eric's death; his reason for being here was proof of that. Wanting to talk to Phoebe only. He needed to know the *why,* and if that meant letting Dockery meet with Phoebe, then that's the way it would go down. "Well, if you want to meet with her, okay. I'll tell her."

Dockery's amazement was plain on his face. "You will?"

"Yeah, I will. And when you *do* tell her? I'll be there, as will her husband. But"—and here he lowered his voice as he looked intently into Dockery's eyes—"if you're gonna give some her bad news about her son, you better fucking warn me, so I can prepare her. Those people been through hell, and I don't want them screwed with, okay?"

"That's cool, Mallen. Okay."

He again looked at the man for a moment. Definitely ex-con material. "It is about Eric, right? Something to do with his time inside?"

"That's right."

"You know who killed him?"

A shake of Dockery's head was his only answer.

"If that's true, then what about his being killed made you come forward now? You know something about it, don't you? Look, I'm just trying to make sense of it. We were friends. The police want to find the prick who shot him, and so do I. Come on, man, the guy had fallen down a hole, but was climbing back out of it! He had everything to look forward to."

Dockery's eyes clouded for a moment. Like he was reliving an old, painful experience. "I can't answer you, man. Sorry."

"Can't? Or won't?" Mallen asked again.

"Look, I'll tell you this, since you're gonna fix it so I can meet the family, okay?" He then fished in his jacket pocket. Pulled out a piece of paper. Scribbled something down on it, then handed it to him. "That's my cell. When you think it's okay with them seeing me, just let me know."

"Ok," Mallen said as he pocketed the paper, handed Dockery back his now-empty gun. "So, how about what you were gonna tell me?"

"It has to do with an apology."

"Apology?" he said, but Dockery was already moving quickly away. Mallen let him go, not thinking he would get any more from the man. He stood there for a moment longer, wondering what Dockery had meant by those last words. Put the paper in his pocket and went back up the street, hoping the Russ household possessed at least two Excedrin.

His knock brought Phoebe to the door. She looked even more tired, if that were humanly possible, and even older than when he'd seen her just last week.

"Yeah, it's true," he said with a faint smile off her look of disbelief, "it's the new me, Phoebe."

"My God, Mark! What happened to you?"

"My past caught up with me is all. Looks worse than it is, Phoebe. Only hurts when I blink."

"Come on in. Come in! Coffee?"

"Sure," he replied as he followed her down the hall to the kitchen. He glanced at the den door, shut tight. "He in?"

"No," came the reply, and he looked over at her. Her voice now had a very sad quality to it.

"What is it?" he asked. Sat at the table. Watched her back as she filled two cups with coffee and brought them to the table. He put a couple spoons of sugar in his, along with some cream.

She watched him over the lip of her mug as she took a sip of her coffee. "How long has it been, Mark?" she asked quietly.

He had to think about that. He'd first gone in the drunk tank just about seven days ago now. Almost a week of being clean. That thought stunned him. "Today or tomorrow will make it a week."

"You believe it will … last?"

He held his mug up in a toast. "Here's to hoping, right?"

"Yes," she replied then, holding up her own mug, "here's to hoping."

They sat for a moment in silence, then he said, "Anything from the police on … his killing?"

"No. Nothing." Anger creeping in now.

"There's still hope," he assured her. To his surprise, she glared at him, like he'd been the one to kill her son.

"Hope? Really? I don't think the police will ever find the man who killed him."

"That's not true—"

"Stop with the empty platitudes, Mark!" she yelled, her voice cutting through the air. "Stop with all the bullshit! Nobody cares! Nobody will do anything!" She caught herself then, looked at him in shock, like she couldn't believe she'd just yelled at a person who'd only come to see how they were doing. Reached out and put her hand on his. "I'm sorry. It's just … "

"I know, Phoebe, I know. Look, it could take some time, but I know the cop that has the case. He's one of the best, most caring Police I've ever known. Trust me when I say that he's working the case to the maximum abilities."

"Thank you," she said in a whisper. Got to her feet and went to the large windows that overlooked the backyard. She stood there for a moment, gazing out.

"There needs ... *needs* to be justice for him, Mark." Then sobs racked her body, and he got up and went to her. She buried her face in his shabby coat and cried. He felt like he was holding a small bird, she felt so frail.

"Phoebe," he said as he guided her back to her seat. "I have to ask again: Besides the personal devil thing, did you notice anything odd in Eric's behavior, in the days leading up to ... what happened?"

She reached over and snagged a tissue from the box that lived on the back edge of the table. Thought for a moment. "We saw him a couple days before. And, well, he did seem distracted, but that—" She stopped then.

"What? What is it, Phoebe?"

"I didn't think about it much at the time. He was spending the night here. Wouldn't sleep in his old room, but slept on the couch. I woke up to use the bathroom. It was just past two. I noticed the lights on downstairs. I found him completely dressed, not sleeping, just peering out the windows. I think he was muttering something to himself, but I couldn't be sure."

That did not seem like Eric at all. That seemed like a scared or paranoid man. "Did you hear what he was muttering?"

Phoebe shook her head. "I wish I had. All I caught was, 'not ever again.'"

Not ever again. He thought about Dockery. About what he'd said. "Hey," he said, "when I was coming up the street, I saw a man pacing back and forth across the street, right in line with this place. It felt ... weird, so I checked it out, and—"

"It's just like Hal told me," she said with genuine warmth. "You *are* still a cop, way down deep inside."

"Sometimes," he conceded. "Phoebe. This man? He said he had to talk to you. Said it had to do with an apology. His name is Dockery. That's all I got. That name ring a bell?"

She thought for a moment, and then shook her head. "No," she said slowly, "that name isn't familiar."

"You sure you never heard Eric mention that name? At all?"

"I'm sorry, Mark, but no. I'm sure I never heard Eric say that name to me."

Well, it'd been a long shot. Maybe Jenna knew that name. He'd have to ask. "He told me that he has to see you. He also said he'd been with Eric, in prison. Told me it was to do with an apology. Would you be up for that? I'll be here, and I'm sure Hal will be, too. It might help the police in figuring out what happened."

She looked up at him then. Very clearly, she said, "Yes. I'd like to meet him."

He squeezed her hand in reassurance. Got to his feet. "Thanks, Phoebe," he said. Gave her his cell number. "If you need anything, just let me know."

As he was leaving the room, she called out to him. He turned. "I'm happy to see you like this, Mark," she said, a small smile briefly crossing her lips. Like a peek of sun behind clouds.

TWENTY-TWO

DOCKERY LIMPED ALONG THE street, ribs aching, face sore. *For a wiry, strung-out white fucker*, he thought, *that guy packed a brick of a punch.* Made his way to the place he shared with his girlfriend. As he went, his chest tightened when he realized he'd probably said too much. But damn it, he needed to see Mrs. Russ. It wouldn't make it okay; hell, nothing could. Maybe it could at least put the mother's mind to rest a bit.

He turned the corner onto his street, and the feeling started again between his shoulder blades. The same feeling he'd gotten that hipped him to Mallen following him. Glanced over his shoulder. All he could see was a dark two-door sedan driving along in the street. Slow. Looking like the owner was hunting for parking.

Or, maybe hunting for something else.

Swore under his breath. Remembered then that Mallen had emptied his gun. *Fucker, you owe me a clip!*

Went to a nearby stoop. Made to tie his shoe. Heard the car pass along the street and keep going. Maybe it was nothing, but his years in the joint wouldn't let him believe that. Something was up.

———

Oberon sat at his breakfast table, coffee near one hand, notebook in front of him. He always pored and pored over his notes, like an archaeologist poring over the Rosetta Stone. His habit of drawing connecting arrows and thought balloons over words left his notes looking like some dyslexic scientific notation that only he could decipher. The phone rang and he picked up the extension.

"Kane speaking," he said.

"Inspector Kane? Saul Lowen, Folsom. Got your message. Sorry it took me so long to get back to you."

"That's understandable. Large establishment you gentlemen run up there."

There was a pause on the other end, like Lowen couldn't figure out if Oberon was making a joke or not. "Yeah, well," Lowen finally said, "it can get busy. Now, what was it you were exactly looking for? Something about two inmates?"

"Ex-inmates. Both were paroled, and now both are dead."

"Shame." He could tell Lowen thought it was anything but.

"I know that both men, Carl Kaslowski and Anthony Scarsdale, were there at the same time. What I need to know is if both men mixed together. Did they know each other?"

There was another pause on the phone. He could swear Lowen put his hand over the receiver for a moment. Mumbled something to somebody. Came back on the line. "You know how many guys we got here? Over thirty-four hundred, on a good day. I don't know if—"

"I understand the difficulty; however, I was hoping that if you could look in their files, maybe there would be a mention of it. They were both the same security risk, so they would probably be housed in the same dorms. I do realize what I am asking, especially with how busy you must be. I'm dealing with two homicides here, and I believe they could be connected."

There was another pause. This time he was sure he heard Lowen whisper something to someone. Then some laughter. "Okay, I hear ya," Lowen said. "I'll have to find the files. I'll get back to you."

Even though he now felt like it would be useless, he asked the question anyway. *Have to at least try, right, Mr. Investigator?* "Do you know how long it might be?"

"Soon. We had a sexual assault on a nurse in the infirmary this morning. I'm a bit jacked up. I'll have it for you soon, like I said."

"Thank you," Oberon said, adding, "it always fills me with warmth when two branches of law enforcement can work together so sympathetically."

"Yeah, okay," Lowen replied, the sarcasm sailing right over his head, and hung up.

Oberon sat there for a moment. Stared out the window at his garden. It was looking a bit shaggy. Badly needed a weeding. A feeling began to grow inside him, stark and hard. Lowen wasn't going to do a goddamned thing to help him. Oh, he might eventually call back, but it would be with a "Sorry, couldn't find a thing." The man wouldn't even bother looking. He sighed. Would have to tackle it another way.

Got up and went to get dressed. He would run a check on both men, see if any of their known acquaintances were on the outside. Maybe one of those people would be able to tell him a thing or two. It would take longer, but if it were the only option, then so be it.

Gato had been sleeping in the backseat of the Falcon when Mallen had returned. His friend had bolted awake, a habit most probably picked up in jail. Gato then got out and went to the trunk, where he pulled out a plastic gallon water container. Bent over, and poured it over his head. Shook off the excess. *That water must've been cold*, Mallen thought as he watched Gato get back behind the wheel of the Falcon.

"You really need some sleep, Gato," Mallen said as he got in and the man started up the car. Gato did a U turn, pointing the hood south, back toward Geary. When they hit Geary, he made a left, back toward the Loin.

It was a few blocks later when Gato finally spoke. "How they doin', *vato*?"

"About like you'd expect." He realized he'd forgotten to ask when Hal would be back. He'd really wanted to see what Hal's take would be on how Eric was acting in the time leading up to his murder. A guy would tell his father things he'd never, ever tell his mother.

He glanced out the window at the local markets, donut shops, and restaurants. The world certainly wasn't more beautiful now that he was off the junk, but it did feel more real. He had to give it that, at least.

"Where you want me to take you now?" Gato said.

"Can you take me back to the Cornerstone?" At Gato's look, he put up his hand to stop him.

"Don't worry, man," he said to Gato. "I'm good. I got Dreamo looking into who sold that junk to Eric. That guy might know something." Left unsaid was the feeling that it might be that maybe no one sold that junk to Eric. That it was a plant. You have to work *every* angle of a case, and that was a fact. The other reason for going back there was to give Bill his cell number. He had to start thinking this way, if the future was going to hold moments like this, where a call might mean a new lead, or a dead end.

The future. He couldn't really remember the last time he'd thought of that particular time frame. He sat back then. Tried to relax as Gato guided the Falcon through the tunnel that ran under Masonic. *Well,* he told himself, *maybe the future will be all right, after all.*

———

The Cornerstone was fairly busy. It was now just after quitting time, so some of the regulars who actually had jobs were in residence. He nodded at Bill as he walked in, took a stool at the far end as usual.

Bill shouted at him, "Usual?"

"A double!" It arrived in short order.

"Dreamo's been asking after you," Bill said under his breath.

That put him back on his heels. "He say that while you were in there pissing, or did he actually come out?"

Bill laughed. "Came the fuck out. He actually was out most of the fucking day. First time I can remember that happening since his mother died."

"Thanks," Mallen said as he took a sip of his drink and slid off the stool. Something was up. Did Dreamo have news?

There was a guy at the urinal. Tall, judging from his back. Big, but not Griffin big. Mallen killed time by washing his hands. Once the guy left, he went to the stall. It was closed up tight. He knocked the secret knock.

And that was when he saw the blood, trailing out from under the stall door. It crept its way toward the rusty drain.

He pushed on the door. Heard Dreamo's foot go up against it. To keep it closed. His mind flipped over then; that was crazy.

"Leave me alone, man ..." said the familiar voice. But it sounded different now. Thicker. The foot slid slowly down the door, tired. The door swung back a little, and Mallen pushed on it the rest of the way. Dreamo sat there, nose bleeding, right eye puffing up swollen, red and ugly. Mallen noticed a couple tiny white objects on the floor—Dreamo's teeth.

"What the fuck happened, dude?" No one, nobody would ever fuck with Dreamo. He was somehow inviolate. If you beat on Dreamo, it was like beating on a priest, as far as the street was concerned. "How long you been here? Didn't B see you come in this way, man? You should've asked for help!"

For an answer, he only got the famous, broken cackle. "Nobody will help another, especially if that other is a dealer, Mal. You know that," Dreamo said as he attempted to push his sagging Mohawk out of his eyes. This was very recent, and—

The man at the urinal ...

Mallen charged out of the restroom and into the main room of the bar. The man wasn't there. Bill watched as he raced out of the bar and into the street. He looked up and down the street, but there was nobody who resembled the back of the person he'd seen. Hell, he hadn't even been paying attention. Damn it! *There's another old muscle that needs to be strengthened again,* he told himself as he went back into the bar and asked Bill for the first-aid kit. He knew enough to know that Dreamo wouldn't want paramedics and cops.

"You see the guy that came out of there, right after I went in, B?" he asked.

Bill shook his head as he handed over the first-aid kit he kept under the bar alongside a Louisville Slugger. "Sorry, Mal."

"It's okay, man. Just a long shot."

"Bad?" Bill asked with a look over at the men's room. Under any other circumstances, it would've been crazy. Absurd.

"Not sure. I don't think so. I'll let you know." He went down the hall and entered the men's room. Dreamo was actually up at the sink. Washing the blood off his face. He rinsed his mouth, the water running a soft red.

"I can take you to emergency, man," he said. "No one has to know it's you."

Dreamo looked over his thin shoulder at Mallen. Spied the first-aid kit. "Naw man. It's good. Not the first I've taken, right? Didn't you beat me once? For shorting you?"

"You wish, asshole," Mallen said. He heard a scraping sound on the door. Smiled. That would be Bill, putting the "Out of Order" sign up. Amazing where our guardian angels came from. He went and sat Dreamo back in his stall. Went to work on the cuts. It was his first time that he could remember ever seeing the man up close, and not through a drugged haze. He was older than he'd originally thought. Thinner, too. There were the tattoos he'd come to know, but had never really studied them. Mystic symbols, astrological signs. Had the tarot card for The Magician on his right forearm. He'd never realized that before. Lots of track scars. *How much longer did Dreamo have?* he wondered.

"Ouch, man," Dreamo said with some heat as he cleaned the cut above the man's right eye. "That shit hurts, Mallen."

"Yeah, it does. Who did it, Dreamo?

A pause. "Didn't recognize him."

"Didn't? Or didn't want to?"

Dreamo glanced at him again. Shook his head. "Didn't."

"Okay. You ask around about Eric at all?"

"Yeah. Came up with shit, man. No one sold him that dope, or that's what's being said. Sorry I couldn't do more."

"You did more than you think, maybe." He put a bandage over the cut above Dreamo's eye. Dug out some aspirin. Held them out to Dreamo, but got only a laugh in return. Mallen had to laugh, too. "Sorry, bro. Don't know what I was thinking." Took a rag that was in the kit and soaked it in warm water. Came back and held it out to Dreamo, who looked at it for a second, then at Mallen.

"Why are you doing all this, man? You're not in my world anymore. I don't get it."

"Take the fucking rag and finish cleaning your face, Dream." As Dreamo did this, Mallen said as he glanced around the room. "You're still a human being. Having been in your world? I can understand you a lot better than I would've had I stayed a cop, you know? And," he added as he put the first-aid kit back in order, "even though you sell horse, you were always straight with me. Never ripped me off. I appreciated that. Every time." Paused for a moment. "The guy that beat on you? What *can* you tell me?"

Dreamo sighed. Reached for his rig, from a secret place behind the toilet tank. "You tell *no one* this is here, okay?" Dreamo said. "Bill would take the hit on it, and I don't want that, man. Dig?"

"I get you," he replied as Dreamo began to cook a shot. His eyes were riveted on the needle. Had it only been like a week? Man … that would feel so good, and then he could—

Dreamo stopped then. Looked at his rig, then at Mallen. Put it away, under the toilet tank. Breathed deeply. "You asked about the guy who beat on me?"

It took a moment to come back to the here and now. "Yeah … yes. I did."

"I didn't see him. He turned off the fucking lights, then busted into the stall and just beat on me. I asked what the fuck, you know? But he never said a word. Strong asshole, that's for sure."

"How many people had you asked about Eric?"

A shrug. "As many as I could handle. Five, maybe seven. Asked some street demons. The word is out there about an ex-cop who fell that *wasn't* you, you know? Nobody is copping to selling some dope to an ex-cop who ended up dead. Why would they?"

Right, he thought, *why the fuck would they*? "And this was what, yesterday? Day before?"

"Both," came the reply. He noted the edge the voice had taken. He'd heard it in his own. Dreamo wanted to shoot. Like now.

Before closing the first-aid kit up tight, he pulled out a couple bandages, along with some aspirin. Laid them on the toilet paper dispenser, maybe just for shits 'n' giggles, but really maybe hoping the guy would use them if he needed to. "Thanks for the help, man," he said as he turned to leave. "If I get my hands on the guy that beat on you, I'll make him regret it, Dream."

He was at the door that led back out into the bar when Dreamo said, "Mallen?"

"Yeah?"

"Thanks for the extra Band-Aids."

Mallen returned to the bar. Bill was busy with a customer but then came over. Mallen gave him back the first-aid kit and the "Out of Order" sign. In exchange, Bill put a double scotch down in front of him with a smile. "On the house, Florence fucking Nightingale! Is he going to be okay?"

"Yeah, as far as I can tell. Just got beat on, is all. He'll be fine." Took a sip of his drink, then looked up at Bill. "B," he said, "why do you care? This guy is committing a crime—a big crime—that could fuck your world all the way to Illinois and back again. I don't get it. I've been coming in here for years, and for like ninety-five percent of that time, I've been copping H in the men's room from Dreamo. Why do you care if he got beat on? Would seem you'd *want* some way to get him out. What's up?" He'd always just assumed that Dreamo "rendered unto Caesar"—gave Bill a little on the side. But that really didn't seem like Bill. If he thought he was going to be surprised by the answer, he was totally blindsided as Bill picked up a glass and filled himself a shot of whiskey. Downed it. Looked around, like to be sure no one would hear. Went to fill the glass again.

"He's my sister's kid."

Mallen couldn't help himself: he glanced back at the men's room door, then at Bill. The world had just taken on an entirely new shape. "Bill," he said, "seriously? Dreamo is your nephew?"

For an answer, Bill downed the second shot. Put the glass in the sink. Nodded. "Yeah. She died about…twenty years ago now? Anyway, Justin…well, he's had it hard. I tried…try to help him. You know how it goes."

"Justin?" Mallen again looked back down the hall. *Justin.*

"I wasn't uncle material, for Christ's sake," Bill continued. "I certainly wasn't going to be a surrogate father. I just want to keep him in the light." Now it was Bill's turn to look down the hall. "I failed. What can I say? I lost him. But goddamn it, I was going to at least make sure he would be as safe as possible." He washed the glass he'd just taken a drink from. Dried it slowly. "What else was I going to do?" Bill continued quietly. "Let him shoot up and deal in doorways? Alleys? He would've been dead years ago."

Mallen held up his glass in toast. Bill waved it away, but there was a smile there. A smile that said, "Thank you for not judging how I worked this out in my head." Mallen finished his drink and slid off the stool. Wrote his cell number down on a napkin. Handed it to Bill.

"Anytime you need to use it, you use it, B." He started for the door. "And thanks for the talk, man. Thank you."

———

It was later than he'd realized as he left the bar. Turning into night now. Cold, with fog lying heavy on the city. Mallen shoved his hands in his coat pockets as he struck off down the street, heading back to his place, not knowing where else to go. Thought back to Bill and Dreamo. How weird and wondrous life turned sometime. Uncle and nephew. Crazy.

He was on the next block when he heard the roar of an engine. Eight cylinders.

A black Escalade screeched around the corner ahead of him, and he knew he was a dead man. The vehicle skidded to the curb as he remembered the gun and dug his hand frantically into his coat pocket. *Too out of practice, idiot!* The front doors flew open. Griffin charged toward him as Jas fanned out in case he tried to run. The look in Griffin's eyes said it all: this was going to be terminal. He finally got the damn gun out and aimed, but the shot went wide. He heard a car window go out. An alarm start. That's all he had time for before Griffin came in, knocking the gun from his hand, grabbing him in a choke hold.

"Now, wait a minute…" he muttered, but didn't get the chance to finish, because he was clubbed in the temple. Proverbial stars then. Barely felt it as he was dragged to the luxury SUV. He was thrown in back face first. Griffin leapt in behind him. Something that felt like a sledgehammer slammed him in the kidneys a couple times. His legs went numb. The door crashed shut behind them. By the time he was able to sit up, the car had already powered away from the curb. He was stuck.

Jas glanced once over his shoulder at Mallen. Spoke to his partner. "Told you it was money well spent. Fuckin' cops, always out for a fucking dollar."

"Long time, no see, guys," Mallen said after finding his voice. "How was prison?"

"Fuck you, civilian," Griffin said and punched him in the face. He tasted blood. Spat it out on the floor.

"Hey, asshole," Jas said to Griffin, "you're going to have to clean that shit up. Gag the narc bastard."

"I was just doing my job," Mallen said. "You woulda done the same, man."

"It's all over for you," Griffin said, and he had to admit, the man was probably right. "I hope you saw your family recently. Be the last time."

A coldness set in between his shoulders. Like a mantle. Sweat broke out under his arms. He looked around the backseat. It was a prison, of course, with no way out. "You won't get away with it," he said, knowing he was lying. Of course they fucking would.

Jas laughed as he turned the Escalade onto Market Street. Headed toward the water. "You know what will happen, if someone even bothered to dig into it?" he said. "They'll find nothing but a recovering junkie who fell back on the spike and OD'd. End of pathetic fucking story."

"Who's going to give a shit about you anyway?" Griffin added. "No one, that's who. You're a piece of shit junkie civilian now. On the bottom of this city's shoe, motherfucker."

Jas tossed something in a baggie over the seat to Griffin. Dread filled Mallen when he saw it was a syringe. Griffin held it up. Grinned. "Maybe I'll shoot this into your tear duct, you undercover son of a bitch."

"What's the matter?" he said, "your mother take your guns away?" There was a forced bravery in his tone. He knew they could tell it was a fucking lie.

"No. Just figured this would be more fun."

Mallen looked out the window. The panic was a growing knot in his stomach. He was just turning it all around. There was too much at stake now to let it end this way. Anna's face was suddenly there in his mind's eye. She would believe the story. Would grow up thinking her dad OD'd on smack. Chris wouldn't even try to say otherwise. Whatever the cops would say would be believed. He *needed* to stay alive! He hadn't felt that way in a very long time. But now he needed to make it to tomorrow. And beyond. He had to find a way out.

The SUV turned onto the Embarcadero. Headed south. There was little traffic at this hour. They pulled up at Pier Three. Parked behind an old van. Jas killed the engine. Both men silently got out.

Griffin stood back as he got out, ready for anything. There was nothing Mallen could think of to do. They were being too careful. They'd taken his gun. But he just couldn't fold it all up and let them have their way.

He had to try something.

Anything.

"Come on, asshole. Move it," Griffin said.

Mallen climbed out. Jas pulled his gun. Held it steady, aimed right for his chest.

They pushed him along the north side of the long, low, crumbling building. The air was heavy with salt. There was the occasional soft splash as a wave hit one of the crumbling pylons that held the up warehouse.

"Watch your step now," Jas said sarcastically. The pier was so dilapidated that a lot of the cement had crumbled away in places, leaving large, dark holes that opened to the cold bay below.

The water would be frigid this time of year. He would have no time to try to swim anywhere. Even if he could manage it under the rush of the huge shoot they were bound to give him, he was as good as dead; if the water didn't kill him, the junk probably would.

They guided him down toward the end. He knew time was running out. He faked tripping, fell to the ground as he kicked out with his right leg. Kicked at Jas's right knee with everything he had. It surprised the man, hit him square in the ACL. The gun fell from Jas's hand and discharged, the shot ringing out over the bay. Griffin swore loudly as he went for his own weapon. Mallen bolted away back toward the SUV. Got only seven feet before he felt Griffin land on his back and drag him down. He tried to rise, but it was too late. Griffin pistol whipped him across temple, stunning him.

Jas limped over, swearing a line of curses. Could barely put any weight on his now-screwed knee. "You okay?" Griffin said.

"I don't think it's broken," Jas said. The small man growled as he punched Mallen in the stomach, which was still in rough shape from his last beating. His insides exploded in agony. He curled up. Tried to breathe. Tried to protect his ribs. He barely registered the fact that Jas might've just busted one.

He felt his coat pulled off his shoulders. His sleeve rolled up. This was it. Now or never. He could swear he heard Anna's voice in his head, whimpering as if she were in a bad dream ...

"Fucking get over here and help, damn it!" He heard Griffin snarl. Felt Jas clutch at his other arm.

"No …" was all he could muster as he, with the last of his strength, fired another kick. It was a blind kick, a kick of sheer panic and desperation, and he felt it connect with something. Jas cried out again and he suddenly felt more freedom, then he rolled away, not knowing what else do to, knowing he only had this one thing he *could* do at that moment: roll. A seagull cried out. The sound echoed through his head and away back toward the beginning of time. Then the rolling ended and he was dropping, falling fast.

The holes in the pier! It felt like he was falling, falling forever. Then he hit a wall of ice, slamming into it at what felt like eighty miles an hour. Then it was quiet, and strangely warm and numbing. He might like it here. Then he heard Anna again, whimpering, calling out for him. He knew he should do something, go and help her maybe, but it was hard to move, and he was so cold, so very cold. Then he heard her voice in his head.

Daddy!

He kicked to the surface, his lungs screaming for air. Broke the water. Above the sound of the waves lapping at the pilings, he heard Jas and Griffin cursing. Saw the flash of a penlight beam. He just had to wait them out, he knew, but how could he? He was already numb from the water's temperature. There was a piling only seven feet away, and he kicked for it, trying to stay quiet and out of the beam of light that skittered over the water. He made the piling, its surface slick, sharp, and grimy, covered with barnacles, algae, and slime. Moved to the far side, to put the piling between him and the hunters. Now he just had to hang on long enough and hopefully leave himself enough energy to find his way out of the water.

It seemed like a year, his body shaking uncontrollably from the frigid water, but the penlight was extinguished, and then he just stayed there until he counted to thirty. He was rewarded by the faint sound of the Escalade's engine starting up and the vehicle driving away.

He'd always been a decent swimmer. Not great, but good enough. His coat weighed him down, but he had no energy to spare to shed it. Spied a dock to his left, looked almost a football field away, but it could've been just over twenty feet. Could he make it? Would he?

Only one way to find out.

The swim was an agony that far eclipsed anything he'd every endured in his life, and that included the withdrawals in the drunk tank. He was down to seconds before he knew he'd succumb to the cold, but he made it and managed to drag his wet, heavy body out of the water and onto the pier, where he lay panting and shivering.

He heard footsteps, but at the moment, didn't give a shit who it was. Only cared if they had a blanket and some hot fucking coffee. A flashlight beam swam over him like a lighthouse giving solace to a lost ship. He managed to reach out, croaking, "Help—" then passed into darkness.

TWENTY-THREE

ERIC CRUMPLED UP THE empty beer can in his hand. Got to his feet. Stood at the rail at the top of the stairs of the northern windmill in Golden Gate Park. Mallen knew what was coming. This had been the place they'd always come to when either one of them had a problem that came from wearing a badge. He knew immediately something was working on his friend. The phone call asking for the meet had felt unusually urgent, uneasy. That wasn't like Eric. To call was to risk Mallen's cover. There was something going on. He knew Eric at least that well. Just like he knew enough to let his friend come to saying whatever he had to say in his own time, his own way.

Eric stood there, leaning against the rail, a black shadow against the night sky. He took a deep breath and sailed the beer can through the air in a great, glinting arc. It reminded Mallen of a falling star. He heard the can whistle through the air, followed by a faint crashing sound as it sailed in through the open back window of Mallen's car.

"Two points for the uniform," Mallen said with a laugh as he clapped his hands. Fuck… he knew he could never, ever have made that shot.

Eric shrugged as he came back over to where they were sitting. Grabbed another beer and opened it. Took a long gulp. Eric was getting pretty drunk, and he still had to drive home.

Again, not like the Eric he'd known.

"Hey," Eric said, "remember that day I had to hit you? Then arrest you? You ever think about that?"

"Sometimes," he replied. That had been last year, but he couldn't help thinking it hadn't been a screw-up. Someone had wanted to make his life… difficult. He'd spent a long time going over it, again and again. Had even made a list of the people he thought might have it in for him. It wasn't long, but it could be considered lethal. Dietrich had set up the raid. Stevens had okayed it. But there were at least four other guys who could've dropped a dime on him, and would've. Not like he'd worked to be anybody's enemy, but sometimes dogs just hated other dogs for no reason, and that was a fact. He'd tried to keep those thoughts away. How could he do his job if he had to worry about not only the bad guys, but the good ones, too? It was too Serpico, and he laughed at that, because he'd wanted to be Serpico.

Just not in this way.

Mallen finished his beer and grabbed another. They sat there in silence for awhile. Eric put his beer down on the wooden planks that made up the causeway running around the windmill. Cleared his throat. Mallen knew that whatever it was that had gotten under Eric's skin, it would be coming out now.

"Mark," Eric said as he leaned his head against the shingled wall. "I don't know if I want to do this anymore."

"Okay. Then stop. But, you gotta know for sure, right? Nine out of every ten Police have felt that—feel that. More than once in their career for sure, probably every fucking day, man. Especially guys on the street, in uniform. Guys like you. Why don't you go for detective or something? You'd make it, easy." And that was the truth: Eric could make detective no sweat. Eric was that good. Better than he was. They had taken different roads, yeah, but they'd both cared. He'd cared about taking down big dealers, stopping the devastation of the drug world. Eric had cared about the guy on the street, just trying to make it through another day so he could protect and provide for his family.

"Eric," he said, then took a drink. "What the hell would you do, if you left?"

A shrug. "Hell, I dunno. Sometimes I just want to…forget about me, and who I am."

"Dude," Mallen said with a chuckle, "you're gonna regret this conversation in the morning, my friend." He took a swig from his can. "Maybe you need to put in for some pussy, or some deskwork? Go and just fill out forms, or maybe fill in a vagina. Take a break."

Eric finished his beer with one long swig. Put the empty back in the paper bag. Not too steady. "I dunno what I need, Mark." Got up then. Paced for a moment. "No," he continued, "I do know what I need."

"Okay. What?"

"I need to do what you do. I need undercover."

That brought him up short. Wasn't what he'd expected at all. "Eric," he replied, "your strength is in being a beat cop. Maybe just for now, sure, but that's the way it seems, don't you think?" The truth of it was that he just couldn't see his friend living the life he did. Something that would be a positive for Eric was that he didn't have a girlfriend for longer than a month. No ties, no weak spots that could be exploited, except inside the cop himself. But still…Mallen just couldn't see it.

Thankfully, Eric nodded. Grinned. "I know, I know," he said as he sat back down. They sat in silence for a moment as the moon rode high above. A car cruised by on King Jr. Drive. Mallen tensed, thinking he might've been seen. He had to be so careful, all the fucking time. It was wrecking his nerves. But as he sat there, he had to admit he was addicted to the rush of these kinds of busts. Maybe that's what Eric felt he was missing out on? Maybe taking down street thugs and notes on robberies had finally paled next to busting guys who sold a ton of dope and thought they were above the law.

"Eric," he said to his friend, "if you are even entertaining the idea of a transfer or leaving the force, you need to deal with that. Really think about it, man. Not everyone is—"

"I know!" Eric shot back. He was angry, the alcohol probably feeding him now like coal in a steam engine. He sighed then, like he'd been beaten at an argument Mallen didn't even know they were having. Sat back down. "You know what my old man would say if I told him I wanted to leave?"

So that was it. That was something Mallen knew very well and dealt with everyday. What would the world say if Ol' Monster Mallen's son didn't love, eat, fuck, and shit the police force? Why, the world would end! Jesus would come down on rubber fucking crutches and smite every Mallen that was still alive, effectively ending the line. He himself would serve an eternity in some whacked-out perdition made up of a booking room and an endless line of public urinaters and prostitutes.

No. This wasn't the life for his friend. He could see that. But now it was Eric who needed to see that. He grabbed the second to last beer. Cracked it open. Took a long slug. The night had been cold, so the beer still was.

"Then quit, man," he said. "If you're that miserable: quit. Fuck whatever anyone else says. Hell man, you're a cop! You're putting your life on the line, right? Not every motherfucker out there can do that, right? If they could, we'd have a much safer society." Took another drag from the beer can. "Or, I guess a police state, yeah?"

TWENTY-FOUR

AND MALLEN WOKE TO light and noise.

Opened his eyes. He was in an emergency room. Knew it immediately by the curtained-off space and the white noise. Took a moment to realize he was in SF General. He knew that by the volume and quality of the white noise. Weird how that could act on the deeper parts of the brain. Like how a peculiar odor could bring back memories.

He'd never been here as a patient, only as someone bringing in somebody. Strangely, he'd never done that as a uniform. That was for the paramedics. After he'd gone undercover, he'd dropped a couple guys at the doors. Had even left Davy inside, in a chair, and told the receptionist his friend really needed help.

That was what he'd *had* to do. That was one of the things that was the hardest about doing what he did. Doing what he *had* to do. Later on, after he'd left the force, he found himself still bringing guys to the emergency room, but then it was walking in, getting it all set with the nurses, then leaving as fast as he could without giving a name, even a fake name. Funny how being undercover he'd had a fake name, but being a junkie ex-cop, he hated giving a fake name. The reason for that had always gone . . . unsolved.

Just chalk it up to the usual junkie bullshit, he told himself. But at least he'd brought those guys here. A lot of other people would've just left them on the street. It was hard, figuring out that thin line between the right and wrong in the junkie's world.

As he looked around now, lying there in the bed, he almost laughed: all the years he'd brought people here, as a cop, or as a junkie, he'd never been here himself. Felt like his journey was now complete, full circle.

There were white curtains on his left and right. Nurses occasionally walked past the open end of his little world, not seeing him, not noticing he was awake. He made a few movements with his limbs. Everything seemed to still be there. Did a visual, just to be sure. Two working hands and arms, that was good. Two working legs. After that, the only thing he found himself caring about was time . . .

How long had he been here?

How much time had passed?

A nurse came into his little cordoned-off space. Short. Tired, but caring. It was then he noticed he had an IV in his left arm. Looked at his right. Recent marks there.

"Your veins weren't up to the challenge," she said as she began to check his blood pressure.

"Yeah, they wouldn't be," he replied. "It's going to take them awhile to heal, you know? Workin' on that."

She looked at him again. Studied him. Dispassionately. *How many strung-out motherfuckers must she see in a night?* he wondered. *Probably more than I ever did when back on the beat,* came the reply. He looked around for his wallet and clothes.

"I'm feeling good to go," he said. "By the way, how long have I been here?"

"The boat captain who found you brought you here about four hours ago." She checked his chart, glanced at him. "If you're … healing, you really need to eat."

"Got it. My clothes?"

She indicated a plastic bag on the nearby metal and cloth chair. He hadn't noticed it. "They're still wet. We're not a laundry service, sorry."

And then he really got it. To them, even with the now-healing holes in his arm, those holes were still there. He'd been … over there. Over the fence somewhere, on that other side, in the darkness. Running away from the light. That was okay, he could understand it. Nobody understands why a junkie becomes a junkie. He smiled at her. "Thank you for your help. I can go, right?"

"Yes. There's some papers to sign, but after that, you can go."

She even helped him sit up. He was feeling pretty good, actually. Like he'd been through an obstacle course and had come out the other side mostly in one piece. "The police were here, earlier," she said to him then. Very softly, so only he would hear.

"Really?"

"Do I look like a liar?" she said, then her expression softened.

He looked down at the bag containing his clothes. "Do you think I have time to catch my death of cold by throwing on my wet clothes and leaving quickly?"

"You might, but only if you sign your release papers."

"Good enough." She left him to get dressed. And as he picked up his cold, salt- and grime-encrusted clothes, he knew that dressing was going to be a fucking misery. Found his cell phone, amazingly still somehow lodged in his coat pocket. Of course it was useless, though, from taking a late-night swim in the bay. Tossed it in the trash. He'd need to get another one. He would've broken down altogether at the thought of the long, freezing slog back to his place had it not been for the news of the police asking after him. *Not now*, he thought, *not yet.* There was work to do, and he had to keep on doing it. That space between him and the needle needed to be maintained, at all costs.

The nurse appeared again, this time with a clipboard. She almost shoved it at him, like she really wanted to help him get the fuck outta Dodge. "I appreciate the special treatment," he told her as he signed his name on every blank line, regardless of what it might mean or what he might owe. He knew he'd make it right, at some point, once he figured out what the hell happened to Eric.

"I don't know what you're talking about," she said, then added quietly, "My sister beat it, two years ago. It was hard. Very hard. But she did. You can, too." She took back the clipboard with the forms. Stood up straight and said loudly, officially, "Hope we don't see you again"—checked the clipboard—"Mr. Mallen."

TWENTY-FIVE

IT WASN'T AN EASY decision for him to make. But really, there was nowhere else to go. The need to lie low and off the grid couldn't be denied. He had to get off the streets for awhile. Maybe Jas and Griffin would even think he'd drowned. That would buy him time. Beyond that? Well, he just needed a rest. Being clean had turned out to be way fucking more stressful than being a junkie, and that was a fact.

He exited the bus downtown. Transferred to another, making his slow way to his destination. Now that he was heading over there, he wasn't so sure about it all. He'd thought about calling first, but in the end he felt it would feel way more dramatic, way more hysterical than just showing up and ringing the bell.

He took a deep breath as he walked up the familiar steps to the door. She'd been good about trimming the ivy on the stairs. Better than he'd ever been. Rang the doorbell. There was no answer and he actually breathed a sigh of relief. But then the light came on. The door opened and Chris was there. She blinked once. Not sure it was him. He tried a smile.

"Hey," he said. "Sorry for not calling. If it's a bad time, I—"

She stepped forward and opened the heavy, wrought iron security gate that kept the rest of the world at bay. "No," she replied, "it's okay. Just a little out of the ordinary, is all." Her eyes went big with fear. "Oh, God … did you take a blood test?"

"No, no, nothing like that. It's, well … complicated. Can I come in and clean up?"

She nodded. He went up the stairs and into the house. In the kitchen, he used the sink to wash his hair of the salt and his arms and hands of whatever the hospital used to disinfect him. Was only too conscious of her gaze when he took off his filthy, crusted shirt. It felt weird to be there, in his old kitchen, using his old sink, after so many years. The water felt sepia-tinted with memories. It was after a moment that he realized Chris continued to watch him intently. "What is it?" he asked.

"Are you … ? You know," she said quietly, evidently trying hard to hide her anger and disappointment.

"No," he said vehemently. "No, no way," he added in a more quiet tone.

She indicated his clothes. "You just look like you've been … forgetting about things again."

He actually found himself smiling at that. Of course that's what she would think with him showing up at this hour, in this state. He hesitated, because the truth wouldn't make her any more relieved. He went and sat down at the table.

"No, I'm not using again," he said as he stared her in the eye. After a moment of staring back at him, she nodded. Let out a breath.

"Okay," she said evenly, "then what happened? Are you in trouble, Mark?"

"Maybe. Yeah, probably." He then told her the entire sequence of events since Oberon had entered his apartment to tell him that Eric had died. And he even told her about Jas and Griffin. Told her everything about what had gone on in his search for the reason why Eric may have been killed. It actually felt *good* to let it all out, almost like old times.

There were moments when she looked like she was going to pop a gasket at him, followed by moments where she stared at him like she hadn't seen him in a long time. When he was finished, he sat back and ran his hand through his wet, stringy hair. "And well, it's gotten a bit hairy, I suppose you could say. And they always say getting clean is good for an addict," he added with a smile.

"And what if something happens to you?" she said. "You're not on the force anymore."

"This isn't what I planned on, sure, but this is Eric. I feel like I owe him some help."

She nodded in response. "I don't know what to say. I guess I should be relieved."

"Relieved?"

"Yes. It's a good sign. If you're involved in this, then you're serious about staying clean." She smirked at him, and he realized it'd been many years since the last time he'd seen her do that. "You just can't help playing a knight in tarnished armor, can you? Damn romantics. You guys kill me."

He laughed then. Long and hard. Again, he was hit with the feeling he wanted to be back here, with her and his little girl. "I was wondering if you'd let me crash in the basement. Somewhere quiet so I could get some rest?" he asked.

"No," she said.

"Oh," he said. "Okay. I understand. Yeah … I mean—"

"Stop," she cut in, "what I mean is that you can have the damn couch. I'll drive you back to your place in the morning. And, well… Anna will get a treat when she wakes up."

"You sure?"

"Yeah," she said. "And I think I even have one or two of your shirts packed away somewhere." She grimaced as she glanced at what he was wearing. "And you should thank me for that, Marky. You look like shit."

She got up and left the room leaving him sitting there, dumbfounded.

Dumbfounded but happy. She still had a couple of his shirts. Maybe he could take that as a hopeful sign.

TWENTY-SIX

ANNA'S SQUEAL OF DELIGHT grabbed him from sleep and dumped him back onto the couch. He woke with a start, instinct kicking in as he reached for a nonexistent gun.

"Daddy!" she said as she leapt on him. He laughed and covered her with kisses. Rubbed his beard on the top of her head. She peeled off a long squeal that hurt his ears. Struggled to get away, but he just hugged her tighter. Noticed that his clothes, which he'd left on the floor just before he'd fallen asleep, had now been cleaned and neatly folded. There was even a fresh, dark gray turtleneck. He hadn't seen that shirt since he'd left. The clothes brought a smile to his face. Chris had always hated him going around in things worn more than one day. His crusty seawater clothes would've set her hair on fire.

"Hey, A," he said as he let go of his daughter. "How's it going, citizen?"

"You smell," she replied. "Don't you shower?"

"Only when I know I won't be seeing you."

She made a face. Struggled to get away again, laughing. He let her go. Smelled his shirt. "Damn," he said with an astonished air, "you were right!"

Chris's cell phone rang from the kitchen. He heard her come in and pick it up. "Hello?" she said, then after a moment, more quietly, "Today? Well, maybe later. I have something I have to do this morning. I'll call you after I'm done. Yeah, I'd like that. Okay. Bye."

He sat there, knowing what the call meant. Heard it in her voice. Could now see all chance of him and Chris getting back together flying out the window like a bird with a new set of wings. After a moment, she walked into the room, phone still in hand. "You heard?"

He nodded. "But I know that I don't have *the right* to hear anything, if you get me." Anna didn't understand what was going on, but got the crashing change in vibe. Sat down next to him. Leaned her weight on his arm. He petted her head. Just like he used to.

"That's true," Chris told him. "But, are you sure? I don't want—or need—to have compartments in my life."

"I don't want to know the particulars. Honest. Like I said: not my business. I do have to say, though, that I'm glad I know."

"Why?"

He got up. "I dunno. You know me: always have to know the exact measurement of the playing field before suiting up. Can you take me back to my place? And really, thanks for letting me crash. I owe ya, okay?" he said, finishing with the best smile he could.

She seemed to appreciate his attitude. Again gave him one of those long looks that used to drive him crazy because she was impossible to read at those moments. Finally she smiled back. Pulled her keys from her nearby purse, saying, "Okay then. Let's hit the road, people!"

———

Just like the last time, he wouldn't let them see his place. Being clean was like windshield wipers for his eyes. The neighborhood was bad enough, but his place was downright embarrassing. Before he got out, he kissed Anna on the cheek. "I'll have a new kite for you, real soon," he said.

"Promises, promises!" Anna said, putting on her best Cockney accent. After he was done laughing, he told Chris one more time how much he appreciated her letting him crash on the couch. She smiled at him, saying, "No matter what's happening in our lives, I want you to know that as long as you're like you are now, you'll have total access to our daughter."

"That's a lot. Thanks." He watched her car until it turned the corner. As if to make sure they got out of the Loin alive. Went down the street and into the corner liquor store. Bought another phone. He noticed that his appearance only reinforced the opinion of the guy behind the counter that he was nothing but a scumbag junkie. He laughed at that as he left, reveling in the fact that it wasn't the truth anymore, no matter what anyone fucking thought.

———

Dockery hung up the phone. Stared at it, shell-shocked. Carl Kaslowski was dead. Couldn't believe it. Man, his woman had sounded all in when she'd told him, heart ripped to pieces. The guy hadn't been one of the bad ones, either. Not an evil one. Def not like that piece of shit Tony S.

Damn, man, he thought. Shot. *That's fucked up. Fuckin' life, man . . . every time you try to get up, it kicks you in the sack again. Fuckin' life.*

The place was suddenly too small to hold him. He needed air. To be out among people. Out free. He said the usual goodbye to his girl. Gave his kid a kiss, then left.

He needed a drink. Should he call his parole officer? No, fuck that bitch. She'd be no help. But he wanted, *needed,* to talk to someone. Anyone. After two blocks, he turned left and went down to the Dark Horse. Ordered his usual and sat at the stick, glumly drinking and thinking. After a moment he looked around, the feeling of being watched kicking in. But there was no one he could point to that looked like they were interested in him. Remembered then that his gun was empty. Mallen had taken the clip. He'd have to get another one, and fast. Felt naked without a loaded beast on him. There was no relaxation in him. Kept going back to Carl's death. Why the hell did shit like that have to go down? The guy was turning it all around. If there was ever a white boy he could look up to, it would have been Carl.

Spent about another hour in the bar, nursing a couple more drinks. He was good and tight by the time he left. *What now?* he wondered. Should he even bother trying to track down some of the other guys? He just wanted to jaw with someone he could connect with.

He walked slowly down Fillmore Street, hands in pockets, lost in thought. His mind barely registered the sound of an engine starting up. Took him a moment to realize he'd heard that engine before. Glanced around the street.

And there it fuckin' was: the small, two-door sedan he'd seen earlier. Right after talking to that Mallen dude.

Could be coincidence, a part of his mind told him. Hell, the city was small. People always running into people. But then again, maybe it wasn't like that. He picked up his pace. Turned on the next block. Headed east to downtown. The car didn't follow him, and he laughed softly to himself for being so on edge. Easy to be that way when you done time.

After another block he decided to go see Soldier. He'd have a spare clip to sell. Kept walking down the street, nice and easy. Was another block on when he again saw the sedan. It had just turned onto the street ahead of him, moving east, in the direction he was heading.

Motherfuck...

Dockery turned on his heel and walked away, picking up speed. The sighting of the car was too fucking weird. Now he had to get to Soldier's. And fast. Walked quickly, crossing back over Fillmore as he went west. The car was rolling up Fillmore toward him. Fucker must've high-tailed it in a double-back. What the fuck? Now he ran, ran at top speed down the street. Soldier's was only ten blocks away. As he ran, he took a jigsaw route: one block up, one block over, one block up, two blocks over in the opposite direction from before. Zigged his way to his goal, always checking behind him. He lost the car two blocks from his destination. Immediately hid on some steps leading down to a dark basement access door of an old apartment building. Lay on the stairs, keeping his eyes just above street level.

Paranoid? Maybe. Wanting to stay alive? Sure as fuck. Waited about another five minutes. Listened and watched. There was no traffic on the street now. Only a passing motorcycle, then a woman strolling by with a baby carriage.

Figured it was safe to go on. He did so quickly, scanning all around him as he went. There was no sign of the car.

———

Oberon checked his notes again. Made sure he had the right place. Looked once more at the building. Hadn't really expected such a nicely kept, Inner Richmond apartment building. They might even be condos in there. Expensive condos. Got out of his car, went to the door. He'd found very little in his search regarding felons who'd not only known both dead men but who were also still out on the street. It had only been in doing some checking with Narco that he'd come up with a couple names. *Thank God for repeat offenders once in awhile*, he thought. Every time a criminal went through the system, they learned a little more about him or her. And sometimes they learned some items regarding their previous time inside.

He entered the building's vestibule. Again, very nice, with subway tile polished a brilliant white. Found the name he was looking for on the glass and brass directory. Pushed the buzzer. A woman's voice answered. Strong and firm. "Yes?"

"This is Detective Inspector Oberon Kane, Ma'am. San Francisco Police. I was wondering if a Mr. Robert Jenks was in?"

There was a pause. "What's this about?"

"Just some routine questions, Ma'am. Let me in please." He hated sounding so formal, but he also hated standing outside a building and speaking to what amounted to a squawk box. It was things like this that made cops nervous, and he was no exception. What was going on inside? Was there someone up in that room dumping drugs down a drain? Hiding drugs? Loading a gun? Strange how something so simple as walking up to a door could be a life-or-death experience.

The lock buzzed open, and he pushed on the heavy oak door. He went up the heavily carpeted stairs to the third floor. Knocked and waited, ears tuned to any noises from the other side that might alert him to trouble.

The door was opened by a man. About six feet, solidly built. Hair cut military short. Wire-rimmed, John Lennon–like glasses. The clothes were business casual for the home. Like something out of a Territory Ahead catalog.

"Robert Jenks?" he asked the man.

Jenks nodded. Smiled as he held out a hand. "Yeah, but my friends call me Bobby, Officer. Care to come in?"

The two men shook hands. Oberon couldn't help but notice that Jenks had a pretty powerful grip, and he didn't think the man was even trying too hard. The flat was done up tastefully. Very neat and tidy. Lots of dark, chocolate-brown leather furniture and heavily lacquered maple. The formal dining room had been given over as an office. The large dining table was now a desk strewn with papers. A white board stood nearby, covered with words such as *persevere*, *integrity*, and *strength*. There were also phrases like "The best way to predict your future is to create it."

Jenks went to the table and picked up a business card. Brought it over to him. Written on it were two lines in a professional, business-type font: *Inner Iron. Bobby Jenks, Motivational Speaker.*

"This is what I've been doing since I got out," Jenks said, proud of his accomplishment. "I'm trying to use my own experience to help others to leverage their lives in a positive and meaningful manner."

"That's impressive, Mr. Jenks," Oberon said as he slipped the card into his coat pocket. "How is it going?"

"Great." Jenks beamed. "I'm opening my first location next week. Renting a storefront and offices over on Union. I'll be able to give seminars there. And, after training two or three hires to run that, I'll be able to personally 'take it on the road', as they say."

"My," Oberon said as he pulled out his notebook, "this must have cost a helluva lot to get going."

A woman entered the room from the kitchen. Incredibly beautiful. Long blonde hair, model-caliber figure. Carried herself well, in a way that made Oberon think she must've gone to some big-shot Eastern college. She smiled at Jenks, kissed him on the cheek. Put her arm around his waist as she studied Oberon for a moment. Then she turned back to Jenks, saying, "I'm going to the market, honey. Need anything?"

"No, I'm good, Kate. Thanks." They kissed. She grabbed keys off a side table and left.

After she was gone, Jenks went to the couch and sat. "Kate's how I was able to start Inner Iron. Her folks have been wonderful to me. It helped that her father felt it would be a good investment. I had to give him one of my speeches, of course. The old dog wanted to see if I could really do it. Gave me the seal of approval, then gave me the check."

Was that a slight inference of derision, Oberon wondered? Couldn't tell, but he made a mental note of it all the same.

Jenks looked him in the eye for a second, then said, "Why are you here, Officer... Kane, was it?"

"Inspector. Yes, Kane," he said, noticing that Jenks didn't offer him a chair. "I'm trying to track down anyone who might have known either a Carl Kaslowski or an Anthony Scarsdale."

At the names, Jenks sighed. Shifted on the couch. "I always thought Carl would be able to stay clean," he said sadly, then started, shocked as the news really sank in. "Wait. 'Might have *known*'? What's happened?"

"They've been murdered, Mr. Jenks. Both by the same gun." The sentence left Jenks with a stunned look on his face. "How well did you know them?"

"Dead? Jesus... Carl? Dead?"

181

"I'm afraid so, yes. You don't mention Scarsdale. You didn't like him as much as Kaslowski?"

Jenks shook his head. "No. Tony was a grimy, craven piece of shit. I had no respect for him. Carl, though, he really didn't belong there. I could tell he was going to turn it around when he got out. It was talking with him, trying to help him, that gave me the idea for Inner Iron. Helped him all I could. Kept the brothers off his ass. It felt good to be able to do some good, especially in there."

"I can understand that." Oberon looked down at his notes for a moment. "You went in for assault?"

"Yes."

"And not your first time, correct?"

"That's right."

"Still reporting to your probation officer on schedule, right?"

"Of course."

"Good to hear it," he said. "Did Kaslowski and Scarsdale like each other? Hang together?"

Jenks thought for a moment. "Not that I remember," he said slowly, "but nobody wants to remember their days inside. You know how it is, right?" Thought some more, then said, "No, I don't *think* they hung out much. But then again, I wasn't around them all the time."

"Of course. Do you think they kept up on the outside?"

"Doubt it. Carl didn't like Tony much, either. On the inside, you do what you need to do to survive. You hang with the people you need to hang with in order to get by. You have to learn to survive in there, any way you can. It's a horrible system we've got going. Overpopulated, underfunded. There's really no *real* way to help the men who are in there. They end up surviving by using each other, exploiting and abusing each other, or … imploding."

"You didn't implode. Kaslowski didn't. Both of you survived."

A shrug. "We were strong enough to realize that what we did inside was *only* for survival. Strong enough to know that once we got out, every day we worked to turn our life around was like an absolution, of a sort." Jenks then stopped for a moment. Remembering. "Hell," he added with a sigh, "maybe that's just what we just told ourselves to stay sane, I don't know."

Oberon looked around the room. It was a place struggling people would give their eyeeteeth for. "You seem to be doing very well, Mr. Jenks. You're a good example for those men inside to follow."

"I was lucky. I found Kate."

"Is there anyone else you can think of that both men knew on the inside and mixed with while they were there?"

After a moment of thinking, Jenks shook his head. "There was a guy they seemed to be around all the time, but I can't remember his name. Black guy. Sorta big. Been awhile now, and I—wait…" He sat there, staring at nothing as he seemed to struggle with remembering. Looked up at Oberon. Smiled. "Dockery," he said. "That was the guy's name. Dockery."

Oberon wasn't buying the memory act, and he made a note next to Dockery's name to that effect. "No first name?"

A shrug. "Sorry, that's all I remember. I think he was local, though. I remember Carl once saying something to me about how Dockery couldn't wait to get home to the Fillmore."

Oberon folded up his notebook. Stuck it in his pocket as he stood. "Don't apologize, Mr. Jenks. You gave me something to go on when I was having the feeling I was chasing a long shot. Thank you for your time." Put one of his cards on the side table. "If you think of anything else, don't hesitate to call me."

"Of course," Jenks said as he led Oberon to the door. "You know, if Inner Iron works out, I'm planning on giving the seminar to young kids who are growing up in problem areas of the city. Hunters Point. The Mission. I think I could really make a difference."

"Well," Oberon said as Jenks opened the door for him, "then I'll be rooting for you."

TWENTY-SEVEN

THERE WAS A SHARP knock on the door, making Dockery jump awake. He'd fallen asleep in his chair, the one he'd turned toward the door. He'd sent his girl and kid to visit her family. Didn't want to take any chances with them, even though he knew shit all about what the hell was going down. Better safe than sorry, though. Like back in Folsom. Had to keep your head on a swivel in that place. You just never knew where a shiv might come from if someone declared your number up. There'd been guys who'd never done nothing to no one there, but ended up dead just the same. Then there were the others, like Eric, who'd come out more fucked up than when they went in. Not everyone in prison was a bad guy, even though the papers liked to write it that way.

Another knock at his door. Dockery pulled his gun out from between the chair pillow and arm. It felt like a real gun again, now that he'd gotten that fully loaded clip. Went to the door. Peered through the curtain. Saw an older-looking dude with silver hair standing there. By the cut of the suit, he could tell the fucker was a cop. But then again, what if it was the dude in the car? What if it was some sort of setup? His mind filled with conspiracy theories and hidden traps that only waited for him to step into and get killed. Another knock. Dockery pulled the hammer back on the gun, then reconsidered. Whatever this guy was going to do, he couldn't do it outside, right there on the street...

———

Oberon stood outside of the frayed Victorian duplex. Checked to make sure he had the correct address. He did. It hadn't taken long to run down Leon Dockery in the computers. Certainly not a model citizen, but society had bred way worse. Still, there was enough violence and repeat offending to make him unhook the catch that kept his sidearm safe in its little nest.

He hoped to get more from Dockery than he'd gotten from Jenks. There was something about Jenks that bothered him. Maybe it was the interchange between the man and his girlfriend. His gut told him it felt forced, like they were performing for him. Maybe it was the man's personality, which he felt also rang false. Or, more likely, maybe he was beginning to be frustrated by the lack of leads. Frustration was bad, he knew, and could lead to poor decisions.

The door opened and a good-sized man stood there. Over six feet, with a heavy build. Knew instantly from the booking photo in Dockery's file that this was the man he'd come to see. Wondered what fight he'd been in recently with that very swollen eye and big walnut on the side of his forehead. Sure looked like he got the worst of it.

"Mr. Dockery?" he said as he pulled out his badge. "My name is Detective Inspector Kane, Homicide."

"Okay," came the cold reply. "What can I do for you, Officer?" There was something about the way the man said it that put Oberon's antenna on alert. Dockery was edgy. Nervous.

"May I come in? I'm looking for people who knew Carl Kaslowski and or Anthony Scarsdale. I've received some information that leads me to believe you might have known these gentlemen."

"Kas is dead?" The shock was genuine, that was for sure. "What's this about, man? I just found out about Tony from his moms. Happen to call her, looking for him." Dockery stood back to let him in. The place was furnished from what looked like various second-hand stores. There was evidence of a child in the home. Dockery went and sat heavily in a overstuffed chair that faced the front door. Oberon stood in front of the fireplace mantel, his back to it as he pulled out his notebook.

"So you did know both men?" Oberon asked.

Dockery still seemed stunned by the news of Kaslowski's death. "I can't believe Carl is dead, too. How'd he die?"

"He was shot, like Scarsdale."

"Same gun?"

"Why would you be interested in that, Mr. Dockery?"

A shrug. "I was just wondering, is all. If it was the same guy. That's all, man."

Oberon studied him for a moment. Seemed an honest answer. "It is, as they say, a definite possibility. What can you tell me about your time with these men?"

"I … I don't know, man. It's just a crazy coincidence, is all, right? That we were inside together, and …" He let his voice trail off then. Shook his head. The shock of Kaslowski's death certainly had the ring of truth to it.

"Just a crazy coincidence?" Oberon replied. "Really? You really think that, Mr. Dockery?"

"Sure," Dockery shrugged. "What else could it be?"

"So you knew both these men well?"

Dockery shuffled a bit in his chair. Another shrug.

"Why don't you want to tell me about your time inside? I've already read your file. I'm just trying to solve a couple murders here. You know that Kaslowski was a new father? His child had—"

"Heck, man," Dockery said, his voice getting an edge to it, "you know that guys don't like talking about their time behind bars. You a cop. You know that."

"Yes, I do know that. But I'm looking at a double homicide. Please don't make me pull my leverage and turn this into something more unpleasant than it needs to be. You know how it goes. I have to visit anyone and everyone who has a history with the victims. We could of course talk downtown, if you prefer."

Dockery sat there for a minute, seeming to get more and more nervous. Maybe it was the mention of going downtown. Repositioned himself in his chair, the weight of his hand pushing down on the cushion. Oberon caught the faint glint of metal. Knew what it was immediately, though he didn't show it. There was no way he could get his weapon out before Dockery got to his. No way at all. A sense of quiet overcame him. Of calm. Everything slowed down. Ice-floe slow. He could feel every tick of the clock. Feel the very energy that lived in the house itself.

Oberon stared down at his notebook for a moment. Tapped the pen on the page as he angled his upper body to get his hand as near as possible to the holster hanging under his left arm. "Mr. Dockery," he said quietly, "would you please stand up and away from the chair?"

Dockery's expression was one of surrender. Shoulders sagged. Brought his hands up as he stood. Eyes had gone opaque. Oberon pulled his Glock from its holster and trained it on him. "Step away from the chair and toward me, please," he said.

"That gun's for my defense, man," Dockery said as he complied with Oberon's command. "I'm being followed. From what you tell me, it might be something to do with Carl and Tony gettin' killed."

"Turn around."

Dockery did as he was told and Oberon pulled out his cuffs. Went to slap one around Dockery's left wrist, intending to pull that arm down without having to holster his weapon. He'd done it that way hundreds of times.

This time it went wrong.

As he reached up for Dockery's wrist, the man—who outweighed him by a good forty pounds—spun around, elbow coming around in an arc that caught him right on his cheekbone. He cursed as he dropped the cuffs and started to fall backward, off balance. Dockery seemed possessed, moving with the speed of a tiger. Maybe he was supercharged with fear at going back into the system. Dockery chopped him on the right forearm and the gun dropped from his nerveless hand. He was then smashed in the face with a huge fist that sent him flying backward into the mantel. His skull crashed into the carved hardwood, sending off a blast of sharp pain and fireworks. Fell hard to the floor, barely able to make out Dockery as the man pulled the gun from his chair. He then kicked Oberon's pistol under the couch, grabbed up a coat, and bolted out of the apartment through the front door.

Oberon got to his feet. Ripped his cell out of his pocket and called in what had just happened. Alerted dispatch to his situation as he dug under the couch to retrieve his weapon, cursing at the wasted precious seconds. Ran out the front door and down to the street. Dockery was nowhere in sight. Figuring the man would run to the nearer end of the block, Oberon bolted to his car and leapt inside, gunning the engine. Tore off in a howl of burning rubber down the street. Brought the car to a screeching halt in the intersection. Her glanced up and down both streets, but the man was nowhere to be seen.

Dockery was gone.

TWENTY-EIGHT

THE FIRST THING MALLEN did when he got back to his place was call Gato. The man picked up on the third ring. "*Si?*" Gato said.

"It's Mallen," he said. "How's it going, G?"

"*Vato!*" came the reply, relief more than evident in his new friend's voice. Could hear traffic noises in the background. His friend was on the road. "Where the fuck you been, man? I've been trying to call you, but it said your number is no longer working. What happened?"

"Remember those two guys I told you about?" He then gave Gato a breakdown on his trip into the bay, and then what happened at the hospital. He left Chris and Anna out of it for now.

As he expected, Gato was pissed. He let loose with a string of swearing in Spanish, then said, "That's it, Mallen. Just say the fucking word and I'll get them found."

Mallen thought about that offer. Longer than he'd expected he would. He needed Jas and Griffin off his back. And how much could Oberon really help him? He needed to tell Oberon about it, sure, but what sort of priority could he actually expect the cop to make it, in the great scheme of things that must be Oberon's world?

"Look," he finally said as he paced the floor of his studio, "I'm giving you the word, but just to *find* them, okay?"

"Well, what good will that do? Finding them won't stop *pendejos* like that. You have to put them down and out. You know that, right?"

"I do. But for now, I just want to know where they're holed up, what their movements are. And this has to be done very quietly, G, okay? They might believe I'm dead, and I want them to keep on thinking that."

"Okay," came the reply. He could tell his friend was disappointed. "You want me to come and get you? You still have that gun? You need another one to keep it company?"

Mallen laughed softly. "What are you, man, a gunsmith? Well, yeah … if you're offering, you know? I'll take better care this time, I promise."

"When do you want to meet up?"

"I gotta find some food, first, so I'll call after that, if that works."

"That's cool," Gato said. They said goodbye, and Mallen put his phone back in his coat pocket. He stood there for a moment, in the center of his dilapidated studio, wondering about how life worked sometimes, putting a person like Gato in his world.

———

He didn't go far for food. After scrounging around his pad for some money, he'd come up with just enough for an Indian buffet joint around the corner. It wasn't great, but at least he could eat a lot for a set price and he wouldn't get ptomaine poisoning. Well, mostly sure he wouldn't. A part of him just didn't want to be seen on the streets too long, if at all possible. Had to chalk that up to his brush with death, in the guise of Jas and Griffin. As he ate at the table farthest from the window, way back in a dark corner, he went over in his mind everything that had happened since Eric's death and his own seeming rebirth. Dockery's appearance, right after Eric's death, meant that he *had* to know something. But what could it be? Could it have something to do with Eric's falling down the rabbit hole of drugs in the first place? He wished again that he'd been a better friend to Eric. He should've listened more or . . . something. Anything.

He pushed away the plate in front of him, like he was pushing away his own guilty feelings over Eric. Left the best tip he could, and walked to the door.

The street felt quiet. Almost subdued. It was late in the afternoon, but not yet the rush hour. As he walked quickly down the street back to his building, he kept on alert for any black Escalades or any other street demons that might look like they were taking an interest in him.

His key was in the lobby door and turning when he heard heavy footsteps rushing up behind him. He spun around to charge at whoever was attacking him.

"Mallen! It's me," Dockery said as he backed off a step, empty hands up at chest level. "Chill, man. It's me. Dockery. Remember?" It was easy to see the man was strung out with frayed nerves. Wound as tight as a guitar string.

"How'd you get my address?" he asked, scanning up and down the street, every sense on high alert as he looked for any sign that might indicate Dockery wasn't acting alone.

Dockery put his hands down. "Did some asking. Was told you sometimes hang at the Cornerstone. The 'tender there, Bill, gave me a general 411 on you. Told me what kind of guy you are. I told him I needed to see you, and bad. He didn't say shit, wouldn't give an address. So, I been cruising this goddamned place for hours, man, askin' after you. Finally got this line on your pad."

"What do you want to talk about that's so urgent? Is it about Eric?"

Dockery nodded, glancing up and down the street nervously.

"What's going on?" Mallen said. "You act like you're being followed or something."

"I am," came the reply. "Some fuckin' car keeps showing up, tailing me."

"You sure?"

Dockery looked at him. "Hell man, I know what being followed feels like. Don't you?"

"I did, but that muscle got a little rubbery. Workin' on building it back up. Why would somebody be following you? You're staying out of trouble, yeah?"

"Tryin', man. Hell, don't most people got reasons for being followed?"

"Good point. So, it's about Eric?"

The man's face showed nerves gone frayed. "I don't know that for sure, but I think so. We done that kid wrong, man. Wrong."

"What do you mean?"

"Me and Carl. Tony, too. There was—" He flinched as a loud truck rolling by backfired. "We gotta do the rest inside," he said. "Not here, okay?"

Mallen nodded. Opened the lobby door...

That was when the shots rang out. Ugly shouts, slicing the air. Dockery's stomach exploded red and he folded to the ground. There was the roar of a car engine. Mallen banked on the fact that Dockery would have his gun, and he was right. Found it in the coat pocket. Ripped it out, bolting to the curb as the air filled with the peel of burning rubber. A dark sedan tore down the street. Maybe a Japanese make. He grabbed his left wrist to stabilize his aim. Fired twice. Heard one bullet hit glass, but then the car was gone, disappearing around the corner.

He cursed then. He should've been more intent on a plate number than doing damage. Ran back to Dockery, who was now surrounded by a few people from the street.

He bent down to check for a pulse. Nothing. Dockery was dead.

———

The street was now a cop-car convention. Seemed like everyone had been sent. There'd been some uncomfortable moments when Homicide found that Dockery's gun had been recently fired, but he held nothing back. Told them exactly what happened. Gave them his background in law enforcement. Some of them had known it. Known him. Seemed they fell into two camps: one was glad to see he was obviously staying clean, the other still despised him for ever falling.

"Why'd you leave the force?" one detective asked him. A small, short Police. Carried a tight, angry expression. Probably pissed at being born short.

"Accidental self-inflicted wound," was his only reply. Hated he couldn't give an ID on the car. It had all happened too fast.

Detective Short Man's Disease looked at him a long moment. Shook his head, then looked down at the yellow tarp covering Dockery's corpse. "Why do you think they were after him?"

"Wouldn't know. I barely knew him. Met him for the first time a couple days ago."

The cop leveled his gaze at him. "You positive there *was* a car?"

"Come on," he replied, "all you have to do is check ballistics. What'd you think? That I talked with Dockery, excused myself to the other side of the fucking street and then shot him, running back just in time for everyone to see me standing over his body?"

"You could've shot him from the street and then tossed your gun down that storm drain right there." A shrug. "You could've then come over and shot off Dockery's gun, and that's all she wrote. All we have is your word you actually spoke with the guy."

"And why would I do all that in the first place?"

Another shrug. "Vendetta? Maybe you owed him? For ripping you off for some drugs, or money, or whatever else gets you people worked up enough to take a human life."

He was about to reply when a vehicle pulled up. Oberon got out. As he came closer, Mallen was surprised to see that he sported a large bandage over his left cheek, and that the other side of his face was swollen dark blue and black. He didn't look happy, either.

With a noticeable limp, Oberon went over to where Dockery's body still lay. Pulled the tarp back. Studied the body. Replaced the tarp. Came over, shaking his head.

Short Man Detective looked about as happy at seeing Oberon as a guy seeing a sore on his prick. "Kane," he said.

"Horton," Oberon said with faint nod. The air changed. Mallen could tell. There were two dogs here now that didn't like each other, not one fucking bit.

"What are you doing here, Inspector?" Horton asked. "I caught this one."

"I know," Oberon replied, "but the body you have here is a man who I was questioning not two hours ago, and who resisted arrest and took off."

"You know him?" Mallen said. "How do you know him?"

Oberon's sigh was legion. "Please do not tell me you know this man, Mark?"

"I don't. I mean, not really. Only slightly. Met a couple days ago."

"Hey," Horton interrupted, "you guys mind if I do the interview? I'm considered pretty good at it."

Oberon's only answer was to take a step back. "Sorry. Of course."

Mallen then had to tell the story one more time, probably because Horton was pissed and just wanted to make Oberon wait like a little bitch at the curb. When he was done telling it all over, Horton folded up his notebook and stalked off without a word, throwing one final glance at Oberon. Dockery's body had been removed by this time. Mallen noticed a couple other detectives still questioning the locals. He walked over to Oberon, who was waiting near the chalk outline of Dockery's body.

"I can't believe Dockery got the better of you," he kidded as he came up, but his friend didn't seem to be amused. "Sorry," he added quietly.

"I must be getting too old for this job," Oberon replied. "Maybe I should pull the pin. Retire to my garden. Long after the significant other I never had."

"What would the city do without its staunchest defender? You gonna be its best gardener?"

"Please quit with the obvious attempts at flattery. I am not buying."

"Okay," he laughed. "What were you doing with Dockery, anyway?"

"I'll ask the questions." Here Oberon looked at him again, like a scientist studying a disease he can't quite figure. "You know what I've realized?"

"What?"

"You always popping up in my cases lately. It's not a trend I wish to continue."

"Trust me: not continuing in that trend would make my fucking day. You want a drink?"

"Yes."

They walked down the street to the nearest bar. One simply named Overflow. He tried to ignore the stares from his neighbors as they left. The place was dark, thank God. The decor was along the lines of an old sea grotto. Blue and green lights. Fake coral all over the ceilings and walls. Fake seaweed crawling up all over everything. Mallen liked it, though his loyalty was with Bill and the Cornerstone.

They went to the stick. An older, hefty Chinese lady took their order. When it came time to pay, Mallen had to look over at Oberon. The cop just sighed. Mumbled something about the weight of the world as he fished out some dollars from his wallet. After both of them were situated and the waitress had left, Oberon then pulled out his notebook. Consulted it. "So," he began, "how again did the man I was arresting earlier today come to be shot on your doorstep?"

"Why were you after him?"

"One would think you were a bit wiser than to repeat your past mistakes so flagrantly," Oberon chided.

"And you'd be right," he replied. Thought for a moment. What to tell Oberon? Took a sip of his drink. "Okay, this is how I know Dockery. I got curious about Eric's shooting. Especially with my name and addy in his pocket. Why wouldn't I be, right? So I think, *I want to look into this.* Dockery shows up outside the Russ house. I just happen to be there, too, wanting to talk to Eric's parents. Happenstance, I think they call it? Dockery won't tell me why he's there. Only that he 'owes Eric's mother an apology.' We tangle about it, but then he splits. I leave it." He took a sip from his glass. Shook his head. "I shouldn't have. Then he pops up on my doorstep, scared and freaked out. Says he's being followed. Tells me that him, and a guy named Carl and one named Tony, did Eric wrong. Real wrong. Was about to tell me why, I think, but then he got dead."

Oberon shook his head. Stared down at the drink in his hand, lost in thought. After a long moment, Mallen asked, "So, what did you have on Dockery?"

"Me? He was clean, for all intents and purposes. I just wanted to know if he knew a couple dead men I have on the books. A Carl Kaslowski, and one Anthony 'Tony' Scarsdale. Got put out when I talked to him. He struck me as an extremely paranoid and scared individual. This individual happened to possess a gun under a chair pillow when I visited. He had the record, so I figured to take him in and press him a bit on his known acquaintances before I booked him for the gun."

"How were those guys killed?"

"Shot, just like Dockery. I have a feeling that the bullet will match up with the other killings."

The old sense of excitement welled up inside his chest again. He was smack dab in the middle of a good case. No way to deny it. And his drive to solve it had taken him over. Hadn't felt this good in years. "Those two other guys? Carl and Tony? Any reports of them saying they were being followed?"

"No, nothing."

"Anything I can do to help?"

"Yes. Stay out of my way. You're doing something on your own, and I'm not happy about that, but I have to say it's better than sticking needles filled with junk into your arm all day. However"— and here he stared Mallen straight in the eyes—"don't do anything to screw up *my* side of it. Are we clear on that point, Mark?"

Mallen glanced down at his drink before answering. Struggled over how to frame the thing he was about to ask Oberon. Fuck it: the only way inside was through the door. "Obie," he said, "let me help you on this."

The detective stared at him for a moment. Laughed without humor. "You are joking, right?"

"Come on. I could help. You know that. Now that I'm clean."

"Now that you're clean," Oberon echoed. Shook his head. "True, but you're not even close to being kosher when it comes to being a detective. No license. No nothing."

"Well, how about this?" he said as he ordered another drink with a nod of his head. The hefty Chinese bartender came over. Winked at him. There was the dull sloshing sound as she filled up his glass, more than what was probably the usual amount. Winked at him again as she walked away. "I'll work *for* you, not with you," he said to Oberon. "Maybe I can dig up something? Like that both Kaslowski and Scarsdale were worried they were being followed, too, maybe?"

Oberon shook his head, took a pull from his glass. Sighed. "It's certainly of interest that Dockery knew both of those dead men, *and* Eric Russ. They all seem to have done time together. I don't like it when cases grow tentacles like this, Mark." Oberon finished his drink. Put the glass quietly put down on the stained and scarred wood. "If you screw this up and draw fire in my direction, I will disown you. Completely. Got it?"

"Got it," he replied with a smile. "I'll just do a little quiet digging. See what I can see, okay? Come on, I'll be a help to you. It'll be just like the old days."

"I am so going to regret this," the detective replied as he shook his head. "I just feel it in my bones. Mama Kane is right now turning over in her grave at her poor son's stupidity."

TWENTY-NINE

Mallen woke to the sound of Anna's whimpering. He got out of bed, Chris murmuring something to him he didn't catch. Probably something about Anna's medicine. Chris had been sick, too—as sick as Anna. Chris's fever had only recently broke. Whatever had brought both his girls down so low had been traveling around the city like a cheap hooker at a convention hotel.

He padded across the hall to the bathroom and got the bottle of red liquid the doctor had prescribed earlier in the day. Grabbed up the teaspoon next to it.

It had been a risk to come home, he knew, but if his little girl was sick like she was, he had to take the chance. He'd received Chris's coded text early yesterday morning, before the sun had come up over the Berkeley hills. He'd been asleep in the loft he lived in, south of Market. The place everyone in his undercover world thought he'd bought with drug money made back east before he'd moved to San Francisco. Luckily, no one had been crashing on his couch, which sometimes happened when one of Franco's gang didn't want to see their old lady, or if they thought maybe the cops might be watching their usual haunts. He knew it must be serious if Chris had sent the text. She wasn't one given to overreacting. That was him more than her.

He went into Anna's room. She'd kicked off the covers to the floor, was sprawled on her back, dressed in the ice blue footie pj's he was so proud he'd bought for her. They had a little embroidered sheriff's badge on the chest, compliments of Chris's handiwork. She whimpered again. Shook her head from side to side. Only four, and already having nightmares. Just like he had been as a little boy. Her lovely face, that little four-year-old face, was scrunched up tight with fear, eyes closed tight, lips quivering as she whimpered again.

"Hey, kiddo," he said softly as he gently laid his hand on her shoulder. "It's okay. Daddy's here."

Her eyes shot open and for a moment, she didn't seem to recognize him. Those blue eyes, with the insanely thick limbal ring. He'd heard a thick limbal ring was a sign of high IQ. It was hard to argue with that, based on what he'd witnessed in his daughter so far. Already so far ahead of other kids her age. Hell, he'd been a Neanderthal at four compared to her. Again: give the props to Chris.

She sat up and reached out to him, and he held her tight for a long moment. The smell of her hair reminded him of a warm day in a berry patch. She was very hot. Was there reason to be concerned, at all her nightmares? The doctor had told them it was normal, that as the child's imagination grew during this early phase, the line between the real world and the magically realistic world often blurred.

"It's okay, rookie," he told her as he laid her back down and then took the cap off the medicine, "the law is here now. He'll make wrongs right."

THIRTY

MALLEN STAYED AT THE bar awhile after Oberon had left, waiting for Gato. He'd called his friend, and if Gato had been pissed before at Mallen being attacked by Jas and Griffin, he was ballistic now that someone got shot right in front of his apartment. Mallen chilled him out, telling him about how it hadn't been a black Escalade, that the gun that had killed Dockery had not been Griffin's .44. He had a moment where he was afraid that Gato was just going to hang up then and there and tear the city apart looking for those two killers, but after he'd blown off some steam, Gato seemed to come back to earth. Mallen was about to ask for a ride out to the avenues again to check on Phoebe and Hal, but Gato had cut him short before he could even ask though, saying to him, "Dude, don't move from where you are. I'll be right there. You need protecting, bro. I'll be right there to the rescue. Where are you?"

Again he wondered about when the Lord had started looking out for recovering junkie, ex-cops so well. He told Gato where he was, and Gato said he was on his way. Mallen sat there for a moment, feeling a little like that guy on *Spenser: For Hire,* and Gato was steadily turning into his Hawk. Laughed at that. Thought about Phoebe and Hal. There were more questions to ask about Eric's time in prison. He was in agreement with Oberon: there was something in those days that linked all the murders together. Had to be.

He sat at the bar and nursed a scotch on the rocks as he thought about what his next moves would, or should, be. Dockery had said he was being followed. Oberon said that, to his knowledge, neither of the other men had been tailed before they were killed. There was no way to know that for sure, though. Had to figure they were, if it was the same gun. Same gun, same MO, same shooter. They'd all been in jail together, with Eric. Eric would've said *something* to Jenna. He had to talk with her again, too. He heard a car horn honk then, an old-style car horn. Looked outside to see the Falcon at the curb, so he slid off the stool, drained the rest of his drink, and left.

Gato was wearing a blindingly white T-shirt and baggy jeans. He also looked like he hadn't slept any more since the last time he'd seen him. When Mallen asked what was up though, Gato only shook his head and mumbled it was wrapped up with his *hermana.* He left it at that, so Mallen let it be and gave Gato their destination.

Traffic was light, making it a short ride over to the Russ place. Gato found parking on the block, the gods of parking being with them today. Mallen strode up to the house and rang the bell. To his surprise, Jenna answered the door.

"What are you doing here?" he asked. She stepped aside to let him in. The air was close. Still, as if the windows hadn't been opened for sometime. Felt like to him like a house waiting to die. "Is everything okay? How're they doing?"

She shrugged. "Phoebe's upstairs in bed, Hal's in his den." Jenna led him down the hall to the kitchen. There was light here, coming in from the west windows that overlooked the backyard. Like he had every time he'd been in this kitchen, because he couldn't help himself, he glanced over at the photos on the fridge: Eric, Eric with Hal, Hal with Phoebe. Happier times.

"He ever come out of the den?" he said.

"Yes." There was something in her manner that he noticed right off as soon as she said it.

"What is it?"

"He's not being there for her. He's being gone. And when he comes back, he smells of alcohol and cigarettes, or fast food. It's frustrating."

"I'm sure it is," he agreed as he sat at the kitchen table.

She looked at him for a moment, toyed with the stem of an empty wine glass. "You look like you've been through the wringer since we last talked," she told him. "You're not...?"

"No," he replied. Smiled. "I'm still good. Just a little bit of my past caught up with me, is all." After a moment, he added, "Jenna, I was going to call you and see if we could meet again, so maybe it's providence that made our paths cross."

"What were you going to call me for? Did you find out anything about Eric?"

"I'm not sure. What I wanted to ask might sound weird, I know. But, Eric ever tell you that he was being followed? Maybe he wasn't even sure. Maybe just *thought* he was?"

She gave him a look like she did indeed think it was a weird question. "Not that I know of, no. Why?"

"Not sure, but there's something strange going on about his death, and I'm not talking about the H and my address."

"What do you mean?"

"Well, there was this guy named Dockery I saw outside this house last week …" He then told her about what Dockery had said to him after they'd fought.

To his disappointment, she shook her head like the name didn't ring a bell. "And he said he knew Eric in prison?"

"Right. Said he wanted to apologize to Phoebe. Told me later, that he, or 'they', had 'done Eric wrong.'"

She thought about that for a moment. "What do you think he meant?"

"Won't be able to find out, now. He was killed last night. Shot right in front of me."

"Oh my God," she replied. "Jesus. What happened?"

He told her how it had gone down. Her eyes were wide by the time he was done. "Oh God, Mark. You could've been killed, too."

He just shrugged that away. "I'm pretty sure I wasn't a target in this. Only Dockery. But, it's *not* just him, either. Two other guys have been shot and killed who knew Dockery in prison. Guys who may have also known Eric. One guy named Kaslowski, the other one Scarsdale."

"Are you kidding? Jesus!" she said, getting up and pacing around the kitchen in her agitation.

"Now, take it easy, okay?" he said. "I know, it's weird. There's got to be some sort of connection. Eric wasn't using, or dealing, so it's not that. I need to ask you about Eric's time in prison again. Really think back, okay? He must've mentioned *somebody*. Nobody goes into the joint and comes out without knowing at least a couple guys. You *have* to form alliances in there, or you're dead. That's just a fact."

"He never talked to me about it, and I never pressed him. I knew it was a painful subject for him. That was obvious, you know?" She went and poured herself a fresh glass of wine from an open bottle on the countertop. She turned to him then and indicated the den. "You could ask Hal. If Eric talked about it, he'd talk about it to his father."

"That's true, thanks." Got up from the table. The door leading to the den seemed somber to him. Like a portal into sadness. He knocked on the door and waited.

"Yeah?" Hal said quietly, his voice a flat tone.

"It's Mallen, Hal."

There was a silence. Then, "Abandon all hope, ye who enter here."

Entering the den felt like entering a tomb. The air was stale with alcohol and cigarettes. The long curtains seemed to have taken on a smoky color, adding to the thin, brown light. It was hard to breathe, or maybe it was his mind playing tricks. He sat down on the couch opposite Hal's dark husk.

"For Christ's sake, Hal," he said as his eyes adjusted to the dim light, "open a curtain or something, yeah?"

The big man stared at him for a moment, a strange look in his eyes. *Is this man going to make it?* he wondered. *Will he and Phoebe be able to live any semblance of a normal life ever again?* As Mallen sat there, he began to strongly doubt it.

"You come here to see me?" Hal asked.

"Yeah," he replied, "and to check on Phoebe. Thought maybe you and me could talk about Eric."

Hal lit up a cigarette. "You know, I used be quit of these, once. Twenty years quit. Now … I'm already up to half a pack a day."

"It's bad for you."

"Yeah. You want one?"

"Sure," he said. Pulled one from the offered pack. Lit it with a match. Hal watched him for a moment, then chuckled quietly to himself.

"What's so funny?"

"Nothin', Mallen. Nothin'. Why do you want to talk about my son?"

"I'm trying to figure out a couple things, is all."

"Like what?"

"A friend of mine is a detective with SFPD. Homicide. He's got a couple killings that might tie together with another man who was shot last night, at my doorstep."

Hal took a long drag of his smoke. Reached over and poured himself a glass of whiskey. Took a sip. "On your doorstep?"

"Yeah. A man who says he knew Eric in prison."

"My son never talked much about his time inside," he said quietly. "Never much."

"When he got out, didn't he ever talk about the guys he knew in there?"

"Only a little, I think. Like I said, not much."

"Did he ever mention a man named Dockery? Leon Dockery? Or Kaslowski? Or a Tony Scarsdale?"

Hal took another drag off his cigarette, and shook his head. "Sorry."

Mallen put his half-smoked cig out in the nearby overflowing ashtray. "Don't be. It's possible I'm totally wrong, but I thought I'd ask anyway."

"What's your next step gonna be, detective?" Hal smirked as he said it. Might've winked, but it was hard to tell in the dimness.

"Don't know. Talk to the people who knew these three men." After a silence, he added, "I think I'm a little worried about you guys."

"Shouldn't be. We're fine."

"Yeah, you look great."

Hal's bulk shook in the gloom as he laughed silently. "I just need to get out once in a while. Clear my head. It's hard now. Very hard."

"Phoebe any better?"

"Better is a relative term, my young friend. I live in hope."

"Don't we all?" Went to the door, "See ya later. Take it easy."

He found Jenna still in the kitchen, washing dishes. They looked like dishes that weren't dirty. She washed with a lot of focus, like there were stains there only she could see. She stopped when he walked in. She picked up the wine glass and took a long pull.

"Don't make a habit of it." He smiled as he came over, indicating the glass.

She turned her eyes on him. "Voice of experience?"

"Hell yes. You think Phoebe's awake?"

"Probably. When I showed up today, she asked if I could give her a hand with the house … do some cooking and cleaning. Said she didn't have the energy, that she just wanted to rest for a while."

He could understand that feeling. He really just wanted to rest, too, but if he was going to keep ahead of The Need, he needed to keep going. Hopefully, one day, it wouldn't be like this. "I'm going to go check on her," he said as he went down the hall and climbed up the carpeted stairs to the upper floor.

The door to Phoebe and Hal's bedroom was open, but like with the den below, the curtains were drawn. However, Phoebe was up, sitting in an overstuffed chair, the floor lamp on, casting a bright light up to reflect off the ceiling. She'd been reading, the open book resting in her lap. She'd been looking at the door as he entered, like she'd heard him downstairs and had been waiting.

He came and sat on the bed near her. Indicated the book in her lap. "What're you reading?"

"Some escapism," she replied. *"Medea."*

He chuckled. "I would read a comic book."

She laughed back. Put the book down. Looked at him. "How are you, Mark?"

"Okay, actually. I think it's going to stick."

She got it. "I'm glad. Happy for you, just like I was for Eric."

"Phoebe," he said, "I know that Eric probably only ever spoke to Hal about his prison days, but I need to ask you to really think hard. Did Eric ever, *ever* tell you he thought he was being followed? This would've been in the days leading up to his death. Anything at all?"

After a moment where she sat there, staring at nothing, remembering back to a time when her son was still alive, she said, "I can't remember anything like that, Mark. I'm sorry. He talked of getting his life back together. Maybe fixing it with Jenna so they could really be together again. Nothing about being followed. Why do you ask?"

"It was just a long shot. There's something going on, with a group of men who all knew each other in prison, and all of them knew Eric. Just trying to make sense of it, is all."

She considered that for a moment. Said, "Are you any closer to the reason he had drugs on him, and your address?"

"No, I'm not. I guess I'm more rusty at the detective thing than I realized."

"He wanted to work undercover at some point, you know?"

"Yeah," he replied, "I knew he was getting burned out on the beat. He had told me once that he wanted to go undercover, but I chalked it up to being burned out on the job. I'd seen it happen a lot, and I hadn't been on the force long." It was true: the burnout rate for cops was horrible. Killed a lot of men.

She looked away. "He'd talked to me about the job. I could see it. I wasn't that surprised when he quit, but I was surprised when he quit and started on...his road." She then closed her eyes. Wiped at them.

Looked back at him. They glinted now, wet with tears. "I'm sorry, Mark," she said, "but I don't want to talk about him anymore."

He got to his feet. "I understand. Sorry to take you away from your book. Take it easy, and I'll check on you guys later, okay?"

"Thank you, Mark."

He made his way back downstairs. Went to say goodbye to Jenna. Found her sitting at the kitchen table, looking out into the garden. She turned to look at him as he approached.

"Hey," she said, "I was thinking about what you asked me. I remember now there was this one guy Eric talked about. Only mentioned him once or twice. Took me a bit to put it all together. The first time he mentioned this guy, he only ever called him 'Woody,' right? Like the woodpecker in the old cartoons?" She looked out at the garden again, saying, "I remember his face sort of lighting up when he said the name. That's what made me remember now, I guess."

"He ever tell you this guy's full name?"

She nodded then, and he pulled out a scrap of paper from of his coat pocket. Almost like it'd been the old days, back on the force. Even had to search his pockets for a pen. Again, just like the old days. Jenna found an old ballpoint under a pile of bills on the table. Handed it to him.

"Wood," she said hesitantly. "Julian Wood."

He wrote it down. "Know where he might be?"

"He's here in the city somewhere, that's all I know. Eric told me a couple times that Julian wanted to meet with him for lunch, but Eric was trying to put him off. Wished the guy would just go away."

"Why was that? Do you know?"

"No. I was amazed he even mentioned him. Once, when he was pretty wasted, it actually sounded like him and Julian had been buddies inside. Looked out for each other. But then he just clammed up and got cold. Cold and sad," she ended quietly, looking down at the floor. "That's it. Just the name. I don't—"

"Hey. I understand. I appreciate you saying this much, trust me."

"Mallen?" she said as made his way to the hall.

"Yeah?"

"Look out for yourself, okay?"

"Don't worry," he replied with a smile. "I've still got that junkie 'flow below the bush line' thing going for me. I know about stayin' under the radar."

THIRTY-ONE

THE DARKENING CLOUDS UP above were heavy. Heavy like how his soul felt as he left the Russ place. The threat of a coming storm was in the air. Found himself welcoming the approaching rain. Maybe it would clean away more than the dirt and grime. He needed a drink. Something, anything, to lift the gloom from his soul.

Gato looked up from the book in his hand as Mallen got in the car. He'd imagined it would've been a bible, but to his surprise, it wasn't. It was a book on creative visualization.

"What, *vato*?" Gato said off his look. "You don't believe that we have the power to change our lives?"

"Of course," he replied as his friend started up the car, "I just figured you thought that was God's job, or something."

The Falcon pulled into the street. Gato said, "it's not God's job to wipe our ass, it's ours."

Mallen had to admit that was a totally correct statement. "Where we goin'?" Gato asked.

"I need a drink. Take me to the Cornerstone." He caught the glance Gato shot him. "And don't worry, man," he continued. "It's all good."

However, as he sat there, the thought of visiting Dreamo for business reasons and not to just check up on him crept into his mind. He shook his head at that. Growled under his voice. He had to admit: he really wanted to shoot. The feeling was hard, sharp, and ugly. He could ignore it while he was thinking or talking to people, but as soon as he sat still, it was there. Like the ticking of a clock he'd tuned out for a while but that was now almost the only thing he could hear.

He kept his eyes focused out the window. Counted people on the street that had grocery bags. When that didn't work, he counted the ones walking. Anything to keep his mind off the junk. It'd been a long time, but not long enough. Maybe it would never be "long enough."

And maybe that was just the way it would be from now on.

If he were strong.

———

Gato decided to come into the bar with him. Like he didn't think it was good idea for Mallen to be alone with the temptation oh so fuckin' close by. Gato was right, too, given Mallen's current mindset.

The Cornerstone was filled with the usuals. There were the same alcoholics (some he knew) and addicts (many he recognized by name) prowling around the place. The joint was jumpin', actually. When he glanced up at the TV he saw the reason why: a big football game. *It must be Sunday*, he thought. Mallen made his way to the bar as Gato found a free table. Bill was so busy he didn't have time for more than a "Hey, get the fuck out!" as he put a double scotch down in front of him and moved on.

He kept an eye on Bill, hoping to get the man's attention, to see if he knew a guy named Julian Wood. The name was pretty singular. Maybe Oberon could help him out with a name search. He thought hard as he went and sat down at the table where Gato was. Nursed his drink.

"What's goin' on?" Gato asked. He obviously wasn't enjoying being in the bar. Kept watching the addicts and shaking his head.

"It's about my friend, is all. I can't figure out why out of all the people he would've run into while doing time, he would only mention *one* guy to anyone."

"Being inside, man? You become a different person. Can't avoid it, you know?"

"That seems to be the only thing everyone agrees on." He took a sip of his drink. "You know anyone doing time up in Folsom?"

Gato thought for a moment. Shook his head. "No man, I don't. Not now, anyway."

Mallen took another sip of his drink. Wondered how Dreamo was doing, if he were in his office, if his face had healed any. Wondered again why someone would beat on Dreamo like that. Maybe Dreamo just didn't want to admit that he had a business rival? Gato shifted at his side. He really wanted to be gone. Mallen looked around the bar then and realized he couldn't blame his friend. Decided not to wait to talk to Bill, as it looked like the bartender was making money and he didn't want to interrupt him. He jotted down a quick note on a napkin, saying he needed info on a Julian Wood, adding his new phone number. Handed the note to Bill with a nod of his head before making his way back to his table.

"Come on, my friend," he told Gato. "Let's get out of here."

The rain had started up. Not a lot, but the temperature was falling pretty rapidly. He dialed Oberon as they walked down the wet street toward the car. The rain felt good on his head, clearing it of thoughts of needles and junk. They were approaching the Falcon as Oberon's voicemail picked up. Left Julian Wood's name and why he wanted to know about the guy. Mentioned he was wondering if there was anyone still inside who knew both Julian and Eric. "Might be something," he said, then hung up.

"Where to now, bro?" Gato asked as he unlocked the driver's side door. He reached over and opened the door for Mallen who slid inside quickly, the rain really starting to pour. *Yeah*, he thought, *where to?*

"I guess home." He needed some down time, and that was a fact. "Thanks again for the ride. You're a godsend," he added with a smile.

Gato laughed in response. "From your mouth to His ears, as my *madre* would say."

———

Mallen asked Gato to drive around the block a couple times. Just to be sure. No black Escalades, but with the rain it was difficult to see if anyone was hanging out in their cars. He told Gato thanks again, and that he'd call.

"Bro," Gato said as Mallen was getting out. "You need that other defender?"

He got it. A gun. Considered for a moment. "Nah. I lost the other one, right? I'm already way in your debt. Thanks though."

"How can a friend be in debt to a friend? Look, I'll find you another gun. Don't worry about it. You'll be helping me one day, just like you're helping those people that live out in the avenues."

"You think?"

Gato nodded. There was a brief glimpse of some sadness there. "Yeah, I do."

"Well all you have to is ask, G. See ya," he said and got out of the car. He glanced up and down the street before going up to his door. It looked all clear, so he made for his lobby door. Got inside and up to his apartment door not meeting anyone. Sometimes the place felt empty, and sometimes it felt like it did now: people barricaded inside their boxes, hoping to keep out an angry and wrathful world.

He came into his apartment and flipped on the light.

The click of the hammer being pulled back was like a slap in the face. There was Jas, sitting on the couch, grinning, his .40-caliber pointed right at Mallen's chest.

"I told Griff to just wait it out," he said as he got to his feet. "Told him you were better than you looked."

"Thanks."

Jas indicated for him to get his hands up. He complied, his mind racing a mile a minute, going over everything in the apartment that could be used as a weapon. Measured distances, trajectories.

"How the hell did you get out of the bay, fucker?" Jas moved closer, standing only about five feet away but blocking Mallen's chance to leap at the table for the old steak knife he used to cut the wood for Anna's kites. It was probably too dull to do shit, anyway.

"I swam. You assholes broke the first rule: always wait to confirm the kill." He looked around his room. His old, derelict, hated room. Strangely, he felt very calm. Like he was outside in the backyard of the house he'd grown up in, waiting for the first snowflake to fall. It was a very different setup from being thrown in the back of a car and driven to the bay. A part of his mind told him that's exactly what they should've done this time, too. "Where is Griff, anyway? Eating babies?"

Jas leapt at him, the gun barrel slapping across his mouth in a flash, the pain stabbing him through his entire head, exploding throughout his entire body. He went down to one knee, spitting some blood out onto the scratched and chipped floorboards. But now Jas was closer, and he knew that was all he'd get.

Jas pulled out his cell. Speed dialed. "Donkey's in the pen," he said with a grin. "Meet in the street." Then he clicked off the call.

And it was all suddenly so quiet. Mallen knew what he had to do, and only seconds to do it in. He thought of Anna, could see her there in his mind's eye, as clear as if she were standing right in front of him. She was the kite that kept him running over the grass on a sunny day.

As Jas shoved the cell back into his pocket, he made his move. Jas wouldn't expect it, and there was a part of him that was also surprised that he remembered any of this shit after trying to kill it all with the needle. He was still down on one knee, and he used that leverage to charge up into Jas, using the top of his head as a battering ram. Pain shot through his neck and spine as the crown of his head connected with Jas's jaw and Jas fell backward, losing his footing on some tissue paper Mallen was going to use for a kite one day.

The gun fell to the ground and discharged. He'd have only minutes now before Griff arrived. Maybe seconds. As Jas fell, he climbed up the man's body, clawing at his clothes, needing to grab at the face. He was rocked by a fist against his temple, then a knee to the groin, but he had to make it. It felt like climbing Everest as he clawed and scratched his way, ignoring the blows. He reached up, desperate, feeling every second go by, no longer aware that Jas was fighting desperately, probably freaking out at the fact that his plan was turning against him.

Eyes. Eyes, nose, throat. His thumbs found the eyes, and he pushed. Pushed and pushed and pushed again. Jas howled, and then he knocked the man's head on the floor a couple times, answered by someone below banging on their ceiling, pissed at the noise.

Gotta love life in the city.

His hands slid down then to Jas's neck. Hard work, being they were slippery with blood. He pressed with his thumbs, pressed like he was crushing an aluminum can. Jas continued to struggle, but then that struggle went weak. The air filled with the heavy odor of shit and piss, an odor that told him he'd survived. He rolled off of Jas's corpse, lay on his back. Jas's phone rung then. The ringtone was Run DMC's version of "Walk This Way."

Probably Griffin wondering why they hadn't come out. He still had to deal with the Griff. Mallen scooped up Jas's automatic, then grabbed the phone. Spoke into it in harsh voice, like he'd been strangled or something. "Fucker got away, Griff!"

"Where to?"

"Dunno! Be down," and he cut off the call. Stood silent then, waiting for the throbbing pulse in his head to calm. Listened for any sirens. None. Maybe the gun going off was a car backfire to everyone. Or maybe that's just what they'd wanted to believe. Everyone was probably figuring that someone else would call it in. Happened that way, everyday, all the time.

He had to go. He glanced around the room one last time. Felt like it was the last time he'd ever see it. Knew then it would be. He had Jas's gun. Went to the corpse and found the wallet. *Wow,* he thought, *Jas was doing alright for himself.* A few hundred, all in twenties and tens. He went and scooped up Anna's nest egg, pocketing it as he ran out. Tossed the wallet down the trash chute. The cops would want to talk to him, he knew, but they wouldn't give too much of a shit over a piece of shit like Jas.

It was then, as he walked calmly down the stairs, that he realized he'd never known Jas's last name.

Walked down to the lobby. The building was still quiet. No sirens from outside, which was good. If they hadn't been heard by now, they wouldn't be. Instead of going out the front door, he made a left and went down the first floor hallway to the door that led to the back of the building. There was a small grassy area there, populated by a few potted plants and an old deck chair left behind by a tenant long since gone. He went to his right, then right again and walked quietly through the hall the garbage men used to come and get the trash bins. Passed the area used by the motorcycle owners who paid an additional $100 a month to park their bikes there, and went to the gate. Peered through it. It was still raining, and very dark out. He could see the Escalade doubled parked.

Griff, waiting like a patient old dog for his master. Joke was on him. Mallen pulled Jas's phone. Dialed 911. Gave the address of his building. Said a killing had happened. Gave Griffin's description and street name, saying everyone on the street knew him as a mad dog. Probably armed. "Oh no! He's—" Mallen said, then cut the call like he'd been suddenly attacked. He popped the battery out and dropped the phone in the grime. Grinned in the darkness. The cowboys would be coming fast now. When the sirens were heard, Griffin would have to leave, not knowing what the hell happened. He laughed at that, feeling better than he'd felt in a long time.

Fuck him. That was life, yeah?

He quietly opened the gate, the pouring rain hitting him like a bucket of water. He walked away from his place, heading against

220

the flow of traffic. He was at the end of the block when he heard the sirens, approaching fast.

———

He spent the night camped out just off Bush Street, in the parking lot of the old neogothic cathedral St. Dominic's. The walk through the rain to get to St. Dom's would've been pure, fuckin' wretchedness at any other time, but not then. He'd welcomed the time to think.

He knew that he'd killed a man. Jas was dead. He knew that fact like someone knew how to add two and two. But, the other side of the ledger told him that that man had wanted to kill him...had *tried* to kill him, with everything he'd possessed. Had even beaten on him just for the joy of giving Mallen pain and anguish. That man would've kept on doing that until he, Mallen, was dead.

But he'd survived. And that's what mattered right now. He'd survived to fight another day.

Killing had never made him feel good. Never had. The three occasions he'd been forced to take a life while as a Police had left him a fucking basket case. They offer up people to talk to, and books to read, but none of that shit can ever help. You've taken a human life. No matter what the circumstances were: you killed someone.

That's a game changer, and that's a fact.

But he had to admit, as he thought more and more about it, that after the long years of scrounging for dope and hiding from the cops and trying to keep on the down-low, it felt...pretty okay...to have sent a message to Griffin and everyone else that he was back.

And everyone would know it, now, too. The news of Jas's death, in Mallen's apartment, would travel. What the outcome of that news would be, he couldn't guess. And right now?

He didn't give a shit.

All he cared about right now was staying as dry and warm as possible, here on this rainy night, curled up under an overhang outside a church. He knew he'd have to be gone early, before school started. He huddled up, listening to the rain, conscious of the weight of Jas's gun in his coat pocket, wondering if Griffin had left in time or had been caught.

The last thing he remembered before he finally fell into sleep was a crack of lightning above, followed by a boom of thunder that felt like God turning a page in a book only He could read . . .

———

His cell rang, almost sending him into the next world. It was early morning, gray and ugly, but at least it had stopped raining. Had no idea how long he'd slept, but it looked like school hadn't started yet. He was stiffer than a board and more cold than he could ever remember being, even after his swim in the bay. *And this was better than shooting nice, warm drugs?* Pushed that thought away as he took a deep breath and answered his cell. "Mallen," he said.

"Hey, Mal, it's Bill." He could hear a TV on in the background. Then a woman's voice, asking Bill something that Mallen couldn't make out. Bill told her to wait a minute. Bill was certainly not at work. It was the first time he'd ever been aware of that side of the man. He'd sometimes figured Bill lived at the Cornerstone, only coming alive when it was time to open, sleeping in some coffin in back after closing time.

"I got your message," Bill continued, "and guess fucking what?"

"Julian Wood's married to your sister."

"Oh, that's funny, Mallen. You should go on TV with an act like that."

"Gotta keep you in stitches, man. How else will you not notice the tab I'm running up on you?"

"Got news for you: it ain't working. Look, all I got right now is that Julian Wood is still living in the city. Don't have an address, yet, but I'm working on it. I'll have it soon."

"Thanks for checking on it for me, okay? I owe you, B."

"Fuckin' got that right, Mallen. See ya," the bartender laughed as he hung up.

He got to his feet, wishing all this had happened during the late summers the city enjoyed. If this had been October, he would've been way happier to be camping out in parking lots, and that was a fact. But now? Now it was March: cold, wet, and dreary.

So, this Wood guy was still in the city. Maybe Obie would be able to get his hands on an address. Maybe his file. It would help to know some background on the only man Eric had ever spoken of with a smile from his prison days. He dialed Oberon's cell as he left the parking lot, conscious of the arriving cars that probably belonged to the teachers, or the priests.

"Detective Kane," Oberon said, picking up on the second ring, voice tight with stress.

"Bad time, yeah?" he replied. "You want me to call back later?"

"Yes, I do. What I've caught might actually have something to do with ... what we discussed earlier."

The hairs on the back of his neck prickled. They always did when something heavy was going down. Monster Mallen's hair had done the same back in the day. "What do you mean?"

"Another gentleman that knew Dockery and friends was attacked at by an unknown assailant."

"Jesus. They get him?"

"No. They got his girlfriend."

———

Oberon shoved his phone into his pocket and turned back to the body. DeJesus was there, nearby, ordering her minions to swab everything, photograph every aspect of the scene. An ambulance siren hit his ears as it took off to UCSF, Jenks in the back with a bad knock on his head and gun wound in his right thigh.

He glanced around the living room again. What had once been a place right out of a house porn magazine was now a war zone. There'd been some fight here. Went and stood by the beautiful young blonde woman lying on the expensive, hardwood floor. Kate was dressed in nothing but a bathrobe, hair still slightly damp. As if she'd stepped out of the shower right before the attack came. But then why was she here, in the living room? The bullet had gone in through the left chest, directly into the heart.

DeJesus came over and stood next to him. Looked down at the corpse. "That sure looks like a .38 entry wound to me."

He sighed. Nodded. "Yes, it does. Give me the ballistics report as fast as you can, okay, Ronnie? I'd really appreciate it."

"You got it, Oberon." She then began her initial inspection of the corpse. It would later be moved to the crime lab and gone over with infinite patience. Ronnie was the best at what she did, and he'd often wished there had been an army of Ronnies in the ME unit.

Oberon took a walk around the apartment, seeing what he could see. Looked like the assailant entered in through the kitchen back door, busting the lock. That would've brought Jenks into the room, possibly. He wouldn't know until he talked with the man. There was blood in the hall. A large patch, then a trail leading to the bedroom. There it just stopped. No, he was wrong. He found a single droplet near the left bedside table. Books on the other side table, mostly on addiction and recovery. The room hadn't been dusted yet, so he took out a pair of rubber gloves and put them on. Opened the near side table drawers. Inside were a pack of cigarettes and lighter, along with a couple novels of the romance bent. A notepad was there, too, the top pages ripped off. He picked it up and held it oblique to the light. To see if he could read what had been written, but it was a no go. Maybe a phone number. Maybe part of a street address. Couldn't be sure. Nothing else had been touched in this room.

Went back down the hall to where Ronnie was working the scene. Stood there a moment, studying the room again, lost in thought. This was all very different from the Kaslowski, Scarsdale, and Dockery killings. Those had all happened out of doors, in open spaces. Kaslowski's death could be considered to have happened indoors, but even then, it was an open parking garage. Maybe this attack on Jenks had nothing to do at all with the other three murders. Maybe he was totally screwed and would have the worst clearing rate of his long career. Maybe he just needed to pull the pin on it all and go garden some acreage somewhere far away from bullets, blood, and people.

THIRTY-TWO

HE NEEDED, AS HIS mother had reportedly been so fond of calling them, a time-out.

Mallen called for a cab and when it showed, finally, he gave the driver the address and climbed in back. It seemed the best place to go and just relax. No one would ever think he'd go *there,* of all places.

As the cab drove along Fulton Street, his thoughts turned back to his mother. He tried not to do that too much. Barely had any memory of her anymore. Most of what he had left were the stories that his father had told him, usually when the old man was more drunk than usual. Ol' Monster Mallen never liked to talk about the shit that mattered or hurt. The topic of his late wife hurt, and that was a fact.

The cab pulled onto a small side road that ran into John F. Kennedy Drive and parked. And there it was: the windmill. Where he and Eric had spent many a drunken night. The rain had stopped, what looked like only for now. The air was filled with the dull, concussive beats from the waves on the nearby beach. He got out, paid the cabbie, and went to the windmill. It hadn't changed, of course.

He hadn't thought it would. The nearby tulip gardens were bare. Tulips were almost here, and he actually found himself looking forward to seeing them. He went and sat on a nearby bench, huddled up in his coat, thinking about the past, and about the pasts he could've had. *What had happened, Eric? Who killed you, man?* Shook his head then. He was too rusty, too out of practice, to maybe ever find the answer to that. He'd been good, once. Pretty damn good. Could he be good again? Well, at least he was clean. There was that, and he had to admit, that was a pretty damn good start.

His cell rang and he answered it. It was Bill. "I've got Wood!" Bill said loudly in his ear, obviously enjoying running the gag out way past its due date.

"You goin' on the road with this comedy routine?" he replied.

"Only if I get free hookers at every stop, Mallen. Only then."

"I'll work on that with your agent, when you get one. So? About Julian Wood?"

"I heard he likes to box over at Jimmy Nielson's old ring. It's a full-fledged boxing gym now. Over on Leavenworth, couple up from Market."

"Okay. Thanks, B. Like I said: I owe ya."

"And like I said: oh so fucking much, Mallen."

———

The gym was right out of *Rocky*. Guys were busy hitting the hard and speed bags. There were a couple of guys in one of the two rings that dominated the room, sparring and working on their foot movement. Looked like feather-weights; two hornets buzzing at each other. His old man had always wanted him to get into boxing, but it just wasn't his thing. Too demanding. One that could really tear your body apart. Funny how a guy could think that, then turn to H, but there it was.

He found one of the trainers, a tall black guy in dirty sweats. Asked him if he knew if Julian Wood was in. The guy looked him up and down before answering.

"What you want with Woody, man?"

"We had a mutual friend. That friend's dead now. Shot dead. I just wanted to talk to him about it is all."

The indicated a doorway with a thrust of his jaw. "He's probably in there, working out. Got a bout day after tomorrow."

"Thanks," he replied. Wove his way through the bodies. The noise of gloves hitting bags or flesh was loud. The doorway led to the weight room. There were no fancy Nautilus machines in here though. This was old school, and then some. Only plates and bars, dumbbells and sweat. Three guys in the room. Two were over at a bench, one spotting the other as he pressed what looked to be a good two hundred eighty pounds. The third was a white dude over by himself in the corner, doing push-ups. Pale skin, chrome dome, lots of tats. Shadow boxed in the mirror after every set, working through combinations and punches, sometimes with five-pound weights in his hands. Looked like a boxer who had a match coming up.

The man watched him in the mirror as he walked over. Certainly had a boxer's eyes. Lasers.

"You Julian Wood?" Mallen asked.

"Who wants to know?"

"My name is Mallen. Mark Mallen. I knew Eric Russ."

Julian turned to face him then. Julian might have been shorter, but he was all muscle. "How'd you know Eric?"

"Old friend, sorta. From his dark blue days."

Julian turned and grabbed a twenty-pound metal plate from the rack. Carried it over to a padded mat. Laid down and did fifty crunches, the weight held behind his head. Mallen had to admit that he was just a little bit jealous right then. Julian finished. Got up and put the plate back. He was sweating now. Wiped at his forehead with a towel he carried in his waistband. "He might've mentioned the name," he said. "What do you want from me? He's dead, right?"

"Yeah. Shot. That's why I'm here. Eric was getting his life back together, by all accounts. He was found with dope on him. Just doesn't figure. Had my address in his pocket, too, though we hadn't talked in some years. Again, just doesn't figure."

Julian went and shadow boxed the mirror for a moment. Shoulders sagged then. Stopped. Looked over at him. "You know his mom?"

"Phoebe. Yeah. Great lady. Was always there with a meal for me when we got off duty."

"You guys were rookies at the same time, right? Him doing the 1-Adam-12, you on the street doing the *Starsky & Hutch*?"

"Yeah. Well, *Serpico* would've be my choice," he said with a smile, trying to lighten the mood.

Had no affect on Julian though. "Makes guys tight, I would guess. Going through being rookies together."

"That's right. Kind of like a trial by fire."

Julian shook his head sadly. Went and sat on a nearby bench. Knocked his fists together hard. "Fuck, man! Eric was good people. Why's shit always gotta happen to good people?"

"I wish I knew, trust me."

"So, what did you want to talk to me about exactly?" The man seemed genuinely shook up by thinking about Eric's death. Like it was hard to focus.

"About Eric. Did you talk much with Eric when you got out?"

"A couple times. On the phone once. Met for coffee once."

"Yeah? I was under the impression he didn't want to talk with you."

"He didn't. Wanted to put the joint way behind him. Can't blame him for that."

"No, you can't."

"Like I said, can't blame him. He had it really fucking hard in there, man. Real hard." Julian's gaze turned to the far wall. Like it was a screen, playing back memories.

"How so?" he asked, suddenly feeling like he was on the verge of hearing something important, something that might make things finally start to fall together.

"You ever been inside?"

"As a customer? No. Only the drunk tank."

"Yeah, as a customer," Julian echoed. "It's a hard world. One you can't fall asleep on. Not at all like all that movie shit."

"And Eric fell asleep?"

"No, man. He didn't. I saw to it that he didn't." Julian looked away. As if looking at something he'd thought long buried and wasn't happy to see. "But I couldn't be there all the time for him," he said, sorrow evident in his voice.

Mallen sat next to him. Checked to make sure no one was around. "What are you saying?" he asked quietly.

"Well," Julian started to say, but stopped. There was a shake of his head. "I don't know, man. Won't solve anything. He's dead. What good is it, you knowing?"

"What good? What you tell me might help find the piece of shit who would shoot him the back. Might bring a little fucking justice to a world sorely fucking lacking in it. That's what good, man."

Julian leaned forward, rested his forearms on his knees. Like he was suddenly tired. "You know what happens in there, man. The shit that goes down when too many guys are inside for too long. You know about the things they do, right? What happens to the new guys that arrive. And arriving a cop? When you get there, it's like every nightmare you ever had. No remorse. I remember the other guys yelling at me, whistling. I knew that they were going to have to fuckin' kill me, man, because it was either that, or they were going to die. You know how fucked up that is, man? Knowing that you got to spend a couple years there, but if you defend yourself, you could end up spending a lot longer? And you can't give in, either. If you do, then it'll never stop. You'll be a marked man. They'll never stop comin' after you, especially if you're a first-timer, or a cop."

The sudden clanging of weights dropping on the floor shattered the air. Someone laughed out. Called someone a pussy. As Mallen sat there, it hit home what Julian was talking about. Being a man, it was the last thing he would've thought of, or probably ever admitted to. The worst violation, hands down. Regardless of gender. The ultimate in the power act, ultimate in the powerlessness for the victim.

"Eric was raped while he was there," he said quietly.

Julian nodded. "Man, Eric was a good guy. He was sorta small, but he could handle himself if the odds didn't get too out of hand. But, he'd been a cop." Julian went and grabbed up a set of twenty-pound weights. Carried them back and slammed them to the floor. The two guys over at the bench glanced over, then went back to their work. "When he got there," Julian said, "I could see how bad it would be for him. I tried to help."

"Why's that?"

Julian looked caught all of a sudden. After a moment relaxed. Fiddled with his weight gloves. "Because it'd been that way for me, my first time inside. You have no fucking idea what it feels like, man. No idea of the pain. The anger. The fuckin' shame and humiliation. And there ain't nothing you can do, either. What the fuck can you do when like four guys, all of 'em big motherfuckers, too, hold you down so they can take turns on you? And you think the guards fuckin' care? No way, man. They don't give a shit. No one does."

Mallen looked around the weight room. Then back at Julian. "This is how you made it through?"

"*Make* it through, man." Julian indicated the room around them. "I dove into something to forget. Boxing works. I can beat the fuck outta someone other than myself for a change. Sometimes I imagine the guy I'm boxing is one of the guys who … I win those bouts by TKO." He smiled.

"But Eric? You tried to protect him? Keep him safe?"

"Yeah, and it took a lot. I paid a lot of guys off so they'd leave him alone. But then one day I couldn't be there for him. They'd been waiting. Prowling. I tried to get them to leave him alone, but got my ass kicked. Only made the shit worse, for both of us."

"Why'd they focus on him?"

"Hell, man, why does a predator go after its prey? Cause it's easy prey. Maybe because he was a fucking cop. How do I know? What difference does it make? I was never so fucking relieved in my life when Eric got sprung. Life was uneventful the rest of my time there, once he left."

"How'd they get to him?"

Julian sighed. "They got me out of the way by getting a bunch of dudes to accuse me of stealing their dope. Those guys beat the crap out of me. Almost killed me. Sent me to the infirmary. I was on the sidelines for a couple weeks. And that was that."

He pictured Eric, attacked and helpless. His heart constricted. "Did it happen more than once?"

A nod. "It must've been a nightmare for him. I tried to set something up for him, some other bodyguards. But this one guy? He had a hard-on for him. *That* fucker was a tough cat. Everyone backed off him. I couldn't do a fucking thing. Hell, maybe that's the other reason I turned to boxing: to try and beat the guilt out of me."

"What happened to the guys that did it? Anything?"

"You kiddin'? Those guys got out when their time was up. Just like I did. But they ruined Eric's life. He barely made it out of there."

"What were their names?" To his surprise, Julian hesitated.

"I can't... can't tell you, man," came the faint reply.

That stopped him in his tracks. Took a moment to realize he'd heard what he'd just heard. "Wait a minute. Why the fuck not?"

The boxer was obviously struggling with something. Hit his fists together a couple times. Growled under his breath as he shook his head. "I just can't," he finally said. "I promised Eric I'd never say a word about it, or about who they were. I've already done a lot more than I'd ever thought I'd do, but hearin' about him dyin', I just..."

"But, it would help," Mallen said. "You don't want to help?"

"Fuck yeah, I do! Of course I fuckin' do. But, I promised him never to say shit, right? He just wanted it to be buried, Mallen. And I take that now as a man's dying wish. You read me on this?" Looked Mallen up and down. Nodded. "Anyway, I think you'll find them on your own, without me sayin' anything about it."

He sat there, not knowing what else to say. If Julian felt this sort of obligation, then he knew he could never get the man to open up. He had no leverage. And, well... he figured he could sort of understand; a promise was a promise. He had to honor Julian's sense of loyalty, and that was a fact. "I hope you're right, about me finding them," Mallen replied. "Look, is there anybody else he might've told?"

Julian shook his head in response. Adjusted one of his weight gloves. "Doubt it. The couple times Eric and I talked, he talked about it, almost like he had to. Like he couldn't stop himself. There were problems, after. Body problems. He told me he told Jenna, but only as much as he could get away with, I guess. Told her that his body had started rotting out from the drugs, and that was why he had so many ... things goin' on."

"I'm really surprised he didn't talk to at least one of his parents. They were a tight family."

"Me too, man. I figured he would've at least told his pops. They sounded like they were real close. Eric idolized him." Julian thought for a moment then. "But maybe that's why he *didn't* say shit to his old man, you know? Maybe it would've been like ... I don't know, admitting you weren't good enough or something."

Mallen nodded. Got to his feet. Extended his hand. "Thanks for the talk, Julian. I appreciate what you told me, and that's putting it mildly."

Julian shook the offered hand. "Hell, man, maybe it was good for me, too. Therapeutic, right?"

"Hope so," he answered with a smile.

Julian sat there, thoughtful for a moment, looking at nothing except maybe memories. "Who knows." He shrugged. "Maybe they're back inside, having it done to them. That's the thing about life, man ... and maybe prison, too: no one preys forever. Even the predator ends up prey."

"Yeah," Mallen said, "that's the truth, isn't it?" Started to walk away, but stopped. Turned back. "Good luck with the fight."

Julian smiled as he picked up the weights. "Wish the other guy luck. He's the one that'll need it."

———

After he'd left Julian, Mallen called Jenna's number. She picked up. Sounded relieved to hear from him. "Thank God it's you, Mallen," she said.

"Yeah? What's going on?"

"I don't know what to do. Neither does Phoebe."

"What do you mean?"

"Hal was out most of last night. Came home about an hour ago, all beat up. Phoebe wanted to take him to the emergency room, but he wouldn't go."

"He say anything at all?"

"No, and we've both asked him a couple times. We don't know what to do."

"You want me to talk to him? He might talk to another guy about it."

"I know Phoebe would appreciate that."

"Okay. I'll be there as soon as I can." He ended the call, then called a cab. Things were happening. He could feel it. The threads were still tangled up, but there was that feeling that even though all the threads were tightening now, they would either become a knot, or he'd pull the right one and they'd all come free. The case was hanging on the proverbial knife's edge, and—

Case? Really? That's what this is, Mallen?

Yes, damn it, came back the answer.

The case.

And again, he was good with that. Very fucking good, actually. He was helping again, trying to help people that needed some help. Would he find out all the answers? Not sure. Did that matter, as long as justice had been served for Eric's parents? Again, he wasn't sure … but he was at work again, had finally crawled from the wreckage of his life to start out on a new road. One he could walk without feeling ashamed or like a piece of shit.

Yeah, he thought. *The case.*

THIRTY-THREE

OBERON TOSSED THE REPORT onto his desk and pulled off his glasses. Rubbed the bridge of his nose until his headache lessened. It was getting late, but here he still sat, going over the Jenks case, wondering for the fifth time that day if he was just getting too damn old to keep up in the job. Tossed the glasses onto the report and leaned back in his chair. Sighed. There were things there, in that case, that bothered him. And he thought he was finally getting close to what they were, just like someone who swings at a piñata and finally brushes it.

And those things that nagged were really two very simple items:

1. The single drop of blood on the bedroom floor.

2. There were no prints anywhere of anybody other than Jenks or his girlfriend.

Jenks never mentioned the attacker wore gloves, even though he'd been asked to describe the person he'd fought hand-to-hand. Oberon couldn't for the life of him imagine a fight where either man didn't reach out to catch himself on a counter, or surface. Somewhere, someplace, that would leave a print. In fact, if you slanted the reported facts a certain way and put the fight between only Jenks and his girlfriend, with no assailant, it could maybe just work. But why would Jenks want to kill his girlfriend? Everyone in the building said they were crazy about each other. The man was rebuilding his life. No one had heard any arguing. However, the building and its units were well made, the walls thick. He might have to have another look. It could be possible a screamfest could happen there and no one would know.

Picked the file back up. Looked again at Jenks's record. There *was* a history of violence there, but he had to admit, it was back in the past. And this foundation and speaking gig he'd started for himself since he got out was indeed some good work. The man had been helping people 24/7 since he'd been released. Well, not right away, actually. There'd been a period of about six months where he'd dropped out of sight, only to appear again with this speaking/life coach career already set up. And why did *that* bother him so much?

Maybe he'd have to pay Jenks a visit again. Talk to him while he was still raw with what had happened. It was just that there were no prints from a third party. The other physical evidence backed up Robert Jenks's story, or appeared to, but again—it was what *wasn't* there that really bothered him. Jenks kept saying he didn't know the man, didn't recognize him; however, with his background and history, nobody should be surprised if some ex-con he'd known inside wanted to get even for something that might've happened in a different kind of place, when he had been a much different person.

Oberon laughed then—he guessed he just didn't like the man. Not at all.

THIRTY-FOUR

IT HADN'T BEEN HARD, of course, to get the junk.

What had been hard was lying to Chris, telling her that he would be away with his crew. She knew what it usually meant: that they were going to make a major buy. This was the job. Getting underneath the wire. Burrowing deeper and deeper into the organizations that bought and sold H in the city. She knew it. But he also knew she was hating it, regretting her decision to follow his play. Hell, what Police's spouse wouldn't have those feelings?

Only this time, there was no major buy. What he'd done was grab a little bag from Punchy, his go-between that stood between him and the street dealers. There were so many levels to travel up, so many more rungs in the ladder as he worked his way up toward the Big Boys. It had been getting pretty hairy, and that's why he'd done what he did. He had to be... authentic. He had to know. No way he'd fuck it up. Ol' Monster Mallen's son? No fucking way.

He'd driven to a Travelodge he'd found down on Highway 1, just south of Half Moon Bay. Taken a room under his street name. And now he sat on the bed, the H in his hand, and the rig on the scarred side table. He'd bought a bottle of Jack Daniels and some sandwiches. Also some Alka-Seltzer. He'd seen a lot of guys puke their first couple times shooting, and he hated to puke. Hoped the seltzer would help that.

Picking up the items for the rig was nothing, of course. There were boxes of needles lying all over Punchy's place, and where that shitbag got them, Mallen could only guess. Probably some strung-out nurse at SF General, wanting to build up some cadre with her supplier. The tubing to tie-off, and something to cook in, the proverbial bent spoon... it was all there for the taking. Just everyday bullshit items that lay around any house in Anonymous USA. Items that could be put to so many other uses. Hell, hadn't he just read about a woman who walked into a fuckin' Walmart and found everything she'd needed to start cooking meth, and had done so, right there in aisle nine? Jesus fuck...

As he sat there on the edge of the bed, looking at the little plastic bag in his hand filled with a drug that had ruined more lives than all the wars fought in the last century, he thought about this whole "drug world" thing. He'd always been amazed at what a great brotherhood this drug world was. How people would share a needle if you needed one—if they soaked it in bleach first, natch. Wouldn't share dope, except rarely, but would for sure share the equipment. Even help you figure out some dough to buy some junk, if they could take their reward out in H.

He needed to know. That was why he was here, in this room. He'd been watching guys shooting and getting high for a long time now and had managed to keep away from doing it. It had been offered to him, more than a couple times. Now that he was an up and comer, he knew shooting would be frowned upon. Who would trust a junkie, right? Guys like Big Z, and Franco... they didn't touch the stuff. They had, back when they were teenagers, but he knew for a fact they didn't now. Now they just moved the pieces on the chessboard, no longer having to spill the blood themselves, or mix it in with the Gold.

He'd tried to pull off pretending to be high a couple times, because he'd had to. He'd actually been drunk, but it just didn't seem, or feel, real. Hell, his father would've probably shot the shit just to see what everyone was so up in arms about. His father would've been able to just walk away after that, so why not him, too? He was Monster Mallen's son, right? He could do this.

Being undercover was everything he'd ever thought it would be: exciting, dangerous as fuck, and way cool. It was like being Serpico, and he had to admit, he loved it. Chris, however, did not. But, to her everlasting credit, she'd given him what he'd needed so he could walk this particular career path. He knew she hated it and worried all the time, even more so since Anna was born. He knew she would only relax if he left undercover work and went and did something like Homicide, where it seemed you rarely pulled your weapon. His argument had been that if he could pull this assignment off, and nab Big Z or Franco, or maybe even the guys above them, then he'd be able to write his own ticket. He'd have his choice of assignments, probably. Hell, Eric was still on the beat. But there was no way he could've done the beat for any amount of time. He'd been only too happy to put on street clothes and go undercover.

He stared at the needle, still in its plastic medical wrapper. Nice and clean and virginal. The spoon was already bent backward, just like he'd first seen in a movie back when he was a kid. The H was in its baggie.

Just heat and serve!

He cooked the shot, just like he'd seen other guys do way too many times. So many people spent so much time trying to escape. Trying to get away. Could he really blame them? The world was fairly ugly, except for his Chris and Anna. He knew what Chris would say if she suddenly barged in and saw what he was about to do. She wouldn't give a shit that he felt he needed to know just so he could better play the role he'd taken on. She wouldn't want to hear that it was for the job, and really... for his safety. And there was a part of him, way down deep, in the furthest part of his mind, that felt she would of course be totally right. But another part of him argued that he needed to be the best actor he could be if he were going to survive the next levels of the organization and come home safely to the both of them.

He tied off. Just like if a nurse had done it to him before giving blood. And in a way, and he smiled here, he really felt that he was giving blood.

Blood for his job.

Blood for his life.

However, putting a needle in your own arm is very different from having a trained nurse do it. He hesitated when he felt the tip press against the vein, that little pinprick that Roger Waters sung about in "Comfortably Numb." But then he let out his breath, and glided in the needle, pushing gently down on the plunger...

———

It wouldn't be until about fourteen months later that he'd realize how stupid and naïve he'd been at that moment. How he'd been bullshitting himself the entire time. How he'd let everyone in his life down, including the ghost of his dead cop father, worse than if he'd just downright pulled a gun and shot himself.

THIRTY-FIVE

JENNA LET HIM INTO the house. She obviously hadn't slept. There were bags under her eyes you could pack for Europe in. She clutched a cup of coffee like it was an oxygen tank.

"He's in the den," she told him. "We've tried to talk to him, but he won't budge. He's already drinking."

"Where's Phoebe? Upstairs?"

A nod. "Trying to get some rest."

"I'll go see him," he added, making his way down the hall.

The den was like the last time he'd been in there. This time though, it felt even heavier. It seemed the strongest light in the room came from the glint off the glass in his hand.

Mallen went to the window and began to pull aside the curtains. Hal spoke up, his voice scratched with alcohol and sadness. "Leave it, will ya?"

"Well, I wanted to see how bad it was."

"It's fuckin' bad, okay? Now will ya leave it?"

"Sure." Put the curtains back. Moved to the bottle and glasses. Poured himself a belt of the vodka. Stood closer now to Hal. He'd been beaten badly about the head and face. Lots of swelling. A black eye coming up. Split lip. Looked like the nose was intact. The front of Hal's shirt was covered in dried blood.

"What the hell happened?" he said as he took a drink.

"How the hell should I know? Didn't see him."

"He got you some good ones on the face, Hal. You saw him."

Hal took a sip of his drink. Agitated. "Looked like your mama, okay? Happy?"

"Other than getting your ass kicked for no reason, how are you holding up?"

"Peachy, kid. The world's all wine and motherfucking roses."

"Come on: so you got your ass kicked. Happens to all of us. Can't tell you how many times I've had my ass handed to me."

"Well, being a junkie, yeah ... I can see that."

"Ex-junkie, Hal. Ex." The man raised his glass in response; an apology for the cheap shot. "Why'd this guy beat you up?"

"I was at a bar," Hal said quietly, "having a drink. I do that now. Being here is ... well, it just is. Anyway, this drunk guy gives me the business while I'm sitting there. Thinks I stared at him or something, I don't know. The bartender calms him down, and after a while I leave. I mean the mood was sorta fucking ruined."

"Yeah."

"So then I'm outside, and he comes out of nowhere and wham! Hits me. Fucking asshole cold-cocked me. Screamed how I'd been staring and did I want to fight?" Took a sip of his drink. "I'm just not that young anymore, ya know?" Shook his head, touching the swollen side of his face. "Different world we seem to find ourselves in these days."

"What bar, man? Some of those down in the Loin can be real holes. Maybe you should only drink north of California Street."

"Why the hell are you asking? You don't believe me?"

He didn't want to say it to the man's face, but no, he didn't. There was something off. Hal was covering up something. All his years on the force and all his years shooting dope while surrounded by liars told him this man was lying about what'd happened to him. The air filled with tension, and that wasn't what he'd expected to be there. He'd come to help. So he changed the subject.

"I think I have some news on Eric. Not sure, but maybe. Spoke with one of the men who did time with him. A sorta friend of his."

Hal took a long drag of his glass. Filled it right up again, the soft sloshing of the liquor a dull sound the dark room. "Yeah? So? That was a part of Eric's life he wanted to forget. I do, too," he added softly.

"Julian Wood. Talked with him for quite a while. Told me some things that might help ease your mind, and Jenna's."

Hal shifted in his chair. "I don't care what you heard. It's a part of my boy's life that was over the day he walked out of that hell-hole. If you want to focus on that part of his life, that's your fuck-ing prerogative, Mallen."

"He told me about the ... about how it was for Eric in there."

"Well, fuck. I thought he talked about how my boy arranged flow-ers while he was inside." Hal wiped at his eyes. Suddenly hauled him-self out of the chair and went to the window. Dragged the blinds open, blinking in the gray light. Mallen could see the tears. Looked away as he took a sip of his drink.

"When did Eric tell you?" Mallen asked quietly.

"When he got out," came the reply.

"Does Phoebe know?"

A shake of the head, then a drink from the glass.

245

"He never wanted her to know. Was embarrassed. I mean, how many people would *you* tell in your life that you'd been forced to take a cock up your ass? Been beaten because you refused to suck another man's dick? He tried to fight 'em, you know. Julian tried, too. Eric told me that. Almost killed the both of them this one time he resisted. Then it was worse. Like on the football field, when one side knows it's bigger and badder than the other? They do what they want, when they want. My God," he said, his voice breaking, "my boy, unable to protect himself. All alone! Nobody did a fucking thing!" he roared. Took a long pull from his glass. Drew a ragged breath before continuing. "His life was broken. Him and me, we worked hard to fix it back up."

Mallen looked down at the glass in his hands. He knew the statistics on the rapes that go on in prison. The dynamics. The fallout. If one guy got to you, then the rest would follow. You'd never be left alone. Ever. "Then you did a good fucking job, Hal," he said, "because Eric did get his life back on track."

"My boy did that. Not me. Those drugs that were found on him? I know that was total bullshit. I *know* it, Mallen!" Was about to take another drink, but stopped. Stared into his glass. Growled, deep in his throat as he put the glass down on the table. "I was there for him, but he did all the heavy lifting. I shoulda—" Stopped suddenly. Picked the glass back up. Filled it, shoulders sagging. Went back to his chair. Fell onto the cushions and sighed.

"Should've what?" Mallen asked.

"Nothing...forget about it." Hal looked down into his glass like he was looking into a deep well and hoping he never found bottom. "I'm not talking about it anymore, okay? I've had enough therapy for today."

Mallen got up. Finished his drink. Put his glass on the side table as he got to his feet. "I have no idea what Eric went through, and I can't know what you're going through now, but I want to let you know that if there's anything I can do to help you, I will."

Hal nodded absently. "Thanks. Appreciate it."

Mallen stood there a moment longer, but there was nothing else to say. He quietly walked out of the room.

Jenna and Phoebe were down at the end of the hall, by the front door. Waiting for him. "What was that all about?" Jenna asked.

"He's just upset. Frustrated."

"Did he tell you about the fight?"

"Just that he got his ass handed to him. For a guy like him, the embarrassment is pretty heavy to carry. He'll … be okay."

She looked down the hall to the den door. "You think so?"

"Hope so, that's for sure." He made his goodbyes and walked out, not liking the feeling inside him.

Felt sort of like leaving a drowning person in the deep end.

THIRTY-SIX

MALLEN PULLED OUT HIS phone as he left the Russ house. Called Oberon.

"Inspector Kane," came the usual answer.

"It's me. Mallen. I might be onto something."

A pause. "Regarding my open murders?"

"I think so, yeah. Can we meet?"

Another pause. "Where and when?"

There was a place on Clement Street he remembered. The Bitter End. Served food. Not seedy. Was out of the way—well, far away from the Loin anyhow. He gave the name to Oberon. "I'll be there within the hour," Oberon replied, then hung up.

It wasn't a long walk, so he just took off east on Clement. Would help to kill the time, and he just needed the air and freedom.

He got to the Bitter End just at the beginning of happy hour. Ordered a scotch and sat at the bar to wait. He didn't wait long. Oberon made good time, given it was the city.

The cop strolled over to him. Slid onto the vacant stool. Ordered a drink from the bartender, then turned to Mallen.

"So? What's going on?"

Mallen took a sip of his drink. "Like I said, it's about those murders you're working on, the guys that knew Eric in jail. There *is* a connection."

"What is it?" Oberon said, trying to keep the excitement out of his voice—it didn't work.

"First you tell me about that last murder you caught. You said it might have something to do with the other ones."

"Well," Oberon began, "there's one Bobby Jenks. He's now a self-help guru, using his time in prison as his pitch. He seems like he really believes it. No," he considered, "He *does* believe it. Like I told you, his girlfriend was killed in an attack that was meant for him."

"And he knew Eric, Scarsdale, and Kaslowski?"

A nod as the bartender came over and deposited Oberon's drink. The cop took a long swig. "So? What's this connection you've found, Mark?"

He told Oberon about what Julian had told him. Told him everything he knew about Eric's time inside. "I know you don't want me involved," Mallen said, finishing up, "but I gotta talk to this Bobby Jenks guy."

"His girlfriend was killed very recently, Mark. Be aware of that."

"I will be, trust me. But he was inside at the same time and place that Eric and the murder victims were. Come on. If you had those facts, you'd be dying for an interview, yeah? He's got to be the key!"

Oberon smiled. Said, "I don't like his story about the intruder. No, I do not. It stinks. He's branding himself into some self-help god, and he's really into it like I said, but . . . I don't know. I'm not saying for sure he's involved in it somehow, but—you know the feeling."

He nodded. "Startin' to, again. You know, I'm starting to believe that Eric had my address because he was coming to try and save me."

"Save you?"

"Sure. He'd done the junkie thing, and then prison. I think he was going to do exactly what Jenks says *he's* doing. I think Eric had my address in his pocket because he was going to come and try to get me off the needle. Get me back to life. I think those vials on him were planted."

"Yes, I can see that." Oberon thought about that a moment. "Strange that, even by dying, he did do that, Mark."

"Beyond strange, I'm thinkin'." He smiled. Finished his drink. "Well, best not let the guy down then, right?"

Oberon nodded his agreement. As both men slid off their stools and made for the door, the cop told him, "Let me know what you think of Jenks. I want to know what your read is of the man."

"You got it."

"And Mark?"

"Yeah?"

A smile from Oberon as he held the door open for him. "Try not to drag my name into it, okay?"

THIRTY-SEVEN

MALLEN DIDN'T MOVE UNTIL Oberon's car was out of sight. Then he walked the half block to the nice, two-story row job. Yeah, money had lived here, he thought as he hit the buzzer and waited.

"Hello?" said a man's voice, tired and solemn.

"Robert Jenks?"

"Yeah. Who is this?"

"My name is Mark Mallen. I'm a friend of Eric Russ's."

There was a pause. He wondered if the guy'd hung up. "I really can't talk. My girlfriend was recently ... recently killed."

"Oh," he said, "I'm ... I'm very sorry to hear that. I hate to press, but Eric was killed, too. Less than two weeks ago. I'm just trying to make sense of it all."

"I really don't think I can see anyone right now."

He couldn't just fold and step away, not with so many chips on the table. "I understand that," he said, "but, it's just that ... well, it's also about Eric's time in jail. About what happened to him in there."

Another pause. "Okay, if it's short," Jenks said, and the lobby buzzer sounded.

Jenks was waiting for him at the door to his flat. The man definitely had the air of someone who'd been in and out of incarceration a few times. It's a look in the eyes, a way of standing. Like a soldier that's seen a lot of war. Mallen extended his right hand and Jenks shook it, wincing a little. He looked down to see that Jenks's knuckles were raw. "Must've been some fight," Mallen said with a smile.

"No fight. Therapy. Sometimes when I work out at the gym I beat on the heavy bag, without gloves."

"Ouch."

"I feel it builds character. Come in," he said as he stepped aside and let Mallen pass. The first thing he noticed was the dining room turned into an office, complete with white board. The room was in disarray but showed signs of being put back in order. The living room, however, was still an untouched disaster.

"You some sort of life coach?" he asked as he read some of the slogans scrawled on the large board. Just like Oberon had told him. All the slogans were very motivational in tone, all very "You TOO can do it!" in nature. There was a steaming cup of coffee on the table, next to a stack of papers that looked recently worked on. "Nothing like work to keep us afloat during tragedy, yeah?"

Jenks went and picked up the cup. Took a sip. "How did you know Eric?"

"We went through the academy together. Were rookies together. He stayed in a squad car, I went undercover."

Jenks sipped at his coffee again. Sat down at the table. Looked Mallen up and down. "Still working undercover?"

"No," he replied with a slight laugh. "I left the force a bit over four years ago now."

"Why'd you leave? The pressure?"

"Let's just say I lost my way."

Jenks nodded, like he understood exactly how Mallen had lost his way, and could relate. Looked down at the work in front of him. "Forgive me, I don't mean to be rude, but what is it exactly you want to know? I'm dealing with a lot here."

"You seem to have a career here talking about dealing with a lot," he replied. "Seems like worthwhile work."

"If I can stop one kid from going to jail," Jenks said as he gazed down into his cup, "or help one guy turn his life around, then my time inside wasn't wasted. So? About Eric?"

Mallen sat down in a spare chair at the table. "I found out that Eric had been repeatedly raped while he was there."

Jenks shook his head sadly. "I hated that part of it. I saw that happen to some guys. More than once."

"You know Julian Wood?" he asked suddenly.

Jenks blinked. Shook his head. "Don't remember the name," he said flatly.

"An Anthony Scarsdale? Leon Dockery? Carl Kaslowski?"

"Why? What do those guys have to do with Eric?"

"I'm not sure, but they're all dead."

"And what the hell is that to you? Sorry for being so blunt, but you're not a cop. Not anyone who has any … authority. What's it to you?"

"No," Mallen replied, "I'm a nobody. Just an ex-junkie cop with a dead friend, who was probably trying to do some good in *his* life. I just wanted answers, is all. Thought you might have some."

Jenks shrugged. "Sorry, I really didn't know them that well. Not really at all. Now, if you'll excuse me?"

It was the way he'd said it. If the man had acknowledged even the thinnest of acquaintances, it might've gone totally different. Folsom was big, but it wasn't China. "Really? Not really at all?"

Jenks looked at him coldly. "Like I said: no. You better go now, Mr. Mallen. If you have a problem, you should go to the police. I have lots of work to do settling my girlfriend's affairs, so if you don't mind?"

Mallen nodded as he got up. "Sorry to bother you. Best of luck with your new career," he said as he made his way to the door.

———

Mallen exited Jenks's building and stood there for a moment, not sure what was next. He thought he felt someone watching him and glanced back quickly at the building. There might have been the flicking of a curtain on Jenks's floor, from a window that would've been their living room window. Maybe not. He took off down the street, hands deep in pockets against the cold, late afternoon air.

Jenks.

Oberon had been right. There was something wrong there. The image of Jenks's knuckles kept appearing in his mind. Whatever he'd hit, he'd hit it a lot. Wouldn't it be crazy if…

The pieces suddenly started to arrange themselves in a brand-new way. In the only way that made any sense. He needed to verify it, and like right away. It would be crazy. A disaster. The world exploding. Decided it was a good time to take up jogging again, and took off at the fastest trot he could manage, given his present out-of-shape state.

———

He got to the Russ house completely out of breath and hot. Wiped at his forehead as he rang the bell. Phoebe came to the door, dressed in jeans and a baggy sweater. Looked wan and tired.

"Good to see you up and about," he said as she let him in. Gave her a hug.

"Well, life needs living, as they say."

He cursed himself then, coming over without checking first. He'd been expecting Jenna. "You send Jenna home?"

Phoebe nodded in response. "She was exhausted. I felt she needed to be home. She's dealing with a lot, too. I told her to spend at least a full day before coming back. She argued with me a little about it, but in the end, went back to her place. It's for the best."

He looked down the hall toward the den. Said, "Hal in?"

"He's resting upstairs. Come on in, I was just about to have a drink."

"I was wondering," he said, working on the fly, "if I can borrow Hal's car?" Off her look, he added quickly, "Only for a day, or so. Look, I know it's a crazy request, but..."—he glanced at the ground, embarrassed—"I don't know anyone else *with* a car."

"His car?" she replied, surprised. Uneasy. "You can't. It's not running. He's been using mine."

"Oh. His isn't running? Nothing major, I hope."

Got a shrug in return. "I don't think so, but I'm not sure. He didn't say. Why?"

"Oh, no reason. Look, I'll just go rent one. I'll come by tomorrow, see how you both are doing." Before she could say another word, he was out the door and down the stairs. Stood near the garage. Checked to make sure Phoebe wasn't at the window, maybe watching him go off down the street in what would've been a weird sort of déjà vu.

He didn't want to do this, but he had to know …

Went and broke in through the side door leading to the garage. Got it open quietly, just like if he'd been doing a B&E while looking for things to pawn. Eric had used to break into the garage too, back when he was just a kid. He said he did it for the kicks, picking the lock with handmade tools. The goal had always been the same: Hal's collection of old *Playboy* magazines. Eric had told Mallen that once, one time when they'd been drunk out at the windmill. How he used to break in and paw over the *Playboy* collection Hal had stuffed away in boxes, way up high where he thought they'd be safe …

Mallen flipped on the overhead. The bare bulb streamed on. Hal's car was under a heavy, dark green tarp. Phoebe's was parked behind it, right at the garage door. A knot tightened in his stomach.

Went to Hal's car. Grabbed up a couple handfuls of the tarp. Yanked it off and to the ground. Underneath was Hal's dark sedan.

The silence seemed endless as he stood there, staring at the nice, neat bullet hole in the rear window. Right where he'd shot it the night Dockery had been killed. Tried the driver's side door. It opened. He leaned in. Followed the bullet path and found the slug still lodged in the dash. Another inch or so higher, and it probably would've gone through the front windshield. Dug the slug out with a screwdriver he found on the nearby tool bench. Clicked the light off. Quietly closed the door behind him as he left.

He went back up the stair to the front door. Knocked again. This time Hal answered. He turned away, going back down to the den. Mallen followed, shutting the door behind him. Phoebe was nowhere to be seen. That made him wonder how much she actually knew. It was all becoming much more difficult, and quickly.

Hal clicked on the desk lamp as Mallen entered. It cast a yellow, brownish light on the floor. Kept Hal's face in shadow as he fixed a drink, then went and sat in his chair. "Car needs a good wash and wax, doesn't it?"

"Yeah," he answered. Hal then brought the gun up from his lap. Then, after another moment that felt like a year, Hal only smiled as he put the gun on the side table. Like the whole thing was a bad joke that had to be humored. "Drink?"

"Sure. Thanks," he replied. Went over to the bar, poured some scotch into a glass. Held it up in toast. "Here's to absent friends and loved ones," he said, then downed half of it. Burned, but in a good way.

"That's a good thing to drink to," Hal replied.

"You wanted to avenge Eric, right?"

A nod. "Those animals ruined my son. He was going okay, making it by. But he was never the same after what happened. Never. They ruined him."

"Those animals? You know, one of them had turned *his* life around. Just like Eric had."

"No!" Hal roared. "No, not like my boy! Don't you fucking try to say it's the same because you know it's not. That guy? The one with the kid? He held my son down, crushing his face into the concrete floor of Eric's cell. Beat my boy like a fucking dog. Fuck him and his turned-around life."

Hal got up then, stalked around the room. Charged up, drinking as he went. "The other ones were just as bad. They all took their turns with him. Dockery was the only one who didn't beat him, but that was the only difference between the four of them."

And that was the piece he'd thought would be there. "Ah," he said. "Jenks."

Hal wiped at his eyes. Went back and sat in his chair. Buried his face in his hands for a moment. Finally looked up at him. "Phoebe found out. Saw the car. We need to protect her, Mallen. We *have* to. She doesn't see it the way I see it. "

"The way you see it? And how *do* you see it?"

"Revenge. Pure and simple. Putting down animals. Like you would any sick dog. Jenks is the last one."

"What happened with him?"

"I went after him, but he tricked me. I was tailing him, but he must've realized it. One second he's there, then he's not, then he's right behind me. Beat the living crap outta me. I know he woulda killed me but too many people saw him. And you know what he told me, as he was beating the crap outta me?"

"What?"

"That he'd worked too fucking hard to have some old bastard tear it all down again. His fucking *reputation* was what he was concerned about." Hal shook his head sadly. "I think it was that bastard who killed my boy."

Mallen thought back to what Jenna had told him, what seemed ages ago. About how Eric had come back one day from the store, a changed man. "He ran into Jenks?"

Hal nodded. "Yeah. The fucker even had the balls to talk to him. Put his arm around my son's shoulder, saying how he'd give him a job if he'd keep his mouth closed. How this one time, he wanted my son to keep his mouth *closed.* Who would buy that self-help, life-turn-around bullshit if it came from a rapist? Threatened Eric that if he said anything, he'd shut him up good. Shove his cock down his throat. Just like 'the old days.' Rip him apart from the inside out. Jenks told my boy that if he told anyone about what had happened in jail, he'd make sure Eric's life was one long nightmare."

"Eric told you this?"

A nod.

It still didn't explain Jenks's girlfriend. Had she found out? It might be possible. But who the hell would kill their girlfriend to keep such a secret? The answer that came back was actually very dark: a lot of guys. "How much of it does Phoebe know?" he asked softly.

Hal wiped tears from his eyes. "Too much."

Mallen sat there, looking down at his drink. Took a long swallow, feeling Hal's gaze on him. Watching him, waiting to see what he'd do.

"Well, what now?" Hal finally said as he suddenly heaved himself out of his chair and went to fix another drink. The man had to work hard to keep his hands from shaking.

"I don't know. I really don't." Mallen kept his eyes on his glass. Didn't know how the fuck to handle it. This man had broken the law. Committed Murder One. Multiple times. No matter the reasons, he'd done it. Confessed to it. The guilty needed to be punished; that was the ever-thin layer that kept societies moving forward. Yeah, it got trampled on all the time, that layer, but it still held. Still managed to do its job.

Mallen stood. Put his empty glass down on the side table. "I'm going now," he said. "You just stay put, okay? Don't say anything to Phoebe until we talk again. I really don't know what I will, or can, do. Yeah, I get what you did. I do. But… hell man, I just don't know."

Hal nodded. Like a child who'd just been told he'd been grounded.

"Don't leave town," Mallen said with a slight smile as he left.

Phoebe wasn't anywhere around as he walked out of their house.

THIRTY-EIGHT

AND IT ALL CAME *down to this…*

Mallen sat in the Commissioner's office, dressed in tie and jacket, trying to look normal. Everyone was present. Captain Stevens, the Commissioner's assistants, even a union rep. Nobody seemed to want this to take too long, but nobody wanted it to go wrong, either. In the end, the Commish only slid a manila envelope across his desk at Mallen. And that was it.

"Inside that," the Commish said in a flat, almost monotone voice, "is your severance package. You did good for us, and we have to honor that, even if"—he glanced at Stevens—"some of us think you shouldn't get shit."

The Commish leaned forward. Rested his elbows on the edge of his desk. Outside it was a sunny spring day. In here? In here is was the end of the road for a cop's career. But instead of talking, the Commish only glanced over again at Stevens. Nodded, then sat back… like he would not be dirtied any further.

Stevens stared at him, disgust more than evident in his eyes. "You," the man said, "go away. Mark? You hear me? We never, ever hear of you again. And we're doing you a favor. You understand that much, right? We could've sent you away... could've made an example of you. But we didn't. And only because, well, you had been so damn fucking good, you prick. Now though? Now you're one of them." He pushed himself out of his chair. Went to the window, hands in pockets. Kept his gaze focused on the street below as he said, "Stay off the radar. You no longer exist to this department. That's all, citizen."

There was nothing to say. Mallen could smell his sweat, the sweat that ran hard down his ribs. All he'd wanted was to fight crime, right wrongs; all he'd done was blow it the fuck up. He deserved this though, he reflected as he grabbed up the envelope and went to the door, part of his mind already wondering how much money they'd given him and would it be enough to keep buying dope to keep away the agony and The Need.

———

And it all came down to this. A note on the front door. At first he was angry; who the hell was she to do this to him? He'd done the homework! Had done the talks with the suits at the bank. He'd been the one that had gotten the down payment financed, along with all that other bullshit that goes with building it all up.

He'd gotten them here.

And now his home was no longer his home? What kind of fucked-up bullshit was that?

Ripped the note off the door. Read it again, still not fully comprehending what it meant, but that would be because the drug still wormed its last tendrils through his body, coaxing and smoothing before the machine reset itself.

"Mark," Chris had written, "I've changed the locks on the doors. I'm doing this because you're an addict. Yes, Mark, you are. I've talked with a lawyer, and he'll be talking to you. IF you clean up, THEN you and I will talk, but I can't have you around our daughter anymore, not in your present state. You know, I was so relieved when they took your job away from you, and made you 'a citizen,' as you loved to call us mere mortals. You shouldn't be out there, armed. Not like you are. Not now. I'll put your things on the street the day after I find this note gone, knowing that you've seen it. You can collect your things then, if you still care enough to do so. We can work out some visitation schedule, but only under supervision, and only if you're not high at those times.

YOU brought us here, Mark. Not me. YOU."

He read the note a second time. It was like everything had stopped, and was quiet. How could she say that it was him that brought them here? Hell, he'd been the one who had put his life on the line for his family. The one who…

…but then there was that voice. It sounded a lot like his father's. Ol' Monster Mallen's. The voice that told him the hard truth, usually when he wasn't looking, maybe even only told him in dreams.

It had been him. He had crashed this out.

He had blown it all to hell.

Mallen crumpled the piece of paper and shoved it into his coat pocket. Turned and walked back down the street. Toward the park. Toward the northern windmill where he had Eric had drunk oh so much beer. He could think there.

God, but he needed to shoot.

———

And it all came down to this. He walked up the sagging stairs, behind the landlord. The man must've been over seventy years old, and strangely he carried a live rabbit nestled in the crook of his right arm. Cooed and murmured at it as they went. Took Mallen a moment to realize that it was actually a live fucking bunny. He had to work to suppress his laugh.

Never rent an apartment high, he figured. Whatever. This was his new life, and fuck it all, this was where he should be now. Anonymous. Derelict like a lost ship in the fog. Fuck it. It would be fine. Sail away to the horizon and hope that one day maybe there would actually be a lip you'd sail over, like in the old drawings of what the world might be like.

The old man had to fight with the lock. Awesome. The door opened and he led Mallen inside. One room. "Bachelor's apartment" was the old phrase, back from like the post–World War II era. Maybe before? One room. Two doorways in the far wall on either side of what had been the Murphy bed closet. Now it was just an empty void used for a clothes closet, judging from the four left-behind bent wire hangers. One of the doorways led to a kitchen, the other to the toilet. Thank fuck at least there was a door to that room, *he thought as he made his way into the bathroom. Checked out the water pressure in the old clawfoot tub. It would do. Went and made sure the gas stove and oven worked. A cockroach crawled out of a crevice in the stove, between the stove door and the body. It leapt to the floor like it was leaping for its life.*

Yeah. This would do. Seemed fitting. Turned to the doddering manager who stood there, whispering to his rabbit. Cooing to it like a loved one.

"It's perfect," Mallen said as he pulled out his checkbook. Used his last check on the security deposit and first month's rent.

THIRTY-NINE

ALL HE HAD LEFT was Gato. He didn't want to intrude in another person's life this way, but he felt there was nothing else he could do. He had no where else to go. Had no idea what had happened since he'd left Jas dead on the floor of his pad. He'd thought about calling Chris again, but then he remembered her answering that phone call. The one he'd overheard. Remembered her voice, the way it sounded as she'd talked. The guy on the other side of that phone was someone she either cared about, or was someone she was *thinking* about caring about. He couldn't do it to her, involve her more.

Gato, of course, had been welcoming. Had even offered to pick him up, but he couldn't go that far. Told Gato he'd find his way to his place. Gato's voice had gone quiet then as he told him, *"Vato,* my *madre?* Not feeling so good, okay?"

"She's not sick, is she? Hey, I can find another roof, G. No worries. If your mother is sick—"

"No, man," Gato replied. "She's just...tired. Her soul is tired today, is all. I'll see you when I see you, bro." And with that, the call went dead.

He took the bus from the Richmond to the Mission. Took him about an hour, but strangely felt good. Like how the normal struggling people lived...not the addicted struggling people.

Gato had been waiting for him. Pulled him aside before letting him go through the door. "Mallen," he said, "my *madre* is asleep, okay? We can't wake her."

Mallen nodded as he went into the apartment. "If this isn't okay," he told Gato, "I can split. I don't want give your mother any worries or problems, man."

But Gato only shook his head at that. "No...we just gotta be quiet. The couch is yours. There's some food in the fridge if you're hungry."

———

They raided the refrigerator and then sat at the table eating. The only sound was the ticking of the mantel clock over the fireplace that didn't work anymore. Gato then excused himself to his room. Said he had some calls to make. He'd thrown a blanket at Mallen, nodded, then went down the hall. Mallen heard him check on his mother, then go to his room. He glanced around the living room for a moment. It was peaceful here, but he felt an underlying tension in the air. What was up with Gato? He figured that at some point, he'd find out. With that, he went to the couch and lay down, trying to forget, if only for a little while, about Eric dying, needles filled with heroin, and what had happened back at his apartment with Jas. About Hal.

And that was when Mallen's phone rang. He looked at the number. The Russes' number. "Phoebe?" he said.

"He's gone," came the strangled voice. It was Phoebe, but she sounded like she'd been crying. "I can't do it, Mark. I can't."

"Do it? Do what, Phoebe?" he said.

"He's gone. Gone after the last one," she told him. Almost a whisper.

"How long ago?"

"Thirty minutes ago. I should've called you sooner, but…"

He got it. He knew what a struggle she must've gone through. "Phoebe," he told her, trying to be as clear as he knew how to be, "You wait one hour, okay? One hour. And if you don't hear back from me or Hal, you call the police and you tell them everything, okay? Everything."

A pause. "Okay, Mark. I will."

"I got this, okay?" he told her. "I'll do my best for you and him, trust me."

Another pause. "Thank you," came the strangled voice, and then the call was ended.

He looked up to find Gato standing there in the doorway, car keys in hand. Without a word, they left quickly. "I hope this won't fuck you up with your mother," he told Gato as they ran down the stairs.

"It's cool," Gato said. "She thinks we're trying to save another junkie."

———

They went to Jenks's place first. Found the lobby door open. Ran up the stairs. Jenks's door was closed, but it opened with a turn of the knob.

266

A battle had taken place here. A big one. It was one big Rage Against Rage Fest, for sure. New blood. But who had won? Hal, Mallen figured. Hal would have nothing left to lose. And Jenks? Well, he would still figure he had everything to lose.

"What now, bro?" Gato asked.

It took only a second, and then he knew. He took off back out the door, saying, "Come on! I'll tell you where!"

————

The Falcon came to a quiet stop at the front of the small access road off of Martin Luther King Jr. Drive. The husk of the north windmill could be seen looming up ahead of them in the darkness. This would be where Hal would end it.

Mallen reached into his coat pocket. Jas's gun rested there, but he kept the safety on. "You armed?" he asked Gato. His friend nodded his head. "You shoot only if Hal looks to get killed, okay? Only then."

"Got it, *vato.*"

"Patrol-level movements," he whispered as he quietly opened the Falcon's door. They stalked off into the darkness, heading west. The crashing of the waves a quarter mile away thrummed in Mallen's head. The air was heavy and wet with fog.

A man's voice then cut through it all, raised in fear, then abruptly chopped off. They headed in that direction.

They found Hal and Jenks on the northeast side of the hulking windmill, in a small grove of trees. There'd been a slight glint of refracted light off of Hal's gun that had led them there. Jenks was on his knees, wrists tied behind him. Fresh bruises on his face. Had something shoved in his mouth to keep him quiet. In the darkness, it took

Mallen a moment to realize that it was one of Jenks's brochures for Phoenix Today. Hal looked over as they approached.

"Don't either of you make a fucking move, or I'll shoot," Hal said, pointing the gun at them.

Mallen could feel Gato tense at his side. He stepped forward, hands where they could be seen. "Easy. I just want to talk, okay?"

Hal didn't seem like he wanted to talk, except maybe in a face-to-face with God. "Go away," he said finally. There wasn't much spirit in it.

Mallen went over to Jenks and removed the gag. Jenks coughed, hard and ragged, as he fought for breath. "Mallen," he finally managed to say, "thank God! Help me. Please! This guy is crazy!"

"I am not!" Hal raged, and before Mallen could stop him, he whipped Jenks across the face with the pistol. Jenks spit out some more blood. Hal brought the gun back for another shot, ready to slap him again.

"Okay, okay! You're not!" Jenks panicked in reply. His eyes went to Mallen. Pleading. Begging.

"You killed your girlfriend, didn't you?" Mallen said to Jenks. It took Jenks off guard.

"No! I didn't. It was a break-in. There was a man—"

"Yeah, there was a man. And that man was you." He got it the rest of it now. Someone building his life back up based on overcoming the evils of prison. Over what prison meant. No one would forgive him for being a rapist. No excuse for that. There was never an excuse for that. "She found out. How, I don't know. Doesn't matter now, does it? But she did. Maybe it was something you let slip. Maybe one of the others contacted you, and she overheard the conversation." He paused then, working out another thing that had nagged at him. "And that explains why you broke into Jenna's place, and mine, yeah?

268

Looking for Eric's notes. He had my address in his pocket, because he was coming to see me, maybe wanting to help me, or needing help, who knows. But you'd found out he was thinking about writing a book, about his time inside. Yeah, Jenna told me that. Maybe you got him to tell you? Or maybe he told you out of defiance, that he had something on you. Told you that when you tried to coerce him into staying quiet, right? But your ego overplayed it all. Eric probably told you to go to hell, so you had to kill him. You thought your girlfriend would be in your corner, but no woman, no *sane* woman, could ever forgive her man raping somebody. Killing somebody. She threatened to talk, yeah?"

Jenks looked at him then, and there was hate there. Hate mixed with the fear. He was thinking, thinking fast on how to work it. "You need to take me in," he said. "I want to talk to a lawyer."

"I'm not a cop, man. Just an ex-junkie on vacation."

"But you're human."

"I have been, at times, yeah."

"Then you need to bring me in."

"Mallen," Hal said from behind him, "back away. Please. I beg you. It was all for nothing if I don't do this."

He turned around, facing Hal, keeping himself between the two men. Gato kept off to the side, hands in his pockets. His friend would follow any lead he laid down, he knew that. He was blessed that way.

"Will it?" he said to Hal. "Eric is still dead. And Phoebe needs you. You've gotten three of them."

"You said he killed his girlfriend. That's wrong."

"It is. People who do wrong have to pay. That's the law. And really, that's just what's fucking right with this world, you know? People who do wrong have to pay. Sure, they don't always do that. Sometimes they

269

get away with murder. But the concept still applies. Still overlays our world."

As he spoke, he thought of Anna and Chris and how frail society's hold was on normalcy. Chaos was the monster under the sheets. The boogeyman man outside at the window, trying to scratch its way in. This normalcy was the delicate balance that everyone worked toward, consciously or unconsciously. Maybe that was why societies were as psychotic as they were: they possessed the collective knowledge that it could all go to hell with just one more murder, one more disaster. It could all come globally crashing down on their heads with just one more flood, one more earthquake … just one more death. Justice was the thing that corrected the imbalance in the scales. That was what he'd been taught. That was what he'd always believed, even now. Even after all his years breaking the law in order to feed The Need.

In the end, the scales had to balance.

He stepped away from Jenks. "See you back at the house, Hal."

"What?!?!" Jenks cried. He tried to yell, but Gato ran over and shoved the gag back in his mouth.

Hal stared at him, uncomprehendingly. "Mallen?"

"You do this thing if you have to. If you need to. But tomorrow? After one last night with your wife? You turn yourself in. I'm sure I know what Eric would've wanted you to do when that sun comes up tomorrow." He took one last look at Jenks, who tried to get to his feet but failed, tried to break his bonds as Hal came and pushed him to the ground.

Mallen walked back the way he'd come, Gato following.

His hand was on the door handle when he heard a small-caliber gunshot. Gato looked back at the windmill, then over at him. Mallen stared at his friend over the roof of the car, giving him the chance to speak. To say anything he wanted to say.

Anything at all.

In the end, Gato only nodded. They then got in the car and drove away.

FORTY

Hal turned himself in the next day.

It was all over the news, the man who'd taken revenge for his son. The morality of it was bandied about in the news for days. Public opinion was mainly with Hal, so they moved the case to another jurisdiction. How it would all come out, Mallen had no idea.

He'd told Phoebe he'd just not gotten there in time. She'd gone silent when he told her, and he wondered if she'd guessed what had really gone down. He then called Jenna, to see how she was doing. She sounded okay.

Like her universe had been righted, at least a little.

———

"Marko, man, you're not really leavin', are you?" Bill had never called him anything close to his first name. Ever. Made him smile. The afternoon sun shone in through the open door of the Cornerstone, like the promise of better days. The bartender put a scotch on the bar in front of him. Mallen noticed that he'd given him a double, gratis.

"For me I guess this is almost a going-away party," Mallen said as he picked up his drink.

Bill chuckled. "Don't expect a lei."

"Not from you, that's for sure."

"Seriously, where you goin'?"

"Don't know. Maybe up to Mendocino for a couple weeks." Months, he was really thinking. Wanted to be far away from the city for a while, and that was a fact. He glanced over at the hallway leading to Dreamo's office. "How's Justin doing?"

Bill picked up a glass. Began to dry it. Seemed to appreciate the question. Shrugged. "Took a couple days off. Don't know where he went, but he wasn't in. He's back now, though." Put the glass away with its now-clean brothers. "You know, I shouldn't say it again for maybe jinxing it, but it's good that you quit riding the horse."

He was about to answer, telling Bill he was crazy for caring, when Oberon walked in. The cop came over and looked down at the two small suitcases near Mallen's leg.

"I must say, I'm amazed you had enough to fill both," Oberon said.

The last of Jas's money had gone pretty far. "One is filled with new-ish clothes. The other is used books. I thought I'd take up reading again."

"And where will you be doing this reading?" Oberon shook his head at Bill's inquiry of what he wanted to drink.

"You know, I'm really not sure. Like I was telling Bill here, maybe Mendocino. Dunno, just … not sure, I guess. I do know I need a change of scenery for a bit. Bad."

"Then I just might have the answer for you, Mark."

"Where?"

"A floating hovel in Sausalito that my mother left me. I can't take care of it. I would never sell it, either, as I of course loved her very much. I was hoping to find someone I could trust to maintain it for me. I would only charge a nominal rent. Just enough to cover the slip fee."

"Jesus, Obie. Why wouldn't you want to live on a boat out *there?* It's heaven."

"Hey Marko," Bill said, "That sounds really pretty nice. I mean, that's a perfect fuckin' fit, isn't it? Close enough, but not so close I get sick of seeing your ugly mug in here all the time, tryin' to beg drinks off me."

"As our esteemed proprietor here has stated," Oberon continued, "this is better suited to you than me. One, I'm a city boy, through and through. Two, I would hate the commute. Three, I get seasick in the bathtub. And four, it's a blessed wreck."

Mallen laughed. Took a sip of his drink. "A wreck, huh?"

"They call them 'floating homes,' but in this case I believe 'floating heap' would be more appropriate. They don't go anywhere, like a houseboat. They just ... well, float."

Mark Mallen gazed down at the amber liquid in his glass. Could this be just what he needed to keep moving forward?

"Come on," Bill urged, "this could be fucking great, man. Do it."

For an answer, he finished his drink. "I promise never to bounce a rent check in a month with an *r* or a *y* in it."

———

Oberon guided his unmarked police car along the 101 and down the hill to Sausalito. Just past town, he pulled off into a parking lot, and the two men got out. Ahead of them stood a long pier. Instead of boats in the slips there were the floating homes. All shapes and sizes. Some were very modern, all glass and chrome. Others were covered in brown shingles and looked decidedly circa 1970.

"I'm not doing you any favors," Oberon said as they walked to the dock gate. "There's a lot of work to be done before you can even start maintaining the place." Oberon unlocked the gate and they walked out onto the wide wooden pier. His friend then handed him a couple keys on a silver ring. He looked down at the small pieces of metal in his hand. Stared around at all the water. A seagull cried out nearby. Yeah, this would be way better than anything he could've come up with on his own. And of course, it was near Anna and Chris. Even though there were too many bad memories here, he still loved the Bay Area. There was just no place else to be.

The home was a small two-bedroom shingle job. And it was just like as described: a fucking wreck. Shingles were missing, windows cracked, and Mallen could swear the whole thing was leaning toward the east. The elements had definitely taken hold. The damn place even had a couple skylights, and a fireplace that might actually work after a month of elbow grease. *Fire and water. Both cleanse the body, and the soul*, Mallen mused. A deck off the upstairs room gave a great view of the bay.

"Well," Oberon asked, "what do you think?"

He looked around. Did a full 360-degree turn. This would make a bad world easier to inhabit. "Okay," he said.

Oberon beamed, his smile wide. "Great. That makes me very happy. You can move in right now, if you like. And if you don't mind camping out until you get the electricity turned on."

———

They'd retrieved Mallen's baggage from Oberon's car, then made a run to the local market, tossing in a side trip to a hardware store. Now they sat on the upstairs deck in a couple of old, rusty lawn chairs, quietly working their way through their third drink. The smell of the ocean was pleasant to breathe. The sound of seagulls filled Mallen's heart. He felt peaceful. Ready to face whatever might come. He laughed at the thought.

"What is it?" Oberon said.

"Just thinking of the future. Caught me off guard."

"Well, maybe you'll need to get used to thinking that way, Mark."

"Maybe," he said as he took another drink.

"Did you hear," Oberon asked, his eyes on his glass, "that Jas was found dead in your apartment?"

"Really?" Off Oberon's look, he added, "Yeah, I'd heard something about that, actually."

Oberon looked away, and Mallen caught the faintest smirk there before he did. "Yes," the cop continued. "Griffin was apprehended a couple blocks away. Won't talk though, except to swear he will piss on your grave one day. You know, the evidence *does* paint a fairly dark picture, Mark."

"I would think it would, Obie." Took a sip of his drink. "Like maybe that Griffin and Jas had a falling out while they were lying in wait to kill me?"

Oberon checked his watch then. Got to his feet. "You know," he said, "that *is* the scuttlebutt downtown. I voted for that scenario, anyway. You know how it is downtown, Mark. It'll be looked into. Who knows?" He went to the sliding glass door that led into what Mallen was already considering his office. Noticed the Police was a little unsteady on his pins.

"You're off duty, yeah?" he said.

"I'm fine. It's this derelict houseboat that makes me stagger."

"Obie?"

"Yes?"

"I owe you my life, a couple times over. Thank you."

"And what would Mother Mallen say," came the reply, "if I let her only begotten child fall prey to a life of debauchery and needles? She'd have my badge, son."

He followed Oberon through the house and out the front door. The last view he had of his friend was of him walking wide-legged down the pier. Like a dog afraid he was going to fall off a narrow log.

———

He slept on the deck that night. Woke up early, just as the sun was rising, his body stiff and hurting, but happy. There was a lot of work to do on the place, but the only thing he really wanted to do was work on a kite for Anna. That's what the trip to the hardware store had been about. He was deep into making a large box kite of bamboo sticks and colored tissue when his cell rang. Expected it to be Gato. To his surprise, it was Bill.

"Mallen," the 'tender said. "Sorry to call you so early."

He looked out the window at the eastern sun shining down on the bay. "I was up. I'm finding I'm loving mornings, go figure. What's up?"

"Well," Bill started, "you gave me your number, right?"

"Yeah, I did."

Silence. After a moment, he said, "Bill? Talk to me."

"You know Helen? Helen Vail?"

Had to think for a moment before it registered. A woman he'd met at the bar a couple times. Nice woman. Worked at the Art Institute over in North Beach. Was raising a teenage son alone. "Yeah, what about her?"

"Not her. Her son, Paul. He's gone missing."

"What do the cops say?"

"Not much. He's just another teenager living in the Loin, gone missing, right?"

"So, they're not doing much?"

"Not really. Problem is, he's got some issues. Sometimes wants to hurt himself, you know?"

"And you're calling me, wondering if … ?"

"Yeah. I mean … Helen's a good woman, and well, I really care for her, right?" Another pause. "We could give you some money for your time, Mallen. You know me, I'm good for it."

"Oh shut the hell up, B," he said. "I'll be right over."

THE END

Photo © Dawn Vail

ABOUT THE AUTHOR

Bay Area resident Robert K. Lewis has been a painter, printmaker, and a produced screenwriter. He is also a contributor to Macmillan's crime fiction fansite, Criminal Element. Robert is a member of Mystery Writers of America, Sisters in Crime, the International Thriller Writers, and the Crime Writers Association. *Untold Damage* is his first novel. Visit him online at RobertKLewis.com and at needlecity.wordpress.com. He lives with his wife in the Bay Area.

ACKNOWLEDGMENTS

You would not be holding this novel in your hands were it not for an incredible group of people:

First and foremost would be my wife of thirteen years and best friend for over thirty, Dawn Vail. Her love, patience, and support over the course of this journey speaks volumes about the beautiful soul that thrives inside her body.

My agent, Barbara Poelle, a wondrous mix of Wolverine and Charles Bukowski. She would go to the mat for me, or to the nearest liquor store to get me a fifth. I couldn't ask for more.

The entire crew at Midnight Ink, in particular Terri Bischoff, Nicole Nugent, Courtney Coulton, and Kevin R. Brown.

To my incredibly supportive family: Sandy, Ed, Sherri, Jim, Siobahn, Garrett, Janet, and Ron. Thank you for loving me as you do.

And my parents, both of whom had a transcendent love of books. My mother, Roz, took me to the library as soon as I was able to read and let me bring home as many books as I could carry, time and time again. For that, and so much more, I will be eternally grateful.